LILAC SKIES

Shivani Bansal has a First Class degree in International Relations and Politics, which has yet to be put to use! She works full time in digital marketing in the charity sector, and also runs a small baking business from home called Sweet Beginnings Bakes. She loves writing story ideas in her Pusheen notebook in her spare time.

She lives in Greater London, and when she's not reading, writing, working, or baking, she can be found dreaming up interior design ideas, and planning holiday adventures.

Lilac Skies is her first novel.

Lilac Skies

Shivani Bansal

First published in Great Britain in 2022 by Orion Dash,
an imprint of The Orion Publishing Group Ltd,
Carmelite House, 50 Victoria Embankment
London EC4Y 0DZ

An Hachette UK company

1 3 5 7 9 10 8 6 4 2

A CIP catalogue record for this book
is available from the British Library.

ISBN (eBook) 978 1 3987 1063 4
ISBN (Paperback) 978 1 3987 1063 4

Printed and bound in Great Britain by

www.orionbooks.co.uk

Nanny, you were the strongest woman I've ever known. Now your strength will inspire others too.

<u>India, 1938</u>

Mango juice dripped down her hands and past her wrists, staining her white kameez.

'Meena! You're all sticky! Ma is going to killllll you!' her brother Himet exclaimed, his eyes twinkling with mischief. Her most playful, yet favourite brother was happy to be the one not in trouble for once.

'I'll clean it up before she sees!' Meena shrieked, throwing the mango skin at him.

He ran off with her brother, Mohan and their two friends, the heavy sun beating down on them. Meena continued to sit in her spot in the shade, the tree branches hanging low around her, creating a secret hideaway. It was mid-May and the heat was almost overwhelming. She peered through the leaves and watched women hang their washing on lines outside their houses; men arriving home from work, their shirts stained with sweat patches. Children ran around playing hide-and-seek and helping their mothers pick the coriander leaves off the stems. Girls and boys cycled by, the creak of their bikes signalling their arrival. The sky was effortlessly blue, without a hint of grey or white clouding it. It was almost turquoise, and the birds soaring through the sky made it look like a painting.

Meena looked down at her now orange sleeves and sighed.

'It's OK, Meena, we can swap,' Parvathi announced, beginning to take off her spotless kameez. Somehow she always managed to stay clean, no matter what.

'Don't be silly. Then you'll get in trouble,' Meena said, while wistfully eyeing up Parvathi's effortlessly clean top.

'I don't mind.'

Meena bit her lip. Parvathi was younger and Ma wouldn't be so angry with her. She shrugged and lifted off her mango-stained top, quickly putting Parvathi's on. Despite their age difference, the top fit perfectly as Ma made them all share clothes. What was slightly tight on Meena was loose and baggy on Parvathi.

Once Parvathi had changed into her kameez, Meena decided they should go back home. The sun remained high in the sky, but it wouldn't be long until her pa came back from work, his footsteps gradually speeding up at the thought of seeing his children. They crawled out from their hiding spot and began the short walk back home. As they passed neighbours, they waved and exchanged greetings. Meena saw her brothers and elder sister ahead of them, kicking stray stones as they walked.

They all entered their home together, the waft of freshly made saag leading them directly into the kitchen.

'Ah, there you all are. Your pa should be home any minute. Clean up for dinner,' their ma said, her eyes taking in their sweaty, slightly dishevelled appearances. Her eyes paused on Parvathi.

'What is that on your sleeves? Did you eat the mango or rub it on your body? This isn't like you to be messy, Parvathi. Go and change, and I want the kameez washed tonight.'

Meena meekly followed Parvathi out of the room, her siblings trailing behind her.

'Meena, come back here.' She was caught. Her ma stood with her hands on her hips. 'Was it you?' She didn't need to say more. Meena's eyes stared into the ground, waiting for the telling off. She nodded. She heard her ma sigh, and then felt her warm presence by her side. 'Come, sit.'

They sat on the refreshingly cool stone floor and her ma began to unravel Meena's bun, combing her hands through her hair.

'The bond you have with your siblings, especially Parvathi, is for life, Meena. She is young, your sister. She will always be there for you. But you must also be there for her. In life, you must lean on each other. We won't also be here, but you will all have each other. Don't take her kindness for granted. Protect her too.'

Meena nodded. Her ma was right. She often let Parvathi take the fall for her. She should do a better job at being a big sister.

The door opened and footsteps entered the room. She ran to hug her pa, his small but strong arms holding her close. Her other siblings ran into the room and they all enveloped him, causing him to laugh and struggle to break free. Once they let him go, he walked over to his wife and kissed her forehead. She smiled.

'I'm home,' he said.

3

Chapter One

The shattering of a plate shocked her out of her daydream. 'What have you broken now, Meena?' a deep voice behind her asked. She turned to see her husband standing tall in the doorway. His veined hands shook slightly, and his towering frame loomed over her. She felt her heartbeat quicken. It had been an accident; she had never been this clumsy before. The fragmented plate glistened white against the red linoleum floor. The design of pieces of fruit around the border of the plate now decorated the kitchen – a shard of banana here, and a piece of pear there.

She felt his eyes burning into her skin, the temperature in the room increasing. Her hands were in fists by her sides, nails digging into her delicate brown skin. This was a new habit she'd picked up – it hadn't existed eight months ago.

As the sun streamed in through the window, casting her body in a warm glow, her thoughts travelled back to where they had been before she broke the plate.

The ruthless sun shining down on her brown skin, burning the sensitive scalp underneath her thick, black hair. The smell of

4

turmeric, cumin and coriander flying into her nostrils, making her stomach rumble with joy at the thought of dinner. Her sister's delicate, small hands plaiting her hair, making sure the tel soaked into every strand . . .

'Are you going to clean that up?'

She felt her head jolt up and winced as her fingernail drew blood in her palm.

'Of course. Sorry, Amar,' she muttered.

She suddenly felt his strong arms around her, his warm lips kissing her on the cheek. He whispered in her ear, '*Koi bat nahi.*' Don't worry. She told herself those words every morning when she awoke in this foreign place, in bed with a foreign man. Her ma used to whisper those same words to her whenever she was frightened. Koi bat nahi, *Meena,* she would say, *you are strong, Meena.*

She smiled to herself and began cleaning up the plate with her ma's words ringing in her mind. Little particles of ceramic stung her hands, but she didn't wince. Amar's shadow was looming over her, and she became more aware of her actions and facial expressions. Suddenly, she felt his arm brush against hers as he stooped down to help her. Electricity soared through her skin and she felt her arm twitch with excitement.

Amar abruptly stood and Meena craned her neck to look up at her husband, his impressive height and broad stature, the nape of his neck slightly darker from the sun. She put her pile of shattered fragments into the bin and took in her husband's appearance. His wide-set eyes, which were the colour of the ground after the monsoon was over – a glorious, shiny, earthy brown. When the sun hit, they turned a deep hazel green. The dimple in his right cheek which became more pronounced when he roared with laughter, usually at his own jokes. Jet black hair, combed meticulously every morning, using just a hint of almond oil. Brown skin that darkened further under the African sun. Tiny bristles of new hair emerging on his upper lip, underneath his long, slightly beak-like nose. His thin face that showed no sign of getting saggy with age. She had been lucky to marry a handsome man.

Meena's face twisted in pain as she involuntarily put her hands back into fists. Small shards of the plate which had been sitting on the surface of her skin now penetrated into her palm. She looked up at Amar, attempting to blink the tears out of her eyes. Without warning, he walked away. She bit her lip and let the tears fall. She would have to pick the shards out of her skin by herself. She tried to brush the tiny daggers from her hands, which only dug them in deeper.

The sound of footsteps made her quickly turn around to dry a tear before it was seen. As she heard feet enter the room, she saw that Amar was carrying a bucket of water. He placed the bucket down on the tiled floor. She lowered down to her knees and had begun to dip her hands in the warm water when she felt his strong hands engulf hers. He loosened out her hands and began to pour the water gently over them. She felt her heartbeat quicken at his touch. She looked up meekly, scared in case her eyes met his. Luckily, he was too enchanted by her hands to notice. His hands had a firm grip on her, helping her to maintain her balance. Her eyes soaked in the small crinkle between his brows which appeared when he was deep in concentration.

The ground met her body without warning as she sharply fell back as Amar abruptly let go of her. His eyes briefly looked into hers and she saw guilt. Or was it sadness? She watched as he hurriedly grabbed the bucket and marched out of the room. Had she done something wrong? Moments later, it all became clear as she heard footsteps approach. Asmita was here. Her mother-in-law.

'Ma, how are you? Would you like some *pani*?' she asked her mother-in-law, while pretending to be cleaning the floor.

'If I need water, I will ask you for it,' Asmita snapped as she sauntered off into her bedroom.

Meena spread her body flat on the kitchen floor as the house shook from Asmita's bedroom door slamming shut. The tiny droplets of blood from her cut hands trickled down her palm. The heat and the sound of birdsong engulfed her body, taking her back to her previous life in India. Her mind drifted to that day over seven months ago when she discovered she was to be married.

She was helping her ma and sister make the dinner. Her ma had been silent all day, barely looking her in the eye. Throughout the day, Meena had felt increasingly sick, her legs becoming wobbly with worry. She wasn't a particularly

7

naughty child, only a bit messy. She left the antics to her siblings.

She looked up to ask her mother if the rice was cooked and found herself staring straight into her mother's round, owlish eyes. Her ma quickly looked down, but not before Meena had seen the look of sadness, despair and longing burning in her eyes, tears threatening to escape into a cascade down her face. Meena heard footsteps approaching.

She turned around to see her pa standing in the doorway, looking lost. 'What's wrong?' she asked, afraid of the possibilities. Was he sick? Had something happened to one of her sisters or brothers? Had they run out of money? She frantically looked from her mother to her father, aching for an answer.

Her ma called Meena's four sisters and three brothers into the room. Parvathi, Priya, Nita, Jiya, Raj, Mohan and Himet. She was surprised to see her elder brother, Mohan, there. Why wasn't he at home with his wife? 'Sit,' whispered her ma. They all sat around the table, the tension in the room so thick that it was hard to breathe.

Her pa spoke in a rush of words, as if he couldn't bear to keep them inside anymore: 'Meena, we have found a husband for you. He has agreed to marry you and we have paid your dowry. The wedding will take place in five days.' As he said the words 'five days', his eyes slowly met Meena's and she felt her lungs become even heavier.

'I don't know him. How can I get to know him in five days?' she exclaimed. 'What if he's old and wrinkly? What if he doesn't like me?' The rush of questions was endless. Nobody had spoken over her. She noticed how they were all looking down, as if they were waiting for her to finish saying

8

her piece. She got up and paced around the room, as if her body were charged with electricity. As she passed the mirror hanging on the wall, she saw something in her own eyes. A look of pure and utter desperation.

'You will not be able to meet him, beti. He will be coming over the day before.'

Confusion took over Meena's mind. Where was he coming from? It did not take five days to travel from one city in India to another. Why couldn't they get married in a year or two when she was ready? She was still a child. She felt like one anyway. She wondered if he was from Pakistan, where her father was from. The question died on her lips as she heard the words: 'He is from Africa.'

Her lungs struggled to find air; her mouth clamped tight. She already knew the answer but still asked: 'Will he be moving to India?'

As a tear fell from her pa's eye, the awful truth dawned on her. She was being sent to live in Africa with a stranger. A different continent. Over 3000 miles away. She was no longer needed here. She was a burden. Betrayal blurred her vision as she ran from the house, desperate to get as far away from her traitors as possible. Parvathi, her youngest sister, chased after her and wiped away the tears Meena hadn't realised were flowing out of her, as if the clouds inside of her had been ripped open and would never drift together again.

The sound of bells startled her from her memories. She heard the local Kenyan man call out for customers. His cart of fresh fruit always looked enticing, but she stayed inside, watching him from the window. At the sound of the bell fading away, she became aware that she was still on the floor. What would Amar and Asmita think if they saw her like this? She quickly stood and brushed the dust off her kameez. The prickling in her hands made her stop. She stared at the small red streams stained on her skin. Noticing the abandoned bucket of water, she rinsed her hands and bandaged them up.

Hindi music began to play, and she heard Asmita singing along. Back home, when her mother sang, they would all hold hands and join in. Asmita's voice travelled around the house, alone in its misery.

The kitchen stood near the back of the house, facing out into the garden. She could turn in that direction and be away from the claustrophobia that engulfed this house. Yet, her footsteps instead took her down the narrow hallway, past her bedroom until she halted at the white door that was at the end of the hallway. Asmita's shrill voice travelled through the closed door, and Meena breathed in the haunting lyrics. Her hand rested on the doorknob. Should she go inside? Maybe they could sing together, like she used to with her own mother. The song finished and Meena stepped back from the door. She walked away, leaving Asmita to revel in her music alone.

As she walked back into the kitchen, she passed by an old photograph of Asmita holding Amar in her arms. He must have been almost a year old in the picture. Her face beamed with pride, her eyes unable to look away from her darling son. Amar's small face looked up at his mother, a grin on his lips. His chubby arms were reaching up to touch her face.

Meena didn't have many photographs – her family could never afford a camera. She marvelled at how a black box could capture such memories, such love between family. She ached to have a picture of her own family. Something she could look at to remind herself of her parents' faces.

She picked up the framed photo of Asmita and Amar and noticed a smaller photograph hidden behind it. She set the framed photo down and picked up the other picture, careful not to damage it. It showed a frowning Asmita in the corner, looking at Amar playing with an older man. Meena held the picture closer to her face. The older man resembled Amar closely, from his tall frame to his pointed nose. That must be his father. She wondered why Asmita looked so angry in the picture. Before she could dwell on it any longer, she heard Asmita's bedroom door open. Without hesitation, Meena quickly put the photographs away and ran out into the garden.

The photograph was etched into her mind. She had never seen a picture of Amar's father before. All she knew was what her parents had told her. Amar's father had been a railway worker for the British Empire in Kenya. When her parents had told her this, she had noticed the look of respect on their faces.

Her parents had also told her that Amar's mother was a widow and to be careful about mentioning her own relationship to her father too often, or the relationship her parents had. As a result of this warning, she never mentioned her parents in front of Amar or Asmita. She often found herself smiling at a memory of her father telling a terrible joke at dinner, or her younger sister stealing bits of food from their brother's plate. If she was asked what she was smiling about, she shrugged. Those memories were hers to keep.

As she wandered out further into the garden, she thought back to her home. The days had flown by then – playing with her sisters, cooking with her ma, helping her pa fix little things around the house. Two of her main passions had been writing and sewing – her dream was to become a famous writer and see her words in every bookstore, her name under headlines in newspapers. She often daydreamed about her books being taught in schools, the children marvelling at her poetic writing skills. Her parents had always encouraged her writing. She now wondered if they had only gone along with it because they knew she would never have that life. Perhaps they had just been trying to appease her until they found her a suitable man to marry.

When she was thirteen, a poem she had written was published in the local magazine. Her teacher at school had mentioned the competition to the class, recommending they all write one poem each and send it in. The teacher had given her a little wink. She had rushed home and spent the evening writing countless poems, trying to make each one better than the last. Her baby sister Parvathi had been her sounding board. She read the poems to Parvathi before bed, editing them as she read them out. Parvathi had been the one to pick the final poem. When she found out she had won the competition, she ran home to her parents and told them the news. The sheer joy on her mother's face was an image she retained in her memory.

She had brought a copy of the paper with the poem in it with her to Kenya. One day, two months ago, Amar had come across it while trying to find a bank statement. She had been about to enter the room, but silently watched from the doorway. Her jaw clamped tight as she watched his eyes skim her words. As he neared the end of the poem, a smile crept across her face as she waited for him to realise that she was the wordsmith. She watched as his eyes lingered on the words, his mouth turned up into a small smile. He carefully put the paper down where he had found it and left the room.

The grass felt soft beneath her feet, and she sighed as the sun stroked her scalp. Her ma would have called her inside and put oil in her hair to stop the sun burning her scalp. She loved the way her ma would sit her down on the floor between her legs, and slowly massage the warm oil into each root of hair. Meena would close her eyes and wish it would never end. As she had got older, she had started to put oil in her ma's hair for her. The first time she had suggested it, her ma had cried. At the time, she didn't know why. She understood now.

The days dragged endlessly here. Amar went to work and Asmita tended to stay inside or go to a friend's house. Countless times Meena had put on a pair of shoes and walked out the front door. Except she never made it past the front yard before turning around and heading back inside. Thoughts would litter her mind on the short walk from the door to the end of the yard. Thoughts that she couldn't shake.

She sometimes saw neighbours in their front yards. She felt their eyes staring at her, judging her. She was a foreigner in their country. This was their land. She was encroaching on it. In their eyes, she was no better than the British. Yet, when Amar left for work, nobody stared at him. When Asmita went to her friend's house, she often saw the Kenyan neighbours wave at her. They had even given Asmita some of the ripe fruit from their garden. So why did she feel everyone watching her whenever she went to leave the house?

She picked up the bottom of her saree and strode to the mango tree. As she thumped down on the ground underneath it, revelling in the shade, she thought about her new country. Nairobi was a beautiful city, reminiscent of home. She could still pick mangoes off the trees, let the heat melt the coconut oil into her hair, and plant fruit and vegetables. The smell of the neighbour's vegetable curry was making her mouth water, transporting her back to her parents' home in Delhi. Although some of the spices were different, the aroma remained near enough the same. She thought she could smell cassava leaves in it. Fresh vegetables decorated with dozens of spices, all perfectly combined to make your mouth water at the sight of it. She also realised that Kenyans ate *roti* too. They were more alike than they realised.

As the sun peaked in the sky, she leant her head against the strong bark of the tree and closed her eyes. Her thoughts drifted back to where they had left off in the kitchen, her sister wiping her tears after discovering she was no longer a part of her family.

Parvathi held her hand and kissed her face. 'Let's go back to Ma. She might change her mind.' Meena looked at her sister with pure adoration. How could she understand? She was too young to know that this was life for women in India. Parents didn't want purposeless people in their house. More mouths to feed. They wanted their children married off, making families of their own, leaving them in peace. She couldn't tell Parvathi that. So, she returned to the dinner table and stated: 'No, I refuse.' Her father had looked up in a mixture of relief and shock. She knew he didn't want her to go; she could persuade him to let her stay.

Her ma, on the other hand, shook her head slowly and said, 'We don't have a choice, beti. *You're too old to stay with us anymore. The neighbours are talking. You need to start your own family soon.' Meena's stomach tightened with the overwhelming sense of betrayal. One of her sisters, Priya, had married last year but that was to a local boy in the next village. She saw her sister all the time, wandering in and out of the house, staying for meals. Sometimes alone, sometimes with her husband. She had known this day would come, had been to the weddings of other girls in the neighbourhood, had witnessed how girls were usually married by her ripe age of eighteen, whereas boys could stay at home until twenty-three or older. Why hadn't she been born a boy? They got to* choose who they married. They got paid to marry somebody's daughter. They could work and earn their own money. They could continue their education. She would forever be dependent on somebody else. On a man.

She had always gossiped with her sisters about what the local bride had done wrong to be married off so quickly. There were often rumours of girls being caught with the neighbourhood boys or showing too much skin, and marriage was their punishment. It was well-known among the village girls that bad girls were sent away to be married because their parents couldn't cope with them anymore. The younger the girl, the worse the crime they had committed. Meena had even seen girls as young as fifteen marrying much older men in the neighbouring village. She remembered wondering, 'What could a child possibly have done so wrong to be taken away so young?'

'What did I do wrong?' she muttered that fatal day, tears threatening to reappear with each word. She felt her parents' tight embrace, felt her father kiss her forehead, his strong arms keeping her safe, telling her she hadn't done anything wrong, she was a good girl. In that moment, the reality hit her that she had precious little time left with her family. Her life would never be the same again.

Chapter Two

She was still half-asleep but could hear low voices near by. She kept her eyes closed, trying to hold onto the last few moments of bliss. She heard glimpses of the mutterings near her but tried to block them out.

'Tell her to wake up! What kind of daughter-in-law sleeps during the day? You need to be firmer with her, Amar. She needs to be taught how to be a good wife.'

'It's OK, Ma, it's a hot day. She must have just fallen asleep.'

'Have I ever fallen asleep in the middle of the day? No. Instead I had to raise you and your sister. Cook for you. Clean the house. Now I still have to do that because your wife is useless. It would have been better just the two of us! Now I have another mouth to feed. It's hard for me, Amar. I'm not young anymore. My hands hurt. My knees are weak. I need help.'

'Sorry. You're right. She needs to learn. I'll wake her now.'

'Meena, wake up. It's time for dinner. What have you made?' a male voice boomed from above.

She opened her eyes, blinking up at her husband. His face was mere inches from hers and she noticed how his lips were slightly uneven. She attempted to disguise her alertness and feigned a yawn. Her nails pressed into her palms and the bandages on her hands began to stain with blood. Her eyes pricked at the wounds she had endured only hours before.

She stood up quickly, her eyes still blurry from sleep. As she made her way to the kitchen, her feet felt heavy, like weights strapped to her body, dragging her downwards. She quickly began chopping onions and tomatoes, without a clue of what to cook. Amar's gaze was upon her, and she felt his intense stare. She watched his eyes travel to her bandaged hands and look sharply away. Asmita had followed them into the room, closely watching her son.

'Meena, I have just come home from a shift at work. Do you think it's fair that I now have to wait for my dinner?'

'I'm sorry, Amar. I fell asleep without meaning to. It won't happen again.'

'You said that the last time! You are my wife, Meena. My wife. You have responsibilities, like cooking and making sure the house is clean for me. I am a kind husband, am I not? Yet you take advantage of me.'

'Amar, I don't mean to take advantage . . . Please don't be angry.'

'Don't be angry? I make money. I have given you a roof over your head. My mother shouldn't feel like she has to cook. She is older. Her hands hurt. It is up to you to look after the both of us. You walk around with your head in the clouds all day, dreaming of a life that you no longer have. This is your life now. You are not a child.'

The tears from cutting the onion mixed with her tears of anguish. She took a deep breath as she had practised before. It helped. She took a few more.

'What are you making?' She turned to see her mother-in-law in the doorway. Of course, she was right there, listening the whole time. Meena pressed one hand over her lips and dug the nails of her other hand into her palm.

'I don't know yet. I am just preparing the *tadka*,' she said, hoping Asmita couldn't sense the wobble in her voice.

She shifted her weight to her left foot and hung her head lower. The sound of footsteps retreating caused her to turn around. Amar had left the room. She met Asmita's gaze. Seconds passed in silence. She saw something in Asmita that she hadn't seen before. Asmita came over and took the knife from her shaking hand. She watched as Asmita expertly finished the onions within seconds, barely even glancing at the chopping board. Asmita went over to the basket of freshly picked vegetables and chose an aubergine by smelling and touching it.

'The vegetable is ripe and ready for picking when the skin is shiny and it bounces back, see?'

Asmita held the aubergine out to show how the skin bounced back when slightly squeezed. There was a light glow of companionship in Asmita's eyes, the first Meena had ever seen.

'Yes, it looks lovely and ripe,' she acknowledged.

A small smile graced her lips. *Maybe things would be OK after all,* a voice whispered in her head. Together, they proceeded to make *aloo bangaan,* one of Amar's favourite dishes to eat. The aromatic smell of spices mixed with potatoes and aubergines welcomed Amar back into the room and he smiled at his wife and mother with surprise and pleasure. Meena glanced at his tall frame leaning against the wall, his deep eyes taking in this unlikely sight.

'It's nice you two ladies are getting along,' he said with a smirk.

Asmita began to smile, her hand continuing to stir the food.

'My two favourite women!' Amar exclaimed as he put an arm around Meena's waist.

She noticed how Asmita's hand tightened around the spatula. Her eyes rested on Amar's arm, and her jaw tightened. She turned and said: 'Well, you chose a wife who can't even cook.'

Betrayal tightened her stomach, and her eyes flashed to Amar's face. She noticed his smile had disappeared and his forehead was wrinkled in frustration. Meena felt words of defence on her lips. They disappeared upon looking at Asmita.

In bed that night, she wondered if this was what the rest of her life would be like. Amar was kind when they were alone. Asmita had shown her kindness today. Yet, there seemed to be a bond between mother and son that she couldn't interfere with. She wanted them to remain close, but she also wanted to be included. Wasn't she part of their family now too?

Amar's snores disturbed her sleep and she silently got out of the bed. She winced as the floorboard creaked, but Amar showed no sign of awakening. She tiptoed to the kitchen. She needed food. There was one thing she could make well, but she hadn't told Amar or Asmita yet. She found the ghee, semolina and sugar and got to work. Within ten minutes, the aroma of fresh *halwa* greeted her nose, transporting her back home. She didn't bother with a bowl. She took the hot pan outside and sat underneath her mango tree. The *halwa* burnt her fingers, yet her hand couldn't help but pick up clumps and let the buttery sweetness sit on her tongue. She leant back and watched the moon shine down, illuminating their garden. She smiled as she slowly ate each bite of the *halwa*, licking her lips in joy.

As she looked down at the nearly empty pan, she bit her lip. Should she eat all of it? She probably should leave some for Amar and Asmita. She put the pan further away from her body. One more bite won't hurt. She put the pan back onto her lap. She savoured the warm pudding, licking the butter off her hands. There was only a bit left in the pan – not enough for Amar and Asmita to share. Her hand hesitated. She thought back to the day she had just had, and without pause, she scooped up the remaining *halwa* and ate it, her eyes closing in satisfaction. Months of being an obedient wife and begging for Amar and Asmita's approval had taken their toll on her. The small act of making food solely for herself had left her feeling revived.

She leant back against the tree and sighed. Her stomach was comforted by its new arrival and her body relaxed into the grass. If only she could stay out here where it was safe and quiet. Her eyes slowly closed, and she let the darkness wash over her. A time later, they were opened by the sun rising in the lilac sky.

She bolted upright, grabbing the pan. She didn't clean up last night! The tap was nearby so she ran the pan under the water, washing off evidence of her deceit. She ran to the kitchen and hurriedly put the ingredients away. Nobody would ever know about her little betrayal. She couldn't help but smile to herself as she slowly got back into the bed beside Amar.

As she awoke later that morning, her stomach curdled. Maybe it was the *halwa*. A groan escaped her lips as she clasped her hands to her stomach. This didn't feel like a simple case of over-eating. Her throat felt tight and she felt a bead of sweat slide down her face. She rolled onto her side and noticed that she was alone in bed. It was a weekday so Amar must have gone to work. It was funny – she still counted the days and weeks as if she had to complete a prison sentence and would be able to return home once her punishment was over. She still hadn't accepted that this was a life sentence.

The bed creaked precariously as she sat up. The nausea continued to hold her body captive, punishing her for her greed the night before.

She took a few deep breaths and closed her eyes. The sun warmed her face, awakening her body. As she splashed her face and her neck with the water warmed by the sun, she thought of how to approach Asmita today. Maybe she could ask her to go into town with her?

The sound of her footsteps broke the stony silence in the house as she walked back inside to decide which saree to wear. Amar had bought her the most exquisite sarees as a gift for their wedding day as per tradition and she had been saving a few for a nice day. She decided today would be that day. Her hands touched a delicate light-yellow saree with silver embroidery on the border. The colour was as if the artist had added a drop of yellow paint into a pure white and mixed it into the beautiful shade of the dahlias blooming in the garden. The material was light and cool, making it the ideal saree for a day as hot as this one. She scraped her hair back into a ponytail and then plaited it down to the end, tying it with a flower from the garden. She dabbed her lips with a deep red colour which emphasised their thickness. A light brush of kohl on the bottom of her eyelids completed the look and she smiled at her reflection in the mirror.

She strode into the kitchen, her shoulders back and her head held high. She noticed Asmita intently reading a letter.

'What are you reading, Ma?' she asked as she wandered over to the table.

Asmita quickly tucked the letter away, muttering, 'Nothing, nothing,' but not before Meena had seen the delicate penmanship. She would recognise that writing anywhere. Without a second thought, she grabbed the letter and skimmed the beautifully written words. Her fingertips gently touched the parts of illegible ink stained with now dried tears. A letter from home. Her ma's exquisite writing swept across the pages, decorating the paper with words she had been aching to hear.

Why was Asmita reading it? She felt tears spring to her eyes at this invasion of privacy. Yet, she also felt her cheeks warm at the thought of her actions. She had grabbed the letter so abruptly. The paper shook in her hands. She tried to sound out an apology. Yet, seeing her ma's delicate writing took over her senses. Words escaped her. Imagine if she hadn't walked into the room at that moment. Would this letter have remained hidden from her for ever?

'You shouldn't read it. It will make you long for home even more. You already spend half your days in daydreams. I was trying to help you,' she heard Asmita say.

Her mother-in-law's words disappeared into non-existence. All she could see were Asmita's pale lips moving, the sound inaudible. Her body drooped and her eyes blurred. A flashback of her ma's beautiful face and her dad's worrying eyes sprang into her mind. She could almost reach out and stroke her dad's soft, dark, slightly thinning hair and kiss her ma's clear, pillowy cheeks. She attempted to refocus her eyes. Asmita seemed to have stopped talking. Meena felt her lip quiver and whispered a quiet 'sorry'. Before the tsunami of tears fell, she ran out to the garden and knelt under her favourite mango tree. The letter said:

My dearest daughter,

We all miss you so much. Parvathi keeps asking when you are coming home. I explained to her that you have a new home now, with a new mother and a husband. She has asked to visit you in Kenya. I wish we could, but it is dangerous to visit another city, let alone another country under British rule. We might not be allowed back home. Or our home might not be here when we come back. We can't afford the tickets for the ship anyway – your father has already asked around. He misses you more than words can say.

I hope you are cooking nice food for your husband and mother-in-law. I am sorry I didn't show you many domestic duties before you left. I wish I had spent more time showing you how to be a good wife. You are a clever girl; I am sure you'll be just fine. Remember, trust your instinct. You will know how much of each spice to put in.

Your siblings miss you too. Your father has been very down since you left. He just wants to know you are safe and happy in your new home.

Things are OK with us, but the British seem to be becoming more aggressive each day. Our neighbour, Arjun, was found beaten up yesterday. Apparently, he asked the white soldier why he couldn't cross a boundary in his own country. He doesn't realise that this is not our country anymore. It belongs to them.

*We do not own our own vegetables, homes, stock —
nothing. If the white man or woman asks for it, it is
theirs. You are a grown woman now; you need to be
aware of these things. I hope it is not the same in
Kenya. I hope you feel safer there. There is talk we
will become independent soon — let us pray for a
brighter future.*

May God bless you always.
Your family

Her own tears mingled with the dry stains on the letter.
She quickly dried them before the letter was completely
smudged and ruined for ever. Her fingers traced the
words and she read them aloud. Her stomach tightened
at the thought of Asmita reading her private letter. To
take the one thing that was meant for her and invade it.

The sound of laughter carried over the fence. Meena
had always been too afraid to go close to their neighbour's garden. What if somebody saw her? Child-like
giggles prompted her to stand up and walk over to the
fence, her letter from home clutched against her heart.
As she reached the fence, she saw two small girls and
an older boy chasing each other around a tree. One of
the little girls was laughing hysterically, the joy of being
chased by her brother lighting up her face. Meena felt
her own mouth open in a wide smirk as she watched
the siblings play.

Without warning, the laughing girl tripped over a
root and fell hard onto the ground. A sharp cry erupted
from her tiny lungs, and within seconds her brother

had picked her up and was cuddling her close. Meena couldn't understand his words, but she felt comforted by them. His voice was calm and reassuring, and soon the little girl was back on her feet. A yell from inside their house had them running indoors, vanishing on demand. Meena strained her neck, trying to see where they had gone. When would they be back? She stood there for several more minutes, until her tired feet took her back under her tree. She sat alone, cradling her letter to her chest.

She looked at the date on the letter. It was dated a month ago! They must be waiting for a reply. She wondered how many other letters they had sent and Asmita had hidden. She rushed to the house and found paper and ink. As she poured her heart out onto the paper, she felt a burden lift from her shoulders. The letter she was writing felt like a warm embrace, lifting her high off the ground and far away from this place. As she wrote, she let her pent-up emotions escape onto the paper:

Dear family,
I miss you all so much. Your letter made me feel the happiest I've been in a long time. Things are not great here. I feel so lost and alone. Amar is always at work and when he is here, he spends more time with his mother than me. I can barely cook properly still but Asmita taught me how to make aloo bangaan. She was horrible to me afterwards though. I know she hates me. I don't why, but she does. Every move I make is

wrong, every kind word I say she thinks is mischievous. They say more family should be joining us soon. I hope not. Two strangers are enough to live with.

The country is beautiful from what I have seen, but tensions are high here too – I don't think the people like us. I don't know why. I don't really go outside. I feel like I am an unwanted guest in their home. I have heard that the British rule here too. Is there anywhere they don't have power? Why do they take the most beautiful countries for their own?

I wake up every morning feeling sick and go to bed every night with a knot in my stomach. I wish you hadn't sent me here. I miss the smell of home. I miss us all crowding round the table, ready for Ma's amazing dinner. I miss Pa's footsteps approaching the door and the joy on his face when he sees us all excitedly waiting for him. I miss Parvathi more than I miss air in my lungs when I can't breathe. I hope she is studying hard and keeping safe.

I am not happy here. Can't I come home? I will not be a burden. I promise. I'll cook and clean and look after you and Pa and Parvathi, Nita, Himet and Mohan. I'm sure Asmita and Amar won't mind if I explain my family needs me.

Love you all,
Meena

She read her words again. The pain seeped through the paper, staining whatever surface it was on. The letter reeked of embarrassment, fear and hurt. She gently stroked its pages and pushed it away from her. She got a new piece of paper and began again:

Dear family,

Thank you for your letter. I miss you all so much, but I am happy here with my new family. They treat me well.

The country is lovely. There is tension here too. I have learnt a bit of Swahili; it is such a beautiful language, like Hindi. I hope to teach you all someday. I learnt it by overhearing conversations and writing the words out in the notebook you gave me. I look the words up in a book I found in the house that translates Hindi, English and Swahili. It's hard but I sound the words out every night to help me remember. I am hoping to become fluent in it so I can go out alone and see more of Nairobi.

Asmita taught me how to make aloo bangaan. It was not as good as your cooking, Ma.

I miss you all.

Love,

Meena

She read the new letter and sighed. She would send this one. Under the mango tree she felt warm and safe, her pa's strong arms around her once again, the smell of her ma's hugs tickling her nose. She would never forget the last hug her ma had given her the day after she had married Amar.

Her mind replayed clips from that day, like a film reel in her mind. Her ma had sewed her the most beautiful saree she had ever seen. A stunning deep red, the colour of the sky after a monsoon had passed and the night was beginning, with delicate gold embroidery creating a border around the gorgeous silk material. The fall of the saree had elaborate gold threadwork of flowers, paisleys and peacocks adorning it. The blouse had three-quarter-length sleeves and a slight v-neckline. She had barely believed her ma had spent so much money and time creating something so beautiful for her. She had cried tears of gratitude, weeping into her ma's arms, the reality hitting her. She was to wear this magnificent saree on her wedding day. The chunni would cover her hair and face, protecting her modesty and ensuring she didn't see her husband properly until after the nuptials. The blouse would protect her bosom, the material wrapped around her like a prison.

A sharp rip startled her into a sitting position. An ostrich had wandered into the backyard again and was silently chomping a portion of her saree, which was unravelling off her body onto the grass. She must have forgotten to pin it the way her ma had taught her. She cried out and flung her arms until the ostrich wandered off. Her beautiful yellow saree ruined on its first wear. She clasped at the material, trying to hold it together. It couldn't be ruined. Not so soon.

Grabbing her letters, she gathered her saree and walked back into the house. Silence penetrated the walls. She was grateful for the loneliness. She carefully unravelled the saree off her body, anxious not to cause even more damage. When she had first arrived at the house, she had set up her sewing machine, a parting gift from her ma. The beautiful Singer had been expensive, but her father had managed to get it cheaper at the market. She had made more back from it than it cost anyway. Her sewing skills had meant that nobody in her family had to sacrifice a meal. It had been a lifeboat for them.

Her sewing machine was one of the very few items she had been allowed to bring here with her. She had begged her parents to be allowed to take it with her but neither had initially agreed. They didn't have the money for a new one. Yet, as she had bade her farewells to her siblings and parents, before leaving for Kenya, her ma had presented her with her sewing machine, carefully wrapped in protective sheets. Meena had gently set it down on the floor, and had hugged her ma tighter than she ever had before. She stared down at the machine, thinking of all the items her ma had created on it. She held back tears and cleared her mind. Her ma needed the machine to sew for her siblings and to make money. She didn't need it. Moments later, she picked up the machine. Her hands trembled as she held the machine out, asking her ma to take it. Her ma refused, her arms not moving from her side. Her father had taken the machine from her hands and set it down on the floor. His arms engulfed her as he whispered in her ear: 'Nothing in this world is more valuable than your happiness. I hope you think of us and our love for you every time you use this machine. Never stop sewing, *beti*.'

She had cradled the sewing machine close to her throughout the long boat journey to Kenya.

Chapter Three

Meena sat at the machine; her foot hovered over the pedal. She leant forward and breathed in its aroma. It still had the smell of home on it. She rested her forehead on it and closed her eyes. She wished she could capture this smell in a bottle and hold onto it for ever.

She breathed in through her nose and let out a deep sigh. If anybody could fix this saree, it was her. She inserted the material into the sewing machine and began to stitch the life back into the garment and her soul. The sound of the machine comforted her overactive heartbeat and relieved the ache in her stomach. The gentle whirring brought her back to simpler times, sewing in her parents' living room, her sisters dancing to their favourite Hindi songs on the radio. '*Na jane kya hai dil ka raaz,*' she began singing, the words flowing out of her as naturally as if she had written the song herself. As she finished up the seam, Asmita strolled into the room.

'Do you have no shame?' she shrieked. 'Sitting there, half naked! Imagine if someone passing by or a neighbour saw you?'

Meena jumped up from the chair. She took a deep

breath and calmed her thumping heart.

'I am inside the house, no one can see me. Plus, I am covered,' she stated, her voice croaking.

She winced as her voice betrayed her. She cleared her throat and stood taller. Moments passed as Asmita stared at her. Meena felt her face begin to weaken and her body begin to sink into itself. She felt Asmita's eyes trail over her body. As she crumbled, she saw Asmita's eyes shine.

'Wait until Amar hears how his wife is flaunting herself to the world,' Asmita said, her chin quivering with excitement.

She strutted out of the room with an over-exaggerated bounce in her walk. Meena felt the tears escape in a flood down her face, staining the corner of her saree with salt water tinged with black kohl. She scolded herself for her own weakness. Why was she so incapable of standing up for herself?

She looked around the room. The wooden bed gathering dust in the corner, the cupboards filled with unknown items. The rug which she hadn't even noticed before. All the items in this room belonged to Asmita and Amar. Even, technically, her sewing machine. The day she had married Amar, she had accepted that everything she owned was now his.

Her stomach churned, and she felt bile rise to her throat. She ran to the bathroom, and everything poured out of her. Her tears of despair intertwined with the involuntary tears that were prompted by her stomach. Her throat burnt with the taste of vomit. She had barely even eaten today. What was there left to come out? She lay on the floor, unable to move or feel anything other than complete hopelessness. She thought about packing her bags and leaving. She didn't have much to take. She could be gone within an hour. These thoughts littered her mind, yet her body stayed still on the bathroom floor.

Her eyelids fluttered and closed as the patterned linoleum tiles swallowed her whole.

Parvathi snuggled into her armpit, so close to her it was as if they were one being, breathing with the same lungs, thinking with the same brain.

'Promise me you won't go, Meena didi. Promise me you won't leave me alone,' Parvathi whispered in her ear.

The tears pricked her eyes and she felt a warmth in her chest.

'Ma says I must go, Parvathi, I don't have a choice. You will be OK; I am the one who will be alone.'

Her kameez felt damp from Parvathi's muffled cries. 'Let's run away. We can be together then. We will come back and visit them one day. They would welcome us back once they realise how horrible life is without us,' Parvathi exclaimed, jumping up with excitement at the prospect of finding a solution.

They both hatched a plot to escape at dawn before their parents and siblings had woken up. They decided they would pack only the essentials — clothes, food and some money. They could figure out the rest. Meena knew in her bones that the idea was stupid and reckless. Where would they go? They would end up in the street as untouchables; or worse, trafficked by the white men. She had seen it all before. Stories flitted around the village on a weekly basis of the treatment of young Indian girls by British soldiers. She would never let Parvathi be treated like that.

She could not put Parvathi in danger; even the thought of it sent goosebumps down her spine, making the thick hairs at the nape of her neck stand on edge. She would rather endure a lifetime of imprisonment in a stranger's house than see her baby sister get hurt.

Parvathi mumbled in her sleep. A surge of power coursed through Meena's veins. She refused to be the girl who was sent away to another country. The girl whose parents were so ashamed of her they didn't even want her on the same continent as them. The girl whose parents had paid another family to take her away. She wondered what her dahej had been – the payment made from the bride's family to the groom's family at the time of marriage. Her family didn't have much; her future husband's family must have been desperate. Whatever it had been, they could surely get it back. She wasn't marrying that man.

She untangled herself from Parvathi, being careful not to wake her. Luckily, her sister was a heavy sleeper. She tiptoed across the room, careful to avoid her other sister's mattress on the floor. Nita was not as heavy a sleeper as Parvathi. She hastily grabbed her schoolbag, weaved by her mother's hand, and slipped out the door. Step one complete.

She knew some money was kept near the mandir, so she snuck outside to their tiny homemade mandir and took the money that was kept there, silently praying for Vishnu's forgiveness. She would pay her parents back one day. Maybe

35

once her novel was published and she was a successful writer.

The last mission was to take food from the kitchen. As she made it to the kitchen, she let out a sigh of relief. No one had heard her.

The glow of the candle was dim, and she struggled to see what food was left on the counter. She put the candle down on the table and lit another one with it. As she settled the second candle down, her eyes noticed something staring at her. She leapt up with sheer fear, nearly dropping the candle and engulfing the kitchen in orange and red flames. Her hands shook as she stared into her ma's tear-ridden eyes, knowing that her last chance of freedom had vanished as quickly as it had appeared.

'I knew you would come down here eventually. Looking for food for your long journey ahead. A journey that would probably lead to your death. I hoped you wouldn't be so stupid, but I know how strong-willed and stubborn you are, Meena.' Her ma spoke with tears running down her face. Meena stared in shock at her ma, words escaping her.

Neither of them uttered another word for what felt like days. What was there to say? Meena felt overwhelmed with shame and fear. Tears fell in an endless stream down her face, drowning her soul until she felt like there was no life left in her. No will to fight. Her mother's voice startled her.

'You don't think I did the same? When I was even younger than you, I was already married to your pa. I had no idea who he was or what he looked like. I was told the day before my wedding day. I married in a plain saree with fear in my heart. I tried to leave that night. My ma knew and she waited for me just as I have waited for you. I hope one day things *change and women have different lives. I hoped we could find a way for you to stay with us, to fulfil your dream of writing. That isn't reality for us, Meena. We don't have money. We don't have power. I can't give you the life you want, even if it is the life you deserve. For now, this is our culture. This is what we do. I love your father now, see? Without him, I wouldn't have you and my other wonderful children. I am thankful to my ma for stopping me from running that day. I hope one day you are thankful to me too.'*

A gentle arm pulled her in tight. The softness of her ma's hug was like a warm blanket wrapped around her, shielding her from the scary world beyond their small home. A world she would soon enter and would never be able to leave.

Meena was awoken by the harsh slam of a door. Why did she keep falling asleep everywhere? In the past week she had felt so drained and ill that every movement seemed to take all the energy out of her. She quickly stood up. Within moments, the room became a carousel around her, spinning so fast she didn't know if she would ever be able to get off. She splashed her face with water from the bucket and walked out of the bathroom. Amar's distinct voice echoed through the house. Her hands tightened into fists. She was strong. She could handle anything.

As she walked out to the porch, the fresh air relieved her headache. Amar was sitting on the rocking chair, nursing a hot cup of chai. His mother was nowhere to be seen.

'My dear,' he said, his eyes crinkling with happiness.

Meena hesitantly sat by his feet and Amar kissed her head.

'I'm glad you're home,' Meena whispered, hugging his lean legs.

His eyes looked down to meet hers. She saw his mouth move as if to say something; then he closed it. A second later, with worry in his eyes, he sighed and asked: 'Are you liking it here?'

The words almost tripped over themselves in her head. There was so much she could say. This was her chance to tell her husband how she felt. She looked up at him. His eyes sparkled in the sunshine.

'I'm OK. Well, maybe I am just a bit lonely,' she muttered.

'Don't worry, my sister will be coming to live with us soon. You will love her.' His voice softened even more at the mention of his sister. She wondered how close they were.

If she were anything like Asmita, then Meena would die of despair.

She had heard stories about Lakshmi, Amar's beautiful younger sister. She looked like a Bollywood star in the photos he had of her. In every picture, Amar had his arm around his sister, both of them beaming at the camera.

'Shall we eat?' Amar asked, after minutes of blissful silence had passed.

She froze. She hadn't made anything.

'Um, OK,' she whispered, slowly walking through the porch to the kitchen.

The red floor tiles felt too hot underneath her feet. She walked over to the stove and hoped there was by some miracle a pot of *sabzi*. Alas, there was nothing. Her face felt as if she had lit a match and the flickering flames were scorching her skin. She turned to Amar.

He looked at her, his eyes unreadable. 'How about we cook something together? I got home a little earlier from work today. We have time.'

The shock left her speechless, words failing to fall out of her mouth. She had never seen Amar cook in all the months she had been here. In fact, he had often voiced his disapproval when she hadn't cooked for him. However, that was when Asmita had been watching over them, her eyes following their every move.

'Don't look at me like that,' he said with a smirk, 'I know my way around a *sabzi*.' She stared in confusion as Amar expertly sliced onions, chillies and ginger before lightly frying them in ghee. 'Carrots or green beans?' he inquired, his face flushed with the heat of the stove.

'Carrots, please,' she said, unsure of what exactly was happening. Months of her being told to cook, yet here Amar was, an experienced cook!

He took her hand as they walked out to the vegetable patch in the garden. They both picked some ripe carrots and walked back to the kitchen in silence. Amar carefully chopped the carrots and added them to the onion mix in the pan. After a tornado of various spices joined the pan, Amar left it to cook and sat down at the table.

'I can make *rotis*?' Meena gingerly asked, hoping he would say no. She hated making *rotis* – who decided they had to be round, anyway?

'We'll have rice. Don't worry,' he stated, his eyes glinting as if he had seen her exact thoughts.

Meena sat at the table beside him, wondering where Asmita had gone.

'She has gone to a friend's house,' Amar said. How did he read her mind like that? 'I think things have been a bit . . . tense here. Lakshmi arrives in a few days – things will be better then. I promise.'

Meena smiled at the thought. Another woman in the house around her age. She shook her head. This was Asmita's daughter. She wouldn't be a replacement sister.

As Amar stood up to make the rice, she saw how life could be. Just her and Amar living in their own home, no arguments, no pain, just love. She could imagine it so vividly, it almost felt real. This was what marriage should be. Two people enjoying each other's company, working together. As she watched him clean the rice, she felt an urge to stand up. Surely, she should be cooking for him. He had been at work all day. Yet, she made no move to help him, but sat comfortably watching her husband make her dinner.

Chapter Four

Days passed and the air felt electric with anticipation. Amar had littered the house with the most beautiful fresh flowers, creating a mix of aromas that made Meena's head spin. A room had been prepared, Meena and Asmita working together in stony silence. However, Meena couldn't help but notice Asmita eagerly looking towards the front door with a glow on her face.

A car carrying Lakshmi's belongings had arrived in the morning with a driver, and Meena and Asmita had spent the afternoon arranging the exquisite sarees into order. Meena marvelled at the various textures – silks, satins, chiffon, lace, cotton, velvet. Dazzling colours that glimmered in the sunlight and diamonds that sparkled in the dark – clearly expensive sarees. What looked to be boxes of gold jewellery joined the collection of sarees.

Amar had been up late the night before, checking everything was in order.

'Meena, did you check we have enough food?'

'Yes, Amar, I checked. We do.'

'Good, thank you. Is the bathroom clean?'

'Yes, I cleaned it.'

'Good. I just want everything perfect for Lakshmi.'

'Amar, how long has Lakshmi been married?'

'Oh, about a year or two.'

'Why did she move to India?'

'The same reason you moved here. Her husband Rajvir lives there.'

'So, why are they coming here?'

Amar gave an exaggerated sigh as if she were a child asking for candy.

'There are opportunities here for business. Her husband is a businessman; he makes good money.'

'Can she speak Swahili?'

'Of course she can, Meena, she was born here.'

'Did she mind moving to India?'

'What is it with all the questions? Surely you can ask her yourself tomorrow.'

Meena looked down and picked at the small cuts on her hands that had almost healed. A few minutes later she heard Amar sigh.

'Come, sit next to me.'

Meena hesitantly got up and sat on the edge of the bed.

'Lakshmi was heartbroken about leaving Nairobi. This was all she had ever known. However, she is very strong. She fulfilled her duty and moved to India without any fuss. She has embraced life there – she goes outside, she made friends.'

'How did your ma handle Lakshmi moving away?'

Amar shifted and closed the magazine that had lain open on his lap.

'She found it . . . difficult. Lakshmi has a lot of similarities to my father. When Lakshmi left it must have felt like losing a part of him again. I know there have been some tensions between the two of you, Meena. I am not blind. However, she is my mother. This is her house. She has withstood a lot of pain in life and now, I want her to be comfortable. Do you understand that?'

Meena nodded slightly, forcing the frown away from her face.

'Lakshmi will arrive tomorrow evening. You'll have a sister to talk to. You're family. You and Lakshmi will get along so well. I promise.'

Amar got under the covers, signalling that the conversation was over. The sun was beginning to set, and the village was cast in a golden glow.

Tomorrow she would go outside of the boundaries of this house. Her mind had prevented her from living her life for far too long. She needed to prove to herself that she could be just as fearless as she had been back home.

As dawn approached, she felt her stomach churn. The thought of leaving the house knotted her intestines into a tight ball, causing waves of nausea to crash over her. She heard Amar get out of the bed and his footsteps echo through the house. Today was the day.

After she washed, she put on her saree and sandals, and let her hair loose from the tight plaits it had been held captive in all night. It was time to see the city she had lived in for months. The city that was now her home. It was late morning and the sun burnt bright in the sky, almost enticing her to see where else it shone. As she took a deep breath, ready to explore a new place, Amar walked into the room.

'Are you OK?' he asked, his eyes taking in her long flowing hair and barely worn sandals.

'I am going out,' she stated, her hands placed on her hips.

Amar stared at her in silence, the idea marinating in his mind.

'Do you want me to come with you?' he carefully asked, his eyes fearful.

She paused. Why hadn't this crossed her mind? The word 'yes' danced on the edge of her tongue. The sound of Asmita singing in the next room made her decision for her.

'No, I am fine. I will be back later.'

She gave him a brief kiss on the cheek as she left the room, sensing his eyes follow her out the door. She couldn't help but smile to herself at the thought of Amar's bewildered expression. Now the question was – where should she go?

She left the front garden, wandering out into a long stretch of road. Left or right? A sign nearby was in English with Swahili written in smaller letters below. She hadn't seen English words in a while, but she was excited at the prospect of challenging herself to remember. She slowly sounded out the words until she understood what they said. 'Fruit and vegetable market' with an arrow pointing left. 'Swimming pool' with an arrow pointing right. 'Shopping mall' with an arrow pointing straight ahead. As she finished reading the final word, she gave a little jump in the air. She had remembered! She could still read English!

She decided to go left towards the fruit and vegetable market. Although Amar liked to grow some vegetables in the garden, they were limited in what they had. She began walking down the dusty road, breathing in the particles as if it was fresh crisp air. She tripped slightly over a bump in the road. She quickly looked around to see if anybody had seen. Of course nobody had seen; she was alone! The thought made her erupt in a fit of giggles. She could trip as many times as she liked!

She walked along the quiet road, taking in the neighbouring homes. They all looked like hers, with neat front gardens and surrounding trees. These houses were unbelievable compared to her home in India. She couldn't believe Kenyans lived in such beautiful homes which weren't piled on top of each other. Each one had surrounding space with trees, flowers and grass. At home, their neighbour's house had practically sat on top of theirs; every word, noise and clatter had been audible. Despite this, you would rarely see a neighbour in their own home – they spent more time visiting other neighbours. Here she rarely heard a peep from any of the houses, each living in their own space and time. As she walked past one particular house, she noticed a lady watering the flowers at the front. She stopped and stared, stunned that another Indian family lived so close by.

The lady looked up and shielded her eyes from the sun. Meena was frozen, unsure of what to do. Should she turn around and pretend she hadn't seen her? She couldn't go back home already. The lady stood on her tiptoes and waved to Meena. Uncertainty gripping her stomach, Meena slowly began walking over to this mysterious desi woman with gorgeous wavy hair flowing down to her hips.

'*Namaste*,' Meena whispered.

The woman stared quietly at her for a second. Suddenly she replied '*Namaste*,' in a voice so loud it made up for Meena's whisper. 'What brings you here then? Do you live around here?' she inquired, speaking a mixture of Hindi and English but with an underlying distinct Punjabi accent.

'Yes, I live down the road,' Meena stated, trying to mimic this woman's enticing mixture of accents.

The desi woman looked at her with an expression of amusement and puzzlement.

'What brings you to this country? You look like you've just come off the boat.'

Meena felt her cheeks burn. She took a step backwards and looked towards the road she had just been walking on. Suddenly, a strong arm was around her, guiding her to sit on the neatly mowed front lawn of this stranger's house.

'Sit,' the woman said, gesturing to the ground.

She disappeared into the house and Meena stared back at the road, only a few steps away from her. It was quite close . . . but before she could finish the thought the lady had returned with a pitcher of water.

'Drink,' she said handing her a glass. 'I did not mean to offend you with my comment. I could just tell you weren't from here. Now tell me your story, *beti*. I can tell you have one.'

Meena took a sip of water, and then the words flew out of her as if she had been holding her breath for months and she could finally exhale.

'I have lived here for nearly eight months now. I woke up one day in my home with my parents and siblings. Days later I was on a ship with a husband I didn't know.' She wept as she continued speaking. 'Each day I feel like I'm walking on eggshells, afraid to ruin the order of the house. Afraid of what will happen to me if I do something really wrong.'

'You may be a wife, Meena, but you are also a person. A human being. A woman. You have your own needs and dreams.'

'Those are a thing of the past. My husband and his mother's needs are what matter now.'

As she talked, the sky began to darken, and the stickiness of the day drifted away. The mystery lady barely uttered a word the whole time, letting Meena speak freely. As Meena's voice tailed off, she gazed into the lady's eyes. She saw her own reflection staring back at her: the grief, the fear, the hope all echoed in this stranger's almond eyes. Moments of comfortable, familiar silence ensued, and the ladies sat underneath the moringa tree, feeling at peace, their hands entwined. Meena felt her shoulders relax and her hands naturally unclench. The mysterious lady broke the silence.

'My name is Shruti. I have a similar story to you, however mine is somewhat darker. I grew up in Amritsar in the Punjab with my parents and an older brother. I was ten years old when I lost both of my parents in the Jallianwala Bagh massacre. My brother and I survived, although my brother was left paralysed by a gunshot wound in his spine.' Tears flowed without grace down her face, soaking her salwar kameez within minutes, the kohl around her eyes creating black smears down her face. 'My mum's brother decided to take me in, but he refused to accept my brother. My brother was left to beg on the streets, and he died only four months later. He had seen a shipment of fresh mangoes arrive and hunger had blinded him. He decided to steal a box. At the most, he expected he might be caught and told off. He didn't realise the mangoes were to be sent to a British sergeant major's wife. He was sent to a prison where he died of malnourishment.

'I did not know this at the time. I grew up with a hole in my heart and an anger in my blood that has never weakened. I searched for my brother for years. When I finally discovered what had happened to him, I wanted revenge. I wanted to see them pay for the lives they took.'

By this point Shruti's body was shaking with rage, tears of sadness turned into tears of outrage. Meena's eyes flowed with the same tears. She had heard about the 1919 Jallianwala Bagh massacre but had been lucky enough to have avoided losing anyone in it. The pictures of the dead bodies had been enough to cause her nightmares for months. As she looked at Shruti's face, she saw the bitterness in it, the pain that would never fade. She couldn't dare to think what it would be like to lose someone you love is such a horrifying way.

Shruti took several deep breaths and continued in a calmer tone, 'When I turned thirteen my uncle said it was time to marry me off. I was only a child. He claimed he could not look after me anymore, that he had been stripped of his resources and had nothing left. That was a partial truth. The whole truth was that the only reason he took me in was to sell me. One day later, I was married to a man fifteen years older than me. That man brought me here when I was seventeen years old, claiming he wanted us to start a happier life here.'

Shruti collected herself again. 'Anyway, ten months ago, my husband disappeared, and I have not seen or heard from him since. I just continue to live in this house and look after the plants. After three months I realised I had run out of money, so I asked around and managed to get a job tending to the crops with a dozen or so Kenyan women. Now here I am, alone in this house.'

Meena was in utter disbelief. How could one woman go through so much pain and still be so . . . alive?

'Do you plan on staying here? Where is your husband?' She had so many questions.

Shruti smiled. 'No, I am going back to India soon. My uncle is sick, and he has written asking me to return to look after him in his final days. I will then live in his house after he has gone. This country is beautiful, but it is not home. We moved here because of the British colony but I refuse to be removed from my own country. This is not my home.

'Also, I do not know if my husband is dead, kidnapped or having an affair. I do not care. I never loved him. I think he met someone new here. He was coming home later and later, sometimes staying out all night. I never asked why. I am content being alone.'

Her absolute honesty and lack of affection for her husband caused Meena to lean away from Shruti. How could you not care about the person you were married to? She blinked quickly and stood up, pins and needles crawling up her legs. She set her hands into a prayer and bowed to Shruti.

'I hope you find peace and joy back home. I should go back to my husband now, but it was lovely meeting you.'

Shruti rose too and gave Meena a deep hug.

'Meena, may you have a life filled with love and happiness. I hope you find everything you are looking for.'

As Meena walked away, she realised she had not even explored the city. She had only walked ten minutes down the road. Yet, she felt she had learnt more in the last hour than she had ever learnt before. She continued to walk down the road, her feet aimlessly wandering. Thoughts littered her mind and she continued in a straight line, with no sense of time until she saw the sky begin to darken and the moon begin to make its daily appearance.

As she walked up the front garden, she saw Amar's silhouette on the porch. 'Where have you been? We have been worried sick. It's been hours! You could have been hurt.'

He drew her into a hug, and she felt her knees give way. Her body leant into his. If her husband disappeared and never returned, she would be completely lost in this world.

Their tight embrace was broken by the shrill of Asmita's voice. 'Where did you go? I almost had a heart attack worrying. You must never leave like that again.'

Meena closed her eyes as she felt Amar move away from her, towards his mother.

'I'm OK. I just went for a walk and met a neighbour. I didn't even go far.'

Amar's eyes brimmed with questions that she knew he would ask when they were alone.

'Come, you must be tired,' Amar said as he led her into the house.

Asmita trailed behind them, her footsteps serving as a reminder of her presence.

'Night, Ma,' Amar said as he closed their bedroom door.

Meena spun around at the sound of the door closing. Amar usually spent most evenings with his mother, sitting together and talking or watching the television. Meena often tried to be with them, perched on the couch, or sitting on the floor if there was no room.

Meena sat on the bed and explained what had happened, eliminating everything she had told Shruti about Asmita and her sadness here. Amar listened quietly, drinking in the story with his deep almond eyes. As she finished the story, he hugged her close.

'Stories like hers are becoming more common. A few men at work haven't come back. Kenyans and Indians.

We all assumed they had found something better, but we fear it might be worse. Your new friend could be in trouble if she is found bad-mouthing the British so carelessly. No matter what they have done, they rule our countries. We need to respect that.'

As she got under the covers next to Amar, Meena's mind was alive with the experiences of the day. Jallianwala Bagh. Disappearances. Independence. She fell asleep with these thoughts playing on repeat in her mind.

The vivid sun opened her eyes. The space next to her was empty. Amar must have got up early. As she rubbed the sleep out of her eyes, she darted upright. Today was the day Lakshmi would arrive. Distant voices travelled to her room. They were here already. She had already planned her outfit, eager to impress Amar's glamorous sister. In a hurry, she splashed some water from the bucket onto her face and quickly wrapped the saree around her. Years of experience and trying on her mum's sarees in private led her to being well-versed in the art of dressing herself in haste, the intricacy of the saree not slowing her at all. She combed her hair in the mirror and effortlessly plaited her hair. She wished she had woken up earlier to prepare better. She didn't look half as beautiful as she had hoped she would.

She took a deep breath and walked through the hallway into the front porch. As her eyes landed on Lakshmi, she took a sharp intake of breath. This woman standing a few feet away was breathtakingly beautiful with a grace that could not be feigned. Meena automatically fixed her posture, suddenly even more aware of her slightly bulging tummy and frizzy hair. Beside the beauty was her husband Rajvir, a slightly older man with an air of power. He had a rigid posture with a mouth that didn't appear to open. He looked like he was trapped in a foreign country and was looking for an escape, while trying to look an inconspicuous as possible. Maybe she had looked the same when she had first arrived. Her eyes drifted back to the silhouette coming closer to her.

All of a sudden, she was right in front of her, even more captivating up close.

'You must be Meena! Wow, you are even more beautiful than the photos,' she said, laughter spilling out of her mouth. Meena hadn't heard genuine pure laughter in a while. She hugged Lakshmi back in an embrace that felt like home.

Lakshmi linked her arm with Meena's and walked towards the house. 'How are you finding it here, Meena?' she inquired, her eyes fixated on Meena's face.

She kept her gaze down, averting Lakshmi's intuitive gaze. 'I am finding it fine, thank you. How was your journey?'

'It was fine! Long but glad to be back home. Amar, where are you?' she called, her breath quickening in excitement.

Amar came bounding out, his face a picture of joy. The siblings embraced and Meena couldn't help but feel a tug in her chest. Her mind wandered to Parvathi. She would do anything to hug her sister close.

She followed them all into the kitchen and braced herself for this new chapter.

Chapter Five

The next morning, she awoke to voices excitedly chattering – a noise she hadn't awoken to since leaving home. The gorgeous aroma of freshly brewed chai teased her nostrils, causing her mind to wake up faster than usual. However, she could also smell the scent of butter and *aloo* (potato) which caused her stomach to churn. Usually, those smells brought her comfort but today they caused waves of nausea. She gingerly sat up and took a few deep breaths. As she swung her legs off the bed, she felt the room spin. She stood up wearily. When she looked down at the floor, she noticed her feet looked slightly bigger. She rubbed her eyes and looked again. They were a bit swollen. She decided to soak her feet with salt later. Her ma always said that was the cure for bad feet.

As soon as she took a step, her stomach betrayed her, and she ran to the bathroom just in time. She had never been a sick child. What was happening to her? As she washed out her mouth and cleaned her face, she looked at her reflection. Her large dark eyes looked withdrawn and puffy, as if she hadn't slept in days. Her usually full, pink lips now looked pale and dry. Her once smooth, caramel skin appeared almost translucent, giving her the appearance of a ghost.

She smoothed down her hair, combing her fingers through the knotted ends. A clump of thick brown hair was left in her hand. How had that happened? She felt around her scalp and a few more strands came out. She held her hands on her head, as if to prevent whatever was remaining from also falling out.

What was happening to her body? Was she sick? Maybe she had a disease. She didn't even know how hospitals or doctors worked in this country. Just as she decided to examine the rest of her body to see what else was amiss, she heard footsteps approaching.

A knock sounded on the door.

'Are you all right, Meena? We made *aloo paratha*. Are you ready to eat?'

Lakshmi's voice eased Meena's distress, but the clump of hair was still in her hand. She attempted to quieten her sobs, afraid her voice would betray her. Suddenly the door opened, and Lakshmi stood in the doorway.

'What's wrong, Meena? Come here,' she said and captured her in a tight embrace.

As she stepped away from Lakshmi, Meena noticed her eyes taking in the strands of hair that had fallen to the floor, her pale skin, the remnants of vomit in the bucket. She wondered how she must look to this perfect stranger. A woman who looked elegant and sophisticated compared to her crumpled reflection.

'Come. We need to sit.'

Lakshmi led her to her bedroom and sat Meena down. Amar's voice boomed down the hallway, asking where they were. Meena closed her eyes and let herself sink into the bed. She heard Lakshmi's footsteps retreat into the kitchen. Muffled voices flowed from the kitchen and soon Lakshmi's footsteps returned.

'Meena, have you not been feeling well lately?'

Meena looked up into Lakshmi's eyes, confused at the question. It was just one time. Well, maybe more than one. This was maybe the second or third time she had been physically sick – on the other occasions she had felt nauseated, but the feeling had passed eventually. She knew the nausea was a result of being away from home and her family. Feeling isolated. Alone. Abandoned.

She had also had spells of dizziness but again, that was because of how unhappy she had been here. That did not mean she was unwell. Lakshmi put her hand on Meena's stomach and Meena cringed away. She knew she had put on a bit of weight during the last month; it was only natural when she was no longer running around with her sisters. Lakshmi took Meena's hands in her hers and squeezed.

'I think you have a baby inside you, *choti*. I think you are pregnant.'

Meena's eyes widened. She felt her stomach somersault. Lakshmi rubbed her hand down her back, and Meena felt herself gradually begin to relax.

She closed her eyes to stop the room from spinning around her. She breathed in and opened her eyes.

The roundabout was going even faster, the room a blur around her. She wanted to get off. She needed to get off.

She had heard the way her parents spoke about the pregnant girls in the village. Though, those were the unmarried ones. She was married. Amar. She had to tell him.

As she looked at Lakshmi's hands cradling her tummy, she felt tears sting her eyes. How should she feel? She had always mothered her baby sisters but that was different from *actually* being a mother. An image of her own mother appeared, and the spinning of the room began to slow. She smiled at the joy her mother would feel at the prospect of a granddaughter.

She felt her face redden at the thought of a daughter. Why had she assumed she would be having a daughter? Yet, as she looked down at her stomach, she couldn't help but begin to pray for a baby girl.

Lakshmi's hand on her back brought her back to reality. This baby was not just hers. It was theirs. A boy could carry the family name, bring respect and money to the household. A girl could cook and clean but then she would marry into another family. They would have to pay someone just to marry her. Still, the thought of a baby girl. Her own little princess.

This world was cruel for girls. It expected everything from them but gave them nothing in return. It broke their backs, while expecting them to hold the world on their shoulders. It told them to be brave in emotion but weak in strength, to be smart enough to cook at home but not smart enough to earn money cooking. It told them to be beautiful but not to show that beauty to the world, only to their husband. It told them to be desirable but frigid, maternal but not emotional, hard-working but not a worker. These thoughts took her back to a memory long buried in her mind.

She was sitting outside with Parvathi, the smell of the chai drifting into their noses. As the chai man called out 'Chai, chai, one rupee, chai,' Parvathi had looked at her with tears in her eyes.

'Didi,' she said, 'the girls at school were talking about something.'

Meena had waited for the rest, but Parvathi was looking at her, expecting a cue to continue. 'Carry on,' Meena said, worry shaking her voice. Parvathi was never like this; she was always a vibrant, chatty girl with a dry wit. She rarely saw even a hint of fear in her baby sister's eyes, yet now they were clouded with it.

'Rahul said his mum had a baby in her tummy. When the baby came out as a girl they cried. Rahul said he never saw the baby again. He said his parents had to get rid of her because they couldn't afford a girl. I don't know what they did to her, but she's gone. Why would they do that to her, Meena? Why wouldn't they want a girl?'

Parvathi's round cheeks were stained with tears, and she was holding on tight to Meena's leg. Meena didn't know what to say. She was only a child herself; she knew little of what the world was like for boys instead of girls. She had heard rumours of people disposing of their babies if they were girls, but it all had seemed a game to scare the girls in the playground. This story sounded real. It sounded terrifying.

Hearing the fear in Parvathi's voice told her there was truth to this story. Parvathi didn't fall for things easily. She wasn't like Meena; Parvathi was resilient and strong-willed. She held Parvathi close, not wanting to lie to her but also not wanting to scare her.

'Do you think Ma wanted to hurt us?' As Parvathi muttered those words, Meena's ma walked out into the street looking for them. She saw the shock and pain in her ma's eyes and knew straight away how much her mother loved them. She would never hurt them simply because they were born female. Her ma walked back into the house, at a speed Meena had never seen. Parvathi was still entangled in Meena's legs and hadn't noticed.

'Come on, we should go inside. Ma would never hurt us. She doesn't believe these things. It's all fun and games anyway. Rahul just wanted to scare you.' Meena wondered if lying to her sister was the best thing to do. Parvathi would grow up one day. She might even have to experience it if she had a baby girl, and her husband didn't want one. Meena reasoned that she would have years to figure things out herself and then tell Parvathi when she knew for sure. There was no point scaring a child when she was barely sure of the truth herself.

Meena led her little sister into the house, a feeling of nausea in her stomach. The smell of a nearby burning prickled her nose. She knew that they burnt dead bodies in their culture; she had seen the processions on the streets. She had even seen a glimpse of a burning when she was younger. Maybe Rahul's baby sister hadn't been born alive. Maybe something had gone wrong, and she had died after she had come out. Maybe they had no choice but to burn her. But just as she had convinced herself of that truth, her mind switched to the alternative. How could someone hurt their baby? That day, she swore to herself that if she ever became pregnant and had a girl, she would treasure her for ever.

As they walked into the house, her ma called them into the main room. Trepidation filled the air as Meena and Parvathi stared at their mother. With a tight jaw, their ma turned to them, a stony look in her eyes that Meena had never seen before. Their mother paused and stated, 'I love you girls just as much as I love your brothers. You are all my babies. I would never hurt any of you. What other families do to their baby girls is something I dread to think about. In this house, we do not discuss these things. You are all my children, and I chose to love all of you. Your father's family may not have been supportive of me having daughters but we have never doubted our love for any of you. Now, never speak of this again.' She swept out of the room and left Meena and Parvathi in awe. Meena silently thanked God for blessing her with such incredible parents. Parvathi switched back to her usual self within minutes, at peace, knowing she was loved. Meena didn't stop thinking about Rahul's baby sister for months after. Every night she included that baby in her prayers. Every night she swore she would love her daughter for eternity, should she ever have one.

Lakshmi calling her name brought Meena back to the present. She noticed that her belly was now free of Lakshmi's hands, and she was sitting alone, with Lakshmi walking around the room. She observed how Lakshmi's footsteps quickly gathered pace as her forehead wrinkled, but then slowed as her face relaxed. This dance continued for several minutes, and soon Meena felt her own thoughts take over.

Her hand rested on her stomach. She gently squeezed. She didn't feel anything. She moved her hands around, circling her stomach. Suddenly, she felt a slight movement. She quickly put her hands back on that part of her stomach and pressed. Another miniscule movement. So tiny that she could have been imagining it.

Images flashed through her mind. A child. A little baby. One that looked like her and Amar, encompassing both of their best features. A tiny, perfect little doll to play with for ever. She felt her heartbeat quicken and her palms sweat. She was broken out of her trance by the sound of Lakshmi's voice.

'We need to check if you are pregnant or just sick, Meena. A lot of women have the signs of pregnancy but are just unwell. I will take you to the doctor tomorrow. I shouldn't have mentioned pregnancy right away. I just had a feeling.'

The prospect of not having the child she had just discovered she had was terrifying.

'No, Lakshmi, I am certain I am pregnant.'

'How can you be certain? You didn't even know a few minutes ago!'

'I felt it.'

'You felt what, Meena?'

'I felt the baby.'

'That's impossible, Meena. It would be so tiny. It probably doesn't even have legs yet!'

Meena kept her lips pursed. Nobody could tell her what she did or did not feel.

'We must tell Amar,' she heard Lakshmi say.

Panic made Meena's voice hoarse. 'No, let's wait until we know for sure. I don't want to get his hopes up.'

The white lie danced on her tongue even after she had said it. For now, this baby was hers. She would hold onto this precious time alone with it for as long as possible.

Lakshmi hesitantly agreed and they walked out to the kitchen.

'Are you OK, Meena?' Amar asked, his forehead wrinkled in concern.

'Yes, just felt a bit unwell but I feel much better now. Thank you.'

As they sat down and ate *aloo parathas*, she examined Amar's behaviour. She noticed how he always ate first, and never waited for anybody else. How he never asked if anybody else wanted the last bit of butter before taking it for himself. How he barely listened to the conversation around the table, too entranced by his own thoughts. Her hand involuntarily rested on her stomach as she questioned what the father of her child would do if he had to look after anyone other than himself.

Thunderous footsteps broke her attention and Asmita strode into the kitchen.

'The bathroom smells. Meena, clean it later. It seems you were the last to use it.'

Anger furrowed Meena's eyebrows. She pursed her lips and carried on eating.

Asmita stared at her, her eyes begging for a reaction. She tried a different tactic.

'So, even my own daughter-in-law eats without me. There is no respect left in this house.'

Power rippled through Meena's body. She felt this child inside of her, giving her the energy and strength to defend herself.

'Why don't you expect the same respect from your own son?'

Silence echoed in the room. Meena dared not look up and carried on eating her food. She stole a glance at the faces around the table. Lakshmi's husband looked shell-shocked, as if he had never heard a woman speak before. A smirk erupted from Meena's lips. She noticed Amar's gaze on her and quickly changed her expression.

She noticed how his eyes had darkened and his fists were clenched. She felt her own hands return to fists, the nails digging into her cut flesh. What must her husband think of her, speaking back to his mother in such a way?

The power of motherhood that consumed her only moments ago now waned. Tense stares around the table and Asmita's frozen expression sucked the last bit of energy out of her.

She tried to catch Amar's eye. He was staring at his plate now, his face a strange shade of red. His hands were visibly shaking. Suddenly, he stood and strode out of the kitchen.

She followed him out of the room. As she walked up to him, he swung round and gave her a look of pure disgust.

'Never talk to my mother like that again. Or you will not have a place to stay any longer.'

She stepped back in shock. Her mind replayed that moment, and she felt her heart sink. She would apologise. It was the right thing to do.

Despite this, she wished she had one person in her corner. Just one person who would tell her that everything would be OK. That she was only human. Her feet ached as she stood there. She suddenly felt overwhelmingly tired. Tired of walking on eggshells for months. Tired of having no one to talk to.

'Amar, why must I be scolded for standing up for myself? Your mother talks down to me every day. I am nothing more than a maid to her. I want to be treated with respect. I am a human being too.'

The anger she felt subsided as she saw the pain on Amar's face. Her body froze in fear. All it would take was one word from him and she could be homeless. She could have nobody. She tried to grab Amar's arm as he went to leave their room. He easily pulled out of her grasp. He stopped in the doorway. She breathed a sigh of relief. He turned around and took a step towards her. His expression had changed to something different – she couldn't quite put her finger on it. Just as she went to hug him, he turned again, putting his back to her. The rejection washed over her.

Without warning, he swung round and hit her. The floor hit her so hard, the breath left her body. Her head knocked against something. She heard the bang but didn't feel it until moments later. It felt like her head had been stomped on, the pain blinding her. Her body was paralysed, unable to move or recognise what had just happened. The stickiness of the floor seeped through her *kameez*, making her feel as if she was glued to the floor. Her eyes were blurry, unable to focus. She thought she heard words but couldn't make out what they meant. Everything felt far away. She felt his body press down on hers, his hand tight on her neck.

She closed her eyes. She hoped when she opened them, this would just be a dream. She slowly opened her eyes after a few breaths. The pain remained. Moments passed. She dared not move. She heard Amar's footsteps retreat and attempted to look up. Her neck protested, her head feeling like it was heavier than her entire body. Her eyes skimmed the room. She was alone.

Chapter Six

Fear jolted her body awake as she felt her stomach. Her baby. What if the baby was hurt? She tried to move but her body wasn't responding. She tried to talk to her limbs using her mind. *Leg – move!* Nothing. *Arm – move!* Nothing. Anxiety washed over her body, the fear of never being able to move again muddying her thoughts. She felt like she couldn't breathe, air struggling to reach her lungs. She took several deep breaths. In. Out. In. Out. Finally, air.

She felt a tingling in her limbs. She just needed to be calm. Her body would follow. She managed slowly to move one leg and then the other. Each movement caused her teeth to grind together, pain hissing through her lips. Despite her back screaming at her, she slowly managed to hoist herself up and sit on the edge of the bed.

Disbelief made her body freeze. She would have thought she was dreaming if her whole body didn't feel so battered. Her neck screamed in agony. There was a pain in her chest that she couldn't place. Was it her heart? Was her heart ceasing to beat?

She heard hurried footsteps approach and soon Lakshmi's almond eyes were staring into her own.

'What happened? Are you OK?' she asked as she put her arms around Meena.

At the lack of Meena's response, Lakshmi filled the silence.

'I wanted to come in straight away, but he said not to disturb you. He said you needed to rest. Him and Rajvir just left – I told Rajvir to keep an eye on him. I would have come sooner, *choti*, I'm sorry. Mum hasn't said a word. She is sitting in her room, I think. Everything happened so fast . . .'

Lakshmi's stream of noise blurred into the background. Meena felt like a stranger looking at a scene before her. She felt as if she was watching a film, but she was in it. The characters weren't real. She wasn't real. She felt no tears on her face, no sob in her throat. She suddenly noticed that it was silent again.

'Did he hurt you?' Lakshmi asked hesitantly, as if she already knew the answer but hoped the question was wrong.

'What if the baby is hurt?' muttered Meena.

Lakshmi held her tight, but she felt as if no number of hugs could put her broken body back together.

'I hear if you bleed then you have lost the baby. Otherwise, you should be fine.'

Lakshmi said the words with such confidence that Meena didn't even think to question her. She slowly walked to the bathroom and took a few deep breaths. The pain surging through her body had paled in comparison to the thought of losing her baby. She was on autopilot. If there was blood, she wouldn't be a mother. If there was blood, she would leave this house and never return.

As she gingerly pulled down her underwear, she kept her eyes closed. Sweat dripped down her brow as she opened her eyes. She stumbled back. Emotions rippled through her.

No blood. The baby should be OK. Sobs erupted from her, animalistic cries that shook her core. Nothing else mattered. Her baby was OK. She walked out of the bathroom and hugged Lakshmi close. What would she have done if Lakshmi weren't here? She held her sister-in-law tight, ignoring the pain rippling through her body. The smell of coconut oil in Lakshmi's hair comforted her.

She eventually let go and stumbled over to the mirror. A mauve bruise was erupting on her forehead from where it had slammed against the floor. She gingerly traced it with her fingers. She grabbed a comb and managed to cover most of it with her hair. The redness around her neck could be covered with a chunni.

She had been lightly punished by her parents before but never hit as hard as she was by Amar. A few taps from her mother. A few hits with a ruler from teachers, although these were rare as she was quiet and bright. She had heard neighbours hitting their wives before, seen women in the village wearing their bruises and scars, some so used to it they didn't even bother trying to cover them anymore. She knew it was potentially a part of being a wife, although she had never seen her father hurt or touch her mother in a threatening way.

Perhaps he was the exception. Or perhaps Amar was an exception.

She gingerly placed her hand on her stomach and pressed lightly. She couldn't feel anything. She moved her hands around and pressed again. Nothing. She kept circling her stomach, her actions becoming more and more panicked. As she was doing this, Lakshmi took her hands in hers and held them tight. Her eyes told her it would be OK.

Soon, Meena got on with her usual daily tasks. She washed the clothes in the bucket outside, picked the ripe fruit and vegetables from the garden, and watered the plants. She tried to ignore the nagging pain in her body. After she had finished her work, she sat under her favourite mango tree and closed her eyes. The African sun bathed her in a warm glow and the pain rippling through her body started to ease. The horizon was beginning to turn her favourite shade of lilac. When she saw the sky turn purple, it made her feel safe. A lilac sky told her everything would be OK.

She hadn't seen any sign of Lakshmi, her husband or Amar in a while. Asmita had been lying in her room the last time she had checked but they had stayed well out of each other's way so far. She had paused outside Asmita's door, wondering if she should go inside. The floor had creaked as she had stood outside, and she knew Asmita had heard. Yet neither woman said anything to the other.

She decided to make Amar's favourite for dinner: chickpea curry with *mung daal* on the side. After a few attempts, she managed to stand up and felt her bones scream in protest. It was like every muscle in her body was telling her to lie back down. She shook off the pain and proceeded to the kitchen. After an hour, with the house smelling of beautiful aromas, she heard the door open. Hesitant footsteps echoed from the porch and stopped at the kitchen doorway. She didn't say anything, waiting for him to say the first word. She heard deep breaths.

'I'm sorry, Meena. I didn't mean to hurt you.'

He came up behind her and gave her a hug so tight her bones felt like they were breaking. An involuntarily squeal of pain erupted out of her mouth and Amar quickly stood back.

'Sorry.'

She smelt the alcohol on his breath. He only drank rarely, maybe once a week on a Wednesday after work. Today he reeked of beer and whisky, his eyes bloodshot with regret. The men back home were usually their most violent after drinking so she decided to proceed with caution. She had seen enough bruised bodies of women in the village to serve her as a warning. In fact, her own pain gave her enough of a warning.

'It's OK. Take a seat and have dinner. I tried my best to make your favourite.'

He took a wobbly seat at the table and she served him *rotis*, the curry and *daal* with fresh mango pickle on the side. He devoured it within minutes, the alcohol fuelling his hunger. She couldn't bear to eat next to him, but she knew leaving the room would upset him more. Plus, the baby needed food.

She decided she would see a doctor tomorrow. Just to be on the safe side.

As she looked at her husband eating, she thought about telling him about the baby. She quickly decided against it. It could tip him over the edge.

Lakshmi's husband Rajvir came into the room.

'Hmm, what is that amazing smell? I'm starving.'

He began piling food into a plate, clearly unaware of the tension in the room. Lakshmi followed in, standing awkwardly in the door.

'Raj, did you ask before taking Meena's food?'

Rajvir looked up, guilt across his face. He stopped shovelling the food into his mouth and stared at the table as if he were waiting for it to answer Lakshmi.

'Carry on eating then. It's a bit late to stop now,' Lakshmi said with a smirk.

Rajvir looked up at her, a smile teasing his face. Lakshmi gave his head a light tap as she walked to the stove. Seeing the obvious love between them made Meena's heart sink. She looked at Amar inhaling his meal, not even noticing that she had barely touched her own plate.

She stood slowly, attempting to erase the pain from her face. Her chunni slid from around her neck as she walked, and she heard Rajvir gasp. She quickly grabbed the material and wrapped it back around her, covering her bruises. She avoided his eyes and carried on walking to the kitchen. She placed her dishes in the sink.

'Meena, let me wash up. Go rest.' Lakshmi said.

As she walked out of the kitchen, she heard Lakshmi's sweet, soft voice again.

'I hope you're OK. Rest up.'

She wondered if Lakshmi's words were a warning to Amar. That if he hurt her again, he would have to answer to his sister. Perhaps her words were a warning to Meena – *be careful what you say*. Either way, she felt defeated. She reached the bedroom and lay on the bed, her body sinking into the thin mattress. The pain was increasing in her body, and she felt tears prick her eyes for the first time that day. She closed her eyes, small droplets running down the sides of her face.

A heavy body sunk into the mattress next to her. A hand grasped her shoulder. She squealed in surprise and instinctively rolled further away. Amar mumbled something.

'What did you say?' she asked.

'Come, we haven't touched in weeks. I won't hurt you ever again. I promise. Let me make things right.'

As Meena heard those words, she felt a tug in her chest. She tried to move away. His hands tightened on her. Fear shook her body and she lay defenceless. She felt his alcohol-infused lips on hers, and let his hands move over her battered body. The taste of whisky washed through her mouth and she tried not to cringe. As she lay there motionless, she felt tears stream down her face.

Chapter Seven

Three days passed and Meena felt on a strange high. Despite her aching body, she was on cloud nine. She had never been treated so well by her husband. Amar had bought her flowers. He had made sure she had eaten properly. He even promised that they would go on a trip to Mombasa soon. Two days after Amar had hurt her, Asmita had joined her under the mango tree while Amar was at work.

'Sitting here is not good for my knees.'

'Shall I get you a chair?'

'No, it's OK.'

Silence had ensued and they had both watched the sun dance across the sky; birds flying in unison, forming a shield to protect their own.

'Meena, my son has a temper. It comes out sometimes. He has a good heart. Please don't forget that.'

Meena felt tears prick her eyes and she picked at her nails. She nodded in response and Asmita gently placed a hand on Meena's arm. They had sat together in silence until Amar had returned home from work. She had watched as Asmita had greeted Amar, her arms hugging his much taller body. She had heard laughter from within the house as mother and son talked about their days, the aroma of fresh food wafting from the kitchen window.

Meena had her doctor's appointment booked for the following day, and then she would announce her pregnancy. Perhaps this would make Amar even more loving.

The chill against her skin opened her eyes. She had fallen asleep under the mango tree again. Her body was still healing, and the constant tiredness was just one of the side effects. She figured it was also just a part of being pregnant. Her eyes were wider than the setting sun as the sky turned a stunning shade of pink mixed with hues of purple. It was one of the most beautiful sights Meena had ever seen. As the sky turned darker, she decided to go inside and start preparing dinner. She knew Asmita had offered to cook again, but there was no harm in helping. Asmita had been cordial towards her recently. She would do anything to keep it that way.

As Meena stood up from her mango tree she felt a sharp pain in her side. She convinced herself it was just cramps due to sitting for a long time. She walked slowly to the house, suddenly desperate to go to the toilet, which seemed strange when she had barely had anything to drink all day. Her underwear felt a bit wet and seemed to spread down her thighs. There was no way she had wet herself! She hadn't done that since she was a child. As she rushed into the toilet, she heard Lakshmi calling her name. She would have to wait; this was far more urgent. How would she clean herself up without anyone noticing? Her face burnt at the prospect of someone seeing her.

As she pulled down her pajami, she noticed the red down her legs and in her underwear. Dark red liquid flowing out of her, cascading down her legs and onto the floor. What was happening?

She closed her eyes and re-opened them. She touched the liquid with her finger, hoping her finger would remain clean. Feeling the stickiness of the blood made her squirm. A guttural cry erupted from her lips as she realised the brutal reality of the situation. She had lost her baby. Within seconds, the door was thrown open and Lakshmi was holding her so tight she felt like she would never breathe again.

'It's OK. It's OK. Let's clean you up, and Raj will drive you to the hospital. Come, it's OK.'

Despite her calming words, Lakshmi's voice shook with emotion. Tears were flowing out of her eyes, but she helped clean Meena up with steady hands. As Meena stood naked in the bathroom, frozen in time, Lakshmi washed the blood off her body. As she watched the burning red blood go down the drain, she felt as if her baby was going down with it. She dropped to the floor, grabbing at the small drain, screaming, 'COME BACK, COME BACK.'

A knock on the door silenced her. Was Amar back already? What would she tell him? Her stomach curdled at the thought of seeing his face. This was his fault. A male voice coughed. Lakshmi called out, asking who it was. Rajvir sheepishly called their names. Both women sighed simultaneously. Lakshmi towelled Meena dry as she yelled through the door, asking Rajvir to get the car ready now. The urgency in Lakshmi's voice sent Rajvir running down the hall. Numbness took over Meena's body. She knew no pain, the crippling ripples in her stomach invisible to her.

She didn't fight Lakshmi's attempts to put her clothes on. Her body was lifeless. Rajvir coughed once again outside the door.

'Come in,' said Lakshmi. 'Help me get her in the car.'

Rajvir looked at Meena and failed to hide his emotion. He saw the red stains on the floor and on Meena's crumpled clothes. He looked at Meena with eyes she would never forget. Pure and unfiltered remorse. Rajvir and Lakshmi struggled to lift Meena from the bathroom floor and carry her to the car. It was as if her body were made of bricks. Just as they managed to get in the car, Asmita's voice rang out from a distance.

'What are you doing? Where are you going?'

Lakshmi looked at Meena and took a deep breath, and yelled that they would be back later. There was no time to waste. Rajvir drove at an alarming speed, Lakshmi's voice speeding him up every time he tried to slow down. Meena drifted in and out of consciousness, the lack of blood as well as the emotional trauma swallowing her into a deep black hole. As they reached the hospital, Lakshmi jumped out of the car and gently shook Meena.

'You need to come out of the car now. The doctor will help you, I promise. It will be OK. I'm here.'

Meena's mind barely registered Lakshmi's voice, as if she were listening through a distant phone line. Her body responded to the voice eventually, getting up and walking from the car to the hospital entrance. Lakshmi followed, and Rajvir stood helplessly by the car, unsure if he was needed or not. Meena looked back at him, silently willing him to stay there. She didn't want anyone else but Lakshmi with her right now.

As Lakshmi hurriedly told a doctor the situation, Meena found herself wandering the corridor. She heard the sound of tears, pain and joy echoing throughout the hospital. New lives coming into the world; others leaving never to return. Life was so fragile – one second you could have two hearts beating inside of you; the next, only one heart remained.

A gentle hand guided her to a wheelchair, and then she was being wheeled through the corridor of sounds. Agonising cries, gentle sobs, near silent tears of joy. The sound of a baby crying hit her harder than Amar's hands had days before. She wondered if her baby had cried inside of her when she landed on the floor. She wondered why she hadn't heard its cries for help. As she was lifted onto a small bed, the yearning for her family became unbearable. She would do anything to have her mother's soft arms holding her tight, to have Parvathi gently plaiting her long hair, making sure she was comfortable. To have Mohan there to tell jokes and make her laugh.

Maybe if she called them and told them what had happened, they would come to Nairobi. Maybe her parents would take her back home and let her stay there forever. As her mind swirled with many different emotions, she noticed a doctor standing over her, talking. She had no idea what he was saying.

She felt a cold gel on her stomach and machines whirring around her. Alien sounds penetrated her brain and she internally screamed for them to stop. What if her baby woke up and she couldn't hear it? What if the machines hurt it? Her body wasn't responding to her mind and she lay completely still like a corpse, her brain shrieking at her to move.

Lakshmi's silhouette came into view in the background, her presence comforting Meena. The doctor suddenly took her hand and asked if she had understood what he had said. She realised he was speaking English. His dark brown hand was wrapped around hers in a way that made her feel completely serene. His soft demeanour made her feel like everything would be OK. His gentle eyes looked into hers, silently speaking, reassuring her. She never wanted this doctor to leave. He said that they would need to give her a check-over and see if everything was OK. What if they noticed the bruises on her body from the fall? She quickly sat up, pain rippling up her side and through her stomach.

'It's OK, doctor, I'm fine. Has . . .' Her voice tailed off. She couldn't bear to say the words. She took a deep breath and tried again. She needed to know.

'Has the baby gone?'

The tears running down Lakshmi's face and the sadness in the doctor's eyes said it all.

Isn't it funny how much our eyes can give away? Two windows to our souls. Without warning, the connection she had felt with the doctor was broken. He had reassured her with his eyes that she would be fine. He had lied to her. She would never be OK again. Why couldn't they save her baby? The grief hit her all over again, the wave sending her drowning in a sea of red. The image of the bathroom drain haunted her mind, the maroon water suffocating her. She drifted off into the red sea, letting her body and mind float in the abyss.

Chapter Eight

Light blinded her. Even with her eyes shut, the light seeped in, causing her brain to hurt. *Someone, please, turn it off!* She needed darkness. Her body gave in and she opened her eyes.

'She's awake! Lakshmi, she is awake.'

Amar's voice made her flinch. What was he doing here? He shouldn't be here. This was her grief. Her loss. Not his. Yet, when she felt his lips kiss her forehead, she couldn't help but want him to hold her tight and not let go. As she became aware of her surroundings again, her body stiffened. Her hand flew to her tummy, hoping some miracle had happened. Maybe they had found a way to save the baby. Her hands pressed her tummy, hoping for some sign. Nothing. Emptiness. She could feel it in her soul. She was alone.

She wondered how much Lakshmi had told Amar. Curiosity took over and she peered over Amar's shoulder to see Lakshmi's face. Her eyes were filled with tears that hadn't yet been spilled, her once rosy face void of colour. Meena felt for her. She had come back home to a stranger in her house and now had to deal with that stranger's problems. Lakshmi was probably hoping for some peace and a happy life in Nairobi. Meena hated herself for stripping Lakshmi of that in such a short space of time.

'Out of the way, please.' An unknown voice was speaking. 'I need to see if she is OK.'

Another doctor edged Amar out of the way and sat gently on Meena's bed.

'Are you feeling OK? We had to sedate you a bit earlier. You were very upset, which is perfectly under-standable. You have nothing to be ashamed of. These are very upsetting circumstances. Unfortunately, you lost your baby but otherwise you seem physically well. We did notice some unusual bruising on your body, but your sister-in-law explained that you had a tumble down the stairs which explains that. You will need to rest for a few days so your body heals. Does that make sense?'

Her voice croaked as she tried to speak. She cleared her throat, took a sip of water and tried again.

'Thank you. I will rest.'

The doctor lightly squeezed her hand and left the room. Lakshmi slowly walked over to Meena.

'Come on, let's get you home.'

As she bent down to help Meena off the bed, she whispered in Meena's ear.

'I'm sorry. Rajvir went back to the house and Amar was there, asking where you were. He brought him straight here.'

Meena couldn't be upset at Lakshmi. It wasn't her fault anyway. None of this was Lakshmi's fault. Meena grabbed Lakshmi's hand tightly and she knew Lakshmi knew that everything was OK between them. She said a silent prayer to the many Hindu gods: *Please rescue my soul. Bring me back to life if you cannot bring my baby. At least bring me back. If I have to stay on this earth, please give me a reason to stay.*

On the drive back to the house, Meena stared out of the window, seeing more of the city than she ever had before. She thought back to the day she had ventured out of the house. Only mere weeks ago. It felt like a lifetime. She once again wondered if the lady was still there, tending to her plants. Maybe she had escaped for a better life for herself. Maybe she had told herself she was going to escape but had stayed trapped in that same house, tending to the same plants, convincing herself that the next day would be different.

As the car pulled up at the house, she realised no one had spoken a word during the whole car ride. Lakshmi was anxiously looking over at her, a toothy smile unable to mask worried eyes. Several hands grabbed Meena, trying to help. She didn't want help. She wanted to walk to her own bed. She slapped their hands away, and swung her legs out of the car, her feet gingerly finding their balance on the ground. She took a few wobbly steps forward. Why wasn't her body working? Lakshmi's safe arms were quickly around her, guiding her inside.

'Why don't you stay with me tonight? Rajvir can sleep on the sofa.' Lakshmi's kind offer somehow seemed cold to Meena, and she suddenly felt a strong urge to break away from her.

'Why? I should be sleeping next to my husband.'

She heard Lakshmi's intake of breath but didn't care. She was married to Amar. He was all she had. As she lay down on her own bed, she closed her eyes, ready for blissful sleep to escape this reality. Darkness soothed her. She floated down into the pool of darkness, grateful for its comforting embrace.

A flash of blood. The drain. Screaming. She sat up so suddenly her whole stomach cramped with pain. She let out a small cry. Amar stirred but did not wake. She was grateful that he did not. His questions would worsen the pain. This was his fault. So, why she wasn't shouting at him? Why did she lean on him when she should be pushing him away? She closed her eyes again. The images came rushing back to her. Pools of blood at her feet. Her kameez stained with red. She opened her eyes again. The light was safer. Her baby was in the dark now. If she went to visit her baby there, she may never return. She must stay in the light.

She reached over to her nightstand and grabbed the book of prayers she used to read every night. Lately she had been ignoring her faith and listening to her favourite Hindi songs to fall asleep to instead. Now, even the thought of listening to those songs caused her pain. She wouldn't stop her prayers ever again.

Chapter Nine

Morning light flooded her eyes. A new day. She gingerly tried to roll over. No sign of Amar. She breathed a sigh of relief and winced as the pain spread across her chest.

She rubbed the sleep out of her eyes and looked around the room. She attempted to sit up, but every muscle cried for her to stop. She took a deep inhalation and tried to swing her legs off the bed, but the pain was too much. She lay there, unsure of what to do. Should she call out to Lakshmi? Or should she just try and get up herself? Moments passed and indecision cramped Meena's brain. Just as she had made the decision to try herself, she heard the jingle of Lakshmi's footsteps. Thank God for Lakshmi and her jingly *ghungroos*. She saw a quarter of Lakshmi's head peer around the door and Meena couldn't keep the smile from gracing her face. The sheer ridiculousness of Lakshmi's popping her head around the door like a child scared to wake her parents caused Meena to erupt in giggles. Bless Lakshmi and her jingles.

Lakshmi bounded into the room, looking equal parts puzzled and joyous. 'What's so funny?' she inquired, putting her hands on her hips.

The look of bewilderment mixed with Lakshmi's tilted head and hands on her hips made Meena giggle more. 'You look like a mixture of my mother and my younger sister. Like you're scared I will tell you off!'

'Well, you can be pretty scary,' Lakshmi said, laughter muffling her words.

Their laughter ended abruptly as Amar walked in the room. Meena's eyes watered at the smell. He looked dishevelled, as if he had been hiking in the mountains for weeks.

He reeked of alcohol and his eyes were bloodshot. Meena felt her heart sink through her stomach. She thought he would be here for her, not drowning his sorrows with strangers. What kind of man had she married? He barely even looked at her as he slumped on the bed next to her, still fully dressed. Meena winced as his arm landed on her side. Surprisingly, her eyes did not well with tears. She felt her fists clench and her jaw tighten. She saw red.

Lakshmi's withering stare calmed her angry thoughts. She felt like hitting him. Shouting at him. Leaving him. Yet, she sat there, glaring at him, her gaze invisible to him. Disgust gave her a sudden urge to get as far away from him as possible.

Lakshmi helped Meena out of the bed as Amar's loud snores provided background noise. As Lakshmi went to follow Meena into the bathroom, Meena turned and stopped her. 'I can do this alone. I need a bit of space.'

She watched Lakshmi hesitantly retreat. As she slowly made her way to the bathroom, she found her feet stumbling over themselves. She involuntarily reached out, only to realise that there was no one there to catch her fall. As she leant against the wall, she heard Lakshmi and Rajvir talking in the next room. At least Lakshmi had someone to support her. Someone she could rely on.

As she cleaned herself in the bathroom, she heard Rajvir ask what the women had made for breakfast. The previous anger rose in her, threatening to explode out of her mouth. She had just lost a baby. A child. Yet, if it were just her and Amar here, she would be expected to make him food. There was a constant expectation that his stomach must be full before hers could begin to fill. That his happiness and comfort came at the expense of hers. Why did a wife become a mother from the moment she signed those marital papers? She didn't experience any of the joys of creating life, she was only burdened with the responsibility of maintaining one. Why did men constantly need a mother, while a girl had to become a mother from the moment she could walk?

Her mind wandered back to her home. The sacrifices her own mother had made. Never failing to fill all her children's stomachs, never showing the pain her back felt when she had to scrub the floors. Never showing her children just how tired she was. Her memory drifted back to one burning hot day in summer when the children had been sent home from school after four children had fainted from heatstroke.

She walked down the street, kicking at the dusty road. Parvathi was trailing behind her, struggling in the heat. Neither of them spoke to each other. Meena was annoyed that Parvathi had drunk all the water without saving her any. How selfish. Who would drink all of the water without asking if anybody else wanted any?

As she had got closer to her house, a strange feeling gripped her stomach. Anxiety made the small hairs on her neck stand to attention. Something felt off. She walked into the house and through to the kitchen, eager to drink some water. Her feet stopped walking and she noticed her mother laying on the floor. She sprang forward and screamed her mother's name, fearing the worst.

Her younger sister, only seven years old whispered: 'Is Ma dead?' She turned and looked into her sister's big innocent eyes and wondered how such a young child knew of death. As she shook her mother awake, knowing nothing of what to do in such a situation, she pondered life without her mother. Her ma was everything. Life would mean nothing without her. She wondered if she would become the woman of the house. The one who held it together. Her older sister Priya was mature but knew nothing of cooking or cleaning. Instead, she spent her days dreaming of marrying a rich man and never having to lift a finger. She was definitely the princess of the household. All these thoughts whizzed through Meena's mind as she tried to shake her mother awake. What had happened to her strong ma?

As her mother groaned and slowly began to lift her body up, she felt a sense of relief like never before. Her ma was her rock. Without her, she didn't know who she was. She was only eleven years old. She needed her for many more years. She left Parvathi and ran next door, shouting for help.

Eventually everyone was crowded outside her house, aching to see what was happening. Several women offered water and food.

Her father came home as soon as he heard and insisted that her mother was not to move. The week ahead was not without struggle. With her ma out of action, her father was lost. He had no idea how to cook, having never had to do it. He had transitioned from his mother doing everything for him to his wife ensuring he had a clean house, fresh clothes and food in his stomach. Now it was his daughter's turn. Meena had no idea how to cook or do anything domestic but she had witnessed her ma doing everything.

That evening, she had to make dinner. Her older sister insisted on helping but ended up causing more mess so Meena eventually sent her away. She took a deep breath and tried to picture her ma cooking. She could figure it out. She stared at the stove for a good ten minutes, unsure of what to do.

She grimaced as her elder brother walked in and laughed at her. She asked him to help but he quickly walked away with a smirk as if the idea of him cooking was completely nonsensical. Tears stung her eyes.

Why would nobody help her? Parvathi had offered to help but Meena hadn't wanted her to get hurt on the stove. Her little hands began to shake as she struggled to cut an onion, her eyes streaming with a mixture of tears and the harshness of the onion. Next were the chillies, which caused her eyes to sting with a burning pain as she rubbed them. After over an hour, she managed to make an aloo sabji but had forgotten to make any rice or rotis with it. She looked at her father, staring at his plate with tears in his eyes. He ate one spoonful and looked up: 'Your ma will be better soon, I hope.' Those

89

were the only words he said. Not one word of appreciation. In his mind, there was nothing to be thankful for — it was her duty. Yet his eyes showed love and Meena knew he was thankful deep down.

As Meena stood with the bucket in her hand, her mind jolted back to the current moment. She had been in the bathroom for a long time, she realised. As she turned away from the sink, she found herself staring at the drain on the floor. That was the last place she had been pregnant. That was where her baby had gone. She fell to her knees and stared at the drain. The next thing she felt were Lakshmi's strong arms holding her up, guiding her to her room. She didn't know how much time had passed.

Days passed and Meena couldn't bring herself to leave the bed apart from when nature called. She had noticed a new curtain covering the bathing area, which was drawn every time she had gone to the bathroom. The first time she saw it, she had cried into it, her tears cascading down the waterproof fabric. It was a reminder of what she had lost in that same place. A reminder of what could have been.

Amar remained in a drunken state, barely making it to work most days. She turned away from him each night, his rancid smell causing her to feel nauseated. When he tried to put his hands on her, she moved away despite her aching body screaming at her to lie still. Some nights she reminisced about his comforting hold and his smile that reached his eyes. His foolish clownery and his sweet whispers. Those were long gone.

More than anything, she missed her home. Her ma would know what to do. Her ma would tell her to get up and continue with her life. *That is what we Dhir women do*, she would say. *We fight, not for ourselves, but for everyone around us. We fight to survive.*

The smell of alcohol signalled his arrival. She shut her eyes, hoping he wouldn't bother to talk to her. She didn't have the energy to convince him to go to sleep. She barely had the energy to do anything these days.

She sensed him looming over her, his stature casting a shadow. The sickening bitter smell of whisky washed over her face as he breathed out. She kept her eyes tightly shut, wishing him away. Her hands relaxed as she heard his footsteps retreat. Gingerly, she opened her eyes and breathed a sigh of relief.

Suddenly, there was a movement across the room. She felt eyes staring at her, and she looked in his direction. He was standing, looking at her from the other side of the room. Tears rolled down his cheeks.

'What have I done to you? What have I done to myself?'

He crumpled to the floor. She had never seen him this vulnerable before. She slowly got out of bed, her bones protesting. They weren't used to moving. She lowered herself to him on the floor, not knowing whether to hold him or not. His arms reached out, grabbing her so tight she couldn't breathe.

'I'm sorry. I will never hurt you again. I will never drink like this again. I swear on my mother's life.'

She didn't want to, but she believed him. His eyes were sincere. She felt her own tears roll down her face and neck, staining her kameez with salt water. How did she know he was telling the truth? How did she know he wouldn't hurt her again? She didn't know. She would have to believe him. She had no other choice. As they lay together on the floor in their room, she felt her body relax into his once more.

When she stood up, her hands entwined with Amar's, she felt a painful pang in her stomach. A reminder of what she had lost. And how she lost it. She shook the fears away, forcing herself to think ahead not behind. People make mistakes. Should they have to spend the rest of their lives seeking forgiveness? She helped him into the bed despite the pain in her limbs and neck.

As Amar lay down on the bed, crumpled in a sleepy mess, she let her feet take her to the garden. The heat engulfed her in a cosy blanket, waking up her tired eyes and weakened bones. She slowly took her cardigan off and let the heat hit her bare skin. She didn't even know how many days she had been bed-bound. She heard Lakshmi's voice in the distance, scolding her husband for one thing or another. Despite the evident frustration in her voice, there was also love and tenderness. She smiled to herself and pictured the scene in her head. Rajvir sheepishly looking at the floor as Lakshmi stood over him, telling him off for putting his socks in the wrong drawer or for cutting the crop down before it was perfectly ripe. She knew Rajvir was petrified of Lakshmi which made it all the funnier. She also knew Lakshmi did it on purpose as she loved seeing Rajvir looking so scared. Lakshmi may have the face of an angel, but she frequently brought out her devilish charm. Either way, the sound of her voice eased Meena's thoughts as she watched the sky fade from blue to pink to lilac to black.

Chapter Ten

Meena's body wandered over to her mango tree. It was in full bloom, beautiful mangoes hanging off it, ready to drop at any point. She could smell their sweet honey scent and for the first time in weeks she felt a strong desire to eat. Her eyes landed on a particular mango, glinting in the striking sunlight. Her mouth salivated at the thought of her tongue tasting the juicy fruit. She had to pick it. Her hands stretched up, but she couldn't reach. She jumped up, ignoring the pain in her stomach. The pain paled in comparison to her desire to eat this mango. She needed it. She tried to jump again, higher this time. The very tip of her fingers grazed it, teasing her. How could she reach this mango? She looked around for something to help her. Nothing. She would have to climb the tree. She had done it all the time with her sisters and brothers when she was younger. It couldn't be that different now.

One of her hands reached around a branch. Sturdy. It would support her. She lifted herself up, surprised at the strength she didn't know she had. While her body still felt tender, it awakened at the thought of movement, of life. She wrapped her legs around another nearby branch. A light breeze swung the mango slightly, teasing it into her eye-line. One branch at a time she climbed until she was so close, she could just about reach it. The overwhelming smell of mangoes mixed with crisp leaves made her head swim in a delightful way. She felt giddy with joy. She leaned forward, grazing it with her fingertips. She just had to reach a little further . . .

'Meena! What on earth are you doing? Do you have a death wish? Get down from there. Oh *Bhai*, I'll get Rajvir. He can help get you down.'

Lakshmi's expression of pure astonishment mixed with confusion and fear brought instant giggles to Meena's lips. She realised how ridiculous she must look. Her body entangled in a tree, trying to reach for a mango when there were plenty she could have reached from below. Her eyes watered with laughter, misting her vision. She heard an outburst of laughter, so poetic it had to be Lakshmi's.

Once she managed to breathe again, she pointed to the mango in question. 'I need that mango!'

Lakshmi looked even more astounded than before. All this for a mango! Lakshmi was now in a heap on the floor, her saree unravelling and laughter turning from poetic to a sound not dissimilar to that of an elephant.

'Why didn't you just use a ladder, *didi*? Like a normal person?' she managed to wheeze out in between fits of giggles.

Meena's body was starting to ache. She knew she wouldn't be able to stay in this tree much longer. The common sense of using a ladder just made her giggle more. In India, they didn't have ladders to use! They just used what they had to hand – usually just their own bodies! She didn't have the mango yet though, so she made the final grab forward and pulled it from the branch. It came off easily, as if it were patiently waiting for her to take it. Now for the journey down.

She gingerly felt for the branches around her. They didn't feel so sturdy anymore. Lakshmi was now looking worried.

'I'll get Rajvir. Wait, *didi*.'

'We don't need a man to help us. Come wait at the bottom of the tree to catch me if I fall.'

Lakshmi stood under the tree, clearly thinking how stupid an idea this was. Meena knew she wouldn't let her forget this. She decided to take the plunge. She threw the mango to Lakshmi and climbed down the tree with the pace of a monkey, but the grace of a rhino. As her feet landed on the floor, she felt a sense of pride. She had done it! The mango was hers. She hugged Lakshmi tightly and they danced around the garden, holding the mango between them.

'Can we eat it now or did you just want it for decoration?' Lakshmi asked.

They giggled their way to the kitchen and shared the sweet mango. It was the best thing Meena had ever tasted. As she looked at Lakshmi biting into the skin, she sensed a feeling in her chest. A feeling she hadn't felt since leaving home. She slowly put her hand on Lakshmi's and held it there.

As she licked the remnants of the mango juice off her fingers, she noticed a sadness to Lakshmi's eyes. She wondered whether to ruin the moment by asking her if she was OK. Just as she decided to see what was wrong – Lakshmi had been her rock, maybe she should be Lakshmi's now – she heard the creaking of a door. Her fists tightened at the thought of talking to Amar.

The echo of footsteps came closer to the kitchen, just as they both polished off the last of the mango. Asmita hovered in the doorway, suddenly seeming a stranger in the house she had never hesitated to control before.

'Ma, sit down. We just finished a mango but I can pick another for you?' Lakshmi said, holding out a chair.

Asmita sat in the chair. 'A mango would be nice. Make sure it's ripe. And pick it properly, using the ladder.'

At this comment, Lakshmi shot Meena a half-amused, half-worried look. Meena hadn't thought anyone had seen them. It seemed Asmita had been silently watching, storing ammunition against her. Lakshmi bolted out of the door, throwing Meena one last look of worry.

'Meena, I have been meaning to talk to you.'

As Meena looked out of the door, anxiously hoping Lakshmi would be quick, Asmita's voice cut across the room.

'Don't go looking for her. She will be a while. You can't hide behind her forever.'

Tears stung Meena's eyes at this accusation.

'She is my sister. I do not hide behind anyone. In fact, it is you I haven't seen much of recently.'

A flicker of surprise crossed Asmita's face. She clearly wasn't expecting such a strong reply.

After a moment of silence, Asmita proceeded as if Meena hadn't spoken.

'My son is not well. You have made him sick. He has never turned to alcohol before. Now you come along and drive him to drink. I don't fall for your games. It is your fault you lost the baby. Nobody else's. You can blame Amar all you want; he was doing what a man should and putting his wife in her place. You, on the other hand, clearly did not fulfil your duty as a mother and protect your baby. If you are given another chance to carry again, you need to be more careful. My son does not need more loss in his life.'

Time had stopped. There was no noise. Everything was completely silent. Meena couldn't even hear her own heartbeat. Asmita thought it was her fault she had lost her baby. She was not seen as a human being, as a woman in her own right. She was simply a vessel created to feed, cater to, and carry her husband's child. If she was not able to do any of those things, she was nothing. Useless. Something to be discarded.

Meena straightened her back and pushed the chair away from the table. The screech across the floor made Asmita wince. Meena revelled in that little victory. Without even a glance in Asmita's direction, she walked out of the kitchen. As she stood in the hallway, she wondered where to go. If she went outside, it would be like she was following Lakshmi. Hiding behind her. If she went to any other room, Asmita could follow her in there. If she went to her bedroom, she had to face Amar.

Amar. She looked back at Asmita's face watching her. She strode to her bedroom and opened the door. Amar's body lay on the bed, seemingly lifeless. Her hands shook as she walked in, closing the door firmly behind her.

At the sound of the door closing, Amar woke up looking dazed. Meena went over to the bed and looked down at him. His eyes crinkled into his familiar smile, a smile she hadn't seen in weeks. She lay down next to him, feeling his arms enclose her. Her skin prickled at the initial feeling of his touch.

The feeling of his hands pressing into her neck, her lungs fighting to find air. The feeling of the cold hard floor smashing into her body. The pain in her stomach that had been her baby dying. The room spun around her, air struggling to reach her lungs.

She tried to quieten her rapid heartbeat. Memories of lying with Amar months ago, their bodies entwined effort-lessly, filtered through her mind. She relaxed her body into his, feeling a heavy weight lift from her limbs. His heavy breathing signalled that he had fallen asleep again. As her eyes fluttered shut, exhausted from the day, she fell into the deepest sleep she had experienced in weeks.

The next morning, as the sun rose in the sky and broke through the crack in the curtains, Meena felt a surge of energy. She rolled over into Amar's arms.

'Morning, *beti*,' he said. 'What do you think about going away for the day?'

'Just us?' she inquired, fearful at the prospect of spending the day with Asmita.

Amar's forehead crinkled in thought. His eyes searched her face, looking for the right answer.

'Yes, just us.'

She breathed a sigh of relief at the thought of a day without Asmita's lingering gaze. Yet, she would be alone with Amar. If his mood switched again, she would have nobody to help her. She closed her eyes, the waves of anxiety rushing over her, causing her to forget how to breathe. This could be good for them, she told herself. They needed time to heal. This could be the start.

As she poured water on her legs, washing for the day ahead, she heard voices travel through the house. Laughter. High-pitched voices. Joy.

As the excited sounds filled her room, she looked in the mirror. Her face looked older already. Tarnished. Withered. Experienced.

She rifled through her wardrobe, looking for the perfect outfit. A saree caught her eye. Her favourite saree that she would wear on birthdays at home. A blue so delicate it looked almost translucent. White peacocks embroidered onto the fall; the rest of the saree beautifully simple. She wrapped herself in it, feeling beautiful for the first time in a long time. She twirled around the room, her favourite Hindi songs playing through her head, fuelling her feet. She plaited her long, thick hair, pinning it into an elaborate bun. A light line of kohl around her eyes and a touch of red lipstick finished her face.

She joined her family in the kitchen. Lakshmi looked radiant, happier even than the day before. Meena silently prayed that it would stay that way.

'Meena! Come join us. I'm making breakfast.'

Meena expertly flicked her saree over her shoulder, allowing her to use her arm freely. She was used to doing this to play or plait her sister's hair. Now she was doing it to cook *aloo paratha*. A year ago, she would have laughed at the idea.

'Here, let me help.'

She noticed Amar staring at her. A blush rose to her cheeks, the idea of him admiring her making her suddenly self-conscious.

The girls giggled as they rolled out *aloo parathas*, trying to make them as round as possible but achieving an array of odd shapes. As Lakshmi rolled one out into what looked like a mango shape, Meena exploded in a fit of laughter.

'Girls, are we actually going to get anything to eat here?' Rajvir's serious voice called across.

This just made Lakshmi and Meena laugh more. Lakshmi imitated his serious voice, attempting to keep a straight face. Amar joined in the laughter at Rajvir's horror. The joy was contagious as even Rajvir began to let out a laugh, struggling to remain in control.

'What's all this noise about?' Asmita's voice boomed from her room. The shuffle of her footsteps caused Meena and Rajvir to abruptly stop laughing. Lakshmi and Amar continued but the laughter was void of the joy it had previously had.

Meena quickly went back to rolling out a paratha.

'Sit, Ma. Here, I have a fresh *paratha* for you.' Meena tried her best to roll a perfect circle.

As she handed the plate to Asmita, her hand quivered. Asmita didn't even spare her a glance and took the *paratha*.

'Very nice *paratha*,' Asmita said.

Meena froze. Did she hear that correctly? Asmita liked something she had made. She turned and looked at Asmita, who continued to stare at her *paratha*.

'Thank you, Ma.'

She struggled to keep the smile off her face.

They ate their *paratha* with ghee and *dahee*, the conversation flowing until it drifted to the subject of the day ahead. Asmita asked why Meena was dressed so nicely. Unsure what to say, Meena looked to Amar for advice.

'We're going out for the day. I thought we could drive to Mombasa for the beach. Maybe stay the night somewhere. Or maybe go to Lake Nakuru for a few hours. I don't think Meena has seen it yet.'

Asmita's eyes sparkled.

'You should have told me. I'll get my things.'

Meena stood up in panic. She looked to Amar to rescue the situation. He continued eating, avoiding making eye contact with her.

Sensing defeat, Meena walked to her room in silence. She sat in front of the mirror and looked at her reflection. She felt as if her face had been redrawn since she got married. It was as if Amar was an artist, pencilling lines into her face, erasing her sparkly brown eyes and painting them a dull black, slowly adding more and more detail to a fresh canvas. She had two options – stay or go. Every bone in her body wanted to stay. Resume her previous position in bed, protected from everyone and everything. She could say she was still in pain, which wasn't untrue. Just as she had made her decision, she thought of the look on Asmita's face if she stayed. It would be pure joy. Joy at the thought of getting her son all to herself, joy at having more ammunition to use against Meena. Joy at Meena's pain. She couldn't let her win. She would go.

She took one last look at herself in the mirror. She refilled her lips, the ruthlessness of the red giving her confidence. She walked back into the kitchen to find Amar and his mother sitting alone at the table, muttering together. Their heads were close, and Asmita had one hand resting on Amar's. Lakshmi and Rajvir were nowhere to be seen.

'Are you ready?'

Asmita looked at her, her mouth open in surprise. Amar cleared his throat.

'Maybe we should go another day?'

He looked from his mother to Meena, desperately seeking an answer. Meena saw something in Asmita's eyes. They were almost apologetic. Could Asmita have reflected on her cruel words? Perhaps even she had realised that they had been too harsh, too unforgivable.

Asmita stood up, the chair scraping across the floor. 'Why don't you two go? I'm not feeling up to it.'

Amar's forehead was crinkled in worry, his eyes following his mother's footsteps. Now the ball was in his court. Meena gingerly put her hand on his shoulder, hoping that would urge him to make a decision. He stood up abruptly, causing the chair to fall back onto the floor with a loud bang.

Chapter Eleven

'Come, let's go. I'll show you around the city,' Amar
said, after taking a few breaths.

As they got into the car, Meena breathed in the
crisp air. The day was warming, and the slight breeze
danced on her skin. Her eyes grazed over Amar's face,
taking in his expression. One of his hands was gently
placed on the gear stick, the other on the steering
wheel. She noticed the prominent green veins along
his hands and arms. Her hand hovered over his. Just
as she was about to feel his skin, she moved her hand
back to her lap.

As they drove along the roads, Meena marvelled at
her surroundings. What a beautiful city! It was quite
developed – more so than her home. She watched
people walking together, families having picnics, children skipping down the street. Amar suddenly bought
the car to a sharp halt.

'They're doing checks. Just stay quiet and let me do
the talking,' Amar said, as he turned down the music
pumping out of the radio.

A British army vehicle was ahead, blocking cars from
continuing down the road. The men in uniform were

sitting on the hoods of their cars, smoking thick smog into the air. She grimaced as they threw their discarded litter onto the floor, grinding it in with their feet. Foul-sounding words escaped their mouths as they laughed in unison as a pair of beautiful black women walked past them. She couldn't help but notice the looks of apprehension on the women's faces.

She watched the car in front of them roll forward to the spontaneous checkpoint. The army man asked the man to roll his window down, his left hand rested on a weapon.

She involuntarily leaned forward, suddenly feeling on edge. The silence caused her to look around. The low volume music had disappeared. She went to adjust the volume and noticed the radio had gone. There was a gap where it once was. She looked to Amar and he slightly shook his head. His clenched jaw and red knuckles gripping the steering wheel answered any questions Meena had. This was not good news.

A black hand emerged from the car in front, handing a licence to the British soldier. He looked it over multiple times, turning it repeatedly in his hand yet not seeming to actually read it. Abruptly, he yanked the car door open and dragged the Kenyan man out of the car. Meena was surprised to see that the Kenyan man made no noise. He looked completely calm, almost vacant. He let the soldier search his pockets and his car, emerging with a stereo and what looked like a bag of grocery shopping. With a simple nod of his head, the soldier walked back to his vehicle, looking through the bag.

The Kenyan got back into his car, started the engine, and drove off without looking back.

Words failed her. That soldier had just stolen the man's belongings and he hadn't said a word. He hadn't protested. Something told her this wasn't the first time he had been treated in such a way by the British.

A knock on the window brought her mind back to the present time. She heard Amar take a deep breath and roll down the window an inch. A further knock on the window. Amar lowered the window more.

'Show me your licence.'

Amar's hands remained steady as he handed the man his licence. Meena noticed her hands were sweaty. She wiped them on her kameez, hoping these men wouldn't harm Amar or her. Suddenly, the hand was giving the licence back to Amar and with a nod of the head they were allowed to continue.

'Is that it? Why did they let us go but take that man's things?'

Amar sighed deeply. 'They target us, but they target Kenyans more. It's disgusting. This is their country. We are sometimes given more freedom than Kenyans. Not much more but a bit. I don't know why, but that is the way it is.'

She watched him bring the stereo back out from beneath the seat and turn up the music. She hadn't even noticed him hiding it there – he must have quickly put it away once he saw the soldiers.

'Come, let's enjoy our day.'

Meena returned a smile, but her heart felt heavy.

'Smile, Meena. You are meant to be enjoying your time with me.'

'Sorry. It just feels wrong. Why do they have so much power?'

Amar sighed and turned the radio down one notch.

'They rule us, Meena. They rule Indians. They rule Kenyans. They rule other parts of the world too. It's just the way it is.'

They continued to drive for another twenty minutes, the radio now blasting Bollywood songs. As Amar parked the car, Meena looked out of the window. They seemed to be near a body of water as people were in swimwear. He hadn't mentioned swimming – she had no idea how to! There hadn't been much opportunity to swim back home. She got out of the car and felt the sun comfort her face, wrapping it in its warmth. She adjusted her saree, which always got skewed in the car.

The scenery was beautiful. Vivid green trees loomed over the tiny people, covering them in a safe blanket from the sun's rays. She could hear birds twittering, singing songs of love to each other. She and Amar began walking through the trees in silence, only hearing the nattering of voices and the calls mysterious hidden animals were making to each other. The trees were so full of life that Meena felt renewed. It was like they were breathing life back into her, sharing their energy. They walked down a manmade pathway, with seemingly never-ending trees all around them, keeping them safe from outside evils. Meena hadn't seen a place so pretty before.

As they continued walking, they came to a wider opening and Meena's footsteps came to a halt. What she saw before her was beauty like she had never seen before. A wide lake that looked as endless as the ocean. In the lake were hundreds or maybe thousands of bright pink creatures.

The lake itself looked like a beautiful sunset; shades of pink splashed across a blue sky. She began to walk again, completely unaware of Amar's whereabouts. She just knew she wanted to get closer. Her breath caught in her throat. These pink creatures were flamingos! They had been her and Parvathi's favourite animal when they were children. She sat down on grass that was so green it looked like it had been painted.

The whole scene looked like a beautiful piece of art, vivid colours splashed on the page, no sign of darkness in sight. She felt Amar sit next to her but didn't have words for him yet. Tears settled in her eyes. Parvathi would have loved this. She would have been so happy. She felt a pain in her chest as she longed for her baby sister. Her baby sister whose memories of Meena faded by the day.

She wished she had something to capture this moment. She heard a click and saw Amar standing with a device aimed at her. It was black and box-like with a circle in the middle. She put her hands up, unsure what this weapon was.

'Calm down, Meena. It's a camera. It takes pictures. So we can look back at this moment.'

She couldn't believe it. She had heard about cameras back home as the white men sometimes had them. She had never seen one up close.

'How did you get this?'

'I found it in the market. I managed to get it at a good price.'

'OK. How does it work?'

'You point it at what you'd like to capture. Press this button and snap! You have taken the picture. Then you can print the pictures and send them to anyone.'

Her heartbeat fluttered at the thought of showing Parvathi the images of the flamingos. She would be astounded! As she leaned back onto her elbows, she saw a family nearby, the siblings playing with each other, completely unaware of anyone but their own bubble of happiness. She cocked her head and watched them play. She couldn't stop the tears from pricking her eyes.

Amar's arm around her shoulders brought her back to the present. She settled into his body, enjoying the feeling of his warmth spreading through her body.

A community of vibrant pink flamingos clashing against the blue of the lake, the vivid emerald of the trees and the bright blue of the sky. She imagined a child holding onto Amar's hand, squealing at the excitement of seeing flamingos. A little boy or girl running across the grass, their little feet becoming muddy. Their little face lighting up at the beautiful scenery in front of them. Small hands wrapped around her finger, leading her closer to the lake, eradicating any fear she had. Just the prospect of a child made her heart swell, feeling five sizes bigger in her chest, squeezing all her other organs out of the way. Her whole body a heartbeat. She looked at the sun shining on Amar's face, giving him an angelic glow as if he were from another earth. Another universe.

As they walked back to the car, Meena couldn't keep the broad smile from her face.

Chapter Twelve

<u>Nairobi, 1947</u>

The sun soared in the sky, illuminating every possible surface in its glow. A roller bird sang into the sky, its lilac breast complimenting the vivid blue heavens above. As it soared into the atmosphere, it let out its harsh *rak-rak* sound. The trees leaves were an emerald green, rich and full of life. Plump juicy mangoes hung off the branches, just waiting to be picked and devoured.

It had been over five years since the day she had visited those beautiful flamingos, revelling in their fuchsia pink glory. She had visited them since, and the feeling of euphoria as she watched them feed and bathe never died. That place made her feel closer to home. Closer to Parvathi. They had continuously exchanged letters, Parvathi's always filled with hometown gossip that left Meena feeling like she still belonged back home.

Meena held the small baby in her arms, overcome with an immense, overwhelming feeling. She shouldn't pinpoint one firm emotion to attribute this swelling in her stomach and the shaking of her hands. A swirl of emotions blurred her eyes. Love. Pain. Fear. Longing.

The tiny human's eyelids fluttered, signalling her imminent need for food. Meena looked around her, feeling frantic. She stared intently at the delicate little face looking for signs of its needs. Her heart slowed down as she noticed that the baby had fallen fast asleep again. She cradled the warm body close, breathing in the scent of her scalp.

A full head of black hair graced her head. Small but thick eyelashes framed her wide almond eyes that shone brown like Amar's. Lips that were slightly too small for her face blew bubbles of spit which somehow made her look even more adorable. She was perfect. Her feet were no bigger than Meena's hand, the little toes on the end spongy from her bath. Her skin was a beautiful burnt caramel, one shade darker than Amar. Staring at this baby's face and seeing Amar's genes made tears fall down her cheeks. Her husband lived through this child. She held her close to her chest, shielding her from the sunlight that was shining through their bedroom window. A small gurgle erupted from the child's lips. Meena felt her pulse quicken. A sound so pure. So innocent.

The sound of familiar footsteps approached, signalling his arrival. She looked up to see her husband walk into the room, his worn-out shoes clicking against the tiled floor. His eyes crinkled as a wide smile graced his face. She had never seen him look so happy. He gently took the baby out of Meena's arms. A tidal wave of emptiness rushed over her. Like her insides had been scraped out and thrown away, leaving just skin and bone.

She couldn't help but stare at Amar as he cradled the child close to his chest. The longing to have the baby back in her arms made goosebumps riddle her arms and legs, causing her to shiver involuntarily. Her nose scrunched at her own frustration with herself. She couldn't fall too deeply in love with this little human. Despite it being over nine months ago now, it felt like only a week ago when Lakshmi had told her the big news Lakshmi was pregnant

During Lakshmi's pregnancy, she remembered hearing her sister-in-law's grumbles about back ache and the baby hurting her ribs. She had found herself spending less and less time with her sister-in-law, her whining making Meena cringe. She would purpose-fully avoid any room Lakshmi was in and leave any she entered. That feeling didn't last long, as her feelings of jealousy were overshadowed with pure protectiveness over Lakshmi and her child.

It was hilarious to watch Rajvir blossom into a father. His usual stern nature was replaced with a look of awe and giddiness every time he laid eyes on his baby. She would watch Rajvir and Lakshmi play with their baby, taking turns to hold her close. She would look up in earnest if the baby began to gurgle or sneeze. Her hands would involuntarily reach out when the baby cried.

As the baby gurgled its way into all their hearts, Meena felt a sense of peace. This child brought comfort to her in a way that nothing else did.

'Meena! Come here!'

She ran quickly to Lakshmi's room, fearful of what she may find. Her heart slowed as she saw Lakshmi with a smile that took over her entire face.

'Look how cute these clothes are! Look at how tiny! We can dress her up like a doll, Meena. She can be our little doll.'

Meena wanted to say so many things. A baby wasn't a doll; it was a baby. She quickly banished those thoughts and walked over to the tiny array of outfits.

'We can do whatever you like, Lakshmi. She is your baby. Amar is with her now. I can tell how happy he is for you. For you and Rajvir.'

She blinked the tears away, remodelling her face into a smile. Her hands folded the delicate clothing, attempting not to hold onto any one piece for too long. As Lakshmi left the room to get a drink, she held a small dress to her nose and breathed in. Her hands fingered the delicate lacework adorning the collar. When Lakshmi returned, she quickly folded the dress into a tiny bundle, barely giving it a second glance.

Chapter Thirteen

The sky was a beautiful shade of purple and pink, causing an ethereal glow over India.

'What a lovely lilac sky.'

Meena looked down at her baby sister and felt pure peace. Staring out across the seemingly never-ending sugar cane field, the emerald green grass meeting the lilac sky as the sun greeted them both, the sisters were completely relaxed. They could hear the sound of cows grazing nearby, and birds nesting in trees above. The contrast of the light lilac sky and the deep green canes made a stunning scene that they could sit and soak in forever. As Meena finished her sugar cane, she pulled a piece of grass out of the soil.

'Don't do that. The grass doesn't like it.'

'Why doesn't it like it, Parvathi? It's just grass. It doesn't feel anything.'

Parvathi looked at her with disappointment in her eyes. 'Of course it feels things. It feels the burning sun giving energy to its body. It feels the tongues of cows as they eat it. It feels your fingertips pulling its roots. How would you feel if you were pulled out of your home and then left? You wouldn't be very happy.'

Meena looked down at her little sister in awe. How could a child possess such knowledge and compassion for inanimate

*things like grass? She had never thought of grass that way.
As a living thing. She guessed it was. It needed food and
water just like she did. She tried to stick the strand of grass
back into the ground.*

*'It's too late now. Once you've pulled something from the
root, there's no saying how much longer it will live. The only
chance it has of survival is if it has some love.'*

*Parvathi picked up the little strand of grass and kissed it.
She held it to Meena's lips so she could kiss it too. Parvathi
laid it down with the other shards of grass.*

'Hopefully now it will live.'

*Meena knew that brief show of love wasn't enough to make
that piece of grass survive. It would need constant attention to
have a chance of surviving. It was kinder to let it die.*

She woke up in a sweat, to the sound of a baby crying.
How many times had she imagined that sound? Now
it was real. Through the thin walls, she heard Lakshmi
sing softly, her smooth voice easing the baby's cries.
Her mind wandered to her dream. Parvathi's small face
staring up at hers. The calm lilac sky encompassing them
in a daydream. Parvathi's words: '*Once you've pulled
something from the root, there's no saying how much longer it
will live. The only chance it has of survival is if it has some
love.*' The words echoed throughout her mind, refusing
to let her drift back to sleep. She looked over at Amar
peacefully sleeping through the noise, and sighed.

Some days, usually about a week after they had an
argument, he came home with gifts. Sometimes a beautiful saree, other times flowers or *barfi*. He whispered

sweet nothings in her ear, kissed her cheeks, cooked her meals. Just as quickly as those things started, they would disappear again.

For the last two years, his brothers had started coming over regularly. They had both temporarily moved back to India but now they were back in Kenya with their wives. Amar's behaviour changed around them. He didn't care that Lakshmi had seen the dark side of him, but he rarely let his brothers see it. Instead, he was caring and nice to Meena. She was expected to make dinner for them, clean up after them and make sure their every need was attended to. However, instead of his occasional cold demeanour, he remained patient and nice. He appeared to be the perfect husband.

She guessed, in some ways, he was. He was a great photographer, documenting some of their best moments. He was a good cook, easing the pressure on her from time to time. He made her laugh when he was in his jolly moods. He bought her beautiful things.

She was aware of the reality of her life. There were two sides to every coin. She was sure she was difficult to live with too. Marriage was about compromise. Even though she never became physical towards him, she knew she deserved his occasional blows. She made stupid mistakes.

She imagined his brothers would be around even more often now they had a little niece to visit. The day she was born, they had all crowded around wanting to know the sex.

'Well, is it a boy?'

'I bet it's a boy.'

'It must be a boy; it has strong genes.'

'Please, everyone. She's a girl. My little girl. Lakshmi said, softly.'

Meena had noticed the looks of disdain and disapproval from everyone but her husband. Amar had scooped up the little baby, holding her in one arm.

The sound of Lakshmi's singing subsided. The house fell into silence once again. Amar rolled back over to his side. Meena breathed.

She thought back to the day Lakshmi had given birth. No water broke. She just felt sudden pains and Rajvir had driven her to the hospital. Amar had driven Meena and Asmita to the hospital straight after. She had heard Lakshmi's cries of pain and then her cries of joy from the waiting room. Rajvir had emerged looking puzzled and vacant, but with his eyes filled with tears of happiness.

On that cloudy day, they had all gone to see Lakshmi cradling her little babe with eyes that shone through the dull room.

Before that day, they had spent hours debating whether it would be a girl or boy, dissecting every myth and superstition they had ever heard. Lakshmi had admitted that she wanted a boy first and then a girl. She wanted a boy to protect his baby sister. Meena knew from experience that girls were better protectors than boys. Girls normally needed protection *from* boys. Girls needed to protect themselves; men usually stuck together. She didn't voice any of her thoughts, however, and instead let Lakshmi daydream about her future son.

Seeing Lakshmi cradle her baby girl tightly in her arms told her all she needed to know. That baby girl was the best thing that had ever happened to Lakshmi and Rajvir. She would be treasured and loved for her entire life. Meena had no doubt about that. Asmita had run into the room late and exclaimed loudly, 'My child, my baby, my grandchild! Let me hold him!'

Lakshmi had calmly looked up into her mother's eyes. 'She's a girl. My baby girl.'

Asmita had halted, surprised at Lakshmi and Rajvir's creation being anything other than what she had imagined. Months of talking about her future grandson and buying blue outfits were now all lost. Seconds passed and silence dominated the room, filling every corner and crevice. Meena had been the one to break it. She had walked over to Lakshmi and peered down at the child's little face.

'She is so beautiful. More beautiful than I could ever have imagined. She has a beautiful soul. Just like you.'

Lakshmi had let the tears flow down her face as Meena put her forehead to Lakshmi's. They stayed like that for a few moments before Lakshmi whispered a 'thank you'. Asmita cleared her throat and strode forward.

'Give me my grandchild then.'

Lakshmi looked in Meena's eyes.

'Hold her, Meena. Hold your little niece. She is both of ours. Whenever you want to, you can hold her, bathe her, feed her. She is ours.'

Meena had taken the bundle into her arms and felt a

feeling she had never experienced before. A completeness. She had only held the baby a handful of times since, but each time brought the same pang to her heart. This innocent being knew nothing of pain, suffering and heartbreak. It just knew hunger and tiredness. And love, of course. It was clear that the baby was devoted to her mother and father. Every time she stared into Lakshmi or Rajvir's eyes, her own eyes shone with pure adoration. They didn't do that when she looked at Meena.

As she continued to stare at Amar holding the baby in his arms, she noticed that the baby's eyes sparkled when they looked at him too. Jealousy gripped her chest. She turned around and lay back down, leaving her husband to cradle his niece.

Chapter Fourteen

Nairobi, 1948

Meena regularly left the house. She had gone back to Lake Nakuru with the whole family a few times, and each time the emerald green leaves and vibrant fuchsia flamingos felt like undiscovered jewels. Their stark contrast always left her speechless, in awe of the beauty surrounding her.

As a new day began, she wrapped her saree around her body and quickly dabbed some red lipstick on. She painted her face in the mirror until she was no longer Meena Varma. Instead, she was Madhubala – an emerging Bollywood actress whose beauty was undeniable. Her brother had written in one of his letters about a movie Madhubala was the star in, and ever since Meena had watched it, she had decided she wanted to be just like her. The performer not only possessed great beauty but also acted in a way that glued your eyes to the screen, relishing in her every move. Her grace was evident even on a grainy black and white television. When Meena put on her own outfit, she told herself she was Madhubala and she could take on anything she wanted.

As Meena strode down the street, she noticed even more British troops than before. In the year that had passed, military personnel had increased in Nairobi. She knew it was no doubt due to India's independence. They had been granted freedom on 15 August 1947. She remembered that day with such clarity, it was like it was yesterday. Increased tensions and fighting in India had preceded an independence movement so strong, even the mighty British Empire couldn't defeat it. It had been due to the civil disobedience movement of Gandhi, she was told. His non-violent approach had spanned decades in India and South Africa. Ultimately, it had been successful. It cost many Indian lives at the hands of the British, but they had finally reached a state of independence and autonomy over their own land.

They had all hugged and held hands when they heard the news. That day, it didn't matter that she wasn't their blood. It didn't matter that she was a barren woman, adding nothing to their household. Nothing else mattered but the fact they were free. Indians all over the world rejoiced together, kissing and hugging each other with a joy that Meena had never witnessed in her lifetime.

However, the Kenyans weren't so lucky yet. You could feel the British fear in the air now. They had lost one of their most valuable countries.

Meena prayed each night that she would get to go home soon. She sat on the bed with her legs crossed, praying to whichever entity would listen. *Please let me see my family. Please let me go home.*

The market was quiet and the produce sparse. She had come too late in the morning. She brushed her fingers across a papaya. The skin was turning brown in the heat, the skin peeling away from its body. Maybe she would wait and come back another day. As she left, she murmured a quiet '*Jambo*' to a group of ladies braiding hair on the pavement. They smiled and shouted '*kuwa na siku njema*' at her. 'Have a good day too,' she had replied, smiling back at them in delight.

Meena kicked at the dusty path and turned back. As she entered the front yard of her house, she decided to walk around and straight into the garden. With her rose-coloured saree brushing against the tips of the grass, she strode towards her favourite spot. She sat down with a bump and leant back, enjoying the safety of the shade.

She stroked the trunk of her beautiful mango tree, caressing its bumps and curves. This tree had stayed with her, through moments of sheer joy, and moments that had brought her to knees, begging God to take her. She sat underneath it, grateful for its comforting embrace.

She hadn't seen her family in over six years. Six long years without her ma's hug, her siblings, fighting, her father's gentle tap of affection. She spent many nights dreaming of them all, especially Parvathi. She would be a teenager now. Nearly an adult. Meena guessed she would be married off soon too. In her letters, Parvathi remained sweet and kind, but with a newfound strength and stubbornness that had appeared in recent years. She didn't see Parvathi settling down so easily!

In the past six years, nearly all of her siblings had got married. Each time she had begged to go. Each time Asmita had denied her the chance.

Parvathi was the last one left. Meena's heart ached, thinking of her baby sister being married off to some man who didn't deserve her. Nobody deserved Parvathi. Her heart was bigger than any man's heart could ever be. The ripe smell of the sticky fruit brought her back to her home in India. As she drifted off under the mango tree, her mind took her back to the past.

She stared out of the window of the train, marvelling at how fast it travelled. They were visiting her father's hometown. His family had fled there amidst rising tensions between Muslims and Hindus and Sikhs. Tensions that her father told her existed due to the British antagonising each side, causing a divide that didn't exist before. Centuries of peaceful coexistence was being erased by white people who had no place in other countries, he said. His words washed over Meena. None of it meant much to her.

Parvathi, only six years old, had been particularly quiet during the journey. Meena had assumed she was just feeling a bit sick because of the motion of the carriage. However, as they came closer to the town, Parvathi started crying. Quiet sobs that nobody else noticed. Apart from Meena. Meena reached her hand out and held Parvathi's. Her brother Himet had also noticed and was gently rubbing Parvathi's back.

'What's wrong, didi?' their ma asked.

'I've been here before. I remember.'

Their ma gave a puzzled look to her husband.

'We haven't been here before,' their pa said. 'You're mistaken. I haven't been back here in years. Since marrying your ma.'

Parvathi shook her head. She wasn't backing down.

'I can prove it.'

She peered out of the window and looked around.

'We need to get off at this stop. Then turn right at the end of the street. There will be a jewellery shop there.'

Meena's father laughed it off but there was a slight tremor in his laugh. He decided to entertain her. As they shuffled off the train, with her father grumbling that this was the wrong stop, they started to walk the way Parvathi had instructed.

'See,' said her pa, once they had reached the end of the street, 'no jewellery shop.'

'Keep walking for a few minutes. It's on the left.'

They continued walking and Meena wondered why he was going along with it. Of course, Parvathi hadn't been here before. And if she had, she wouldn't remember every street. Or a jewellery shop for that matter. She didn't even own any jewellery!

Meena's apprehension soon became shock. There it was. A jewellery shop. On the left side of the road. They all stood together in silence, every one of them too afraid to speak. Even Parvathi looked uneasy at her own knowledge. Ma was the first to break the ice by sighing heavily. Meena looked up at her and wondered what she was thinking.

'Come,' said her ma. 'We'll go inside.'

They all crossed the road and stood outside the jewellery shop. Meena turned and noticed Parvathi was a few steps behind them.

'Come. This is because of you.'

Parvathi started shaking.

'I used to live here, Meena. I used to live here. I remember this shop. I remember the flat above it. It was my home.'

Meena hugged her sister and struggled to find the right words to say. Himet put his arm around them both, with Nita and Mohan trailing slightly behind. She thought Parvathi was crazy. Although she had known where this shop was. There was no way she could have known that.

Meena held her sister's hand as they entered the shop. The owner greeted them with a warm smile, taking in the sudden appearance of this large family in his shop.

'Salamu alaykum, *my friends. Welcome to our shop.*' He smiled at each of them until his eyes rested on Parvathi. He crinkled his forehead and rubbed his eyes. Meena noticed his eyes suddenly looked watery.

'One second please.'

The man disappeared behind the counter. Meena's ma wandered around the store, looking at the shiny pieces of gold. Nita joined her, her eyes sparkling at such stunning pieces of art.

'Sorry. This is my sister, Amana' the man said as he emerged with a young woman by his side. She looked no more than twenty years old, her black hair tied into an elaborate braid over her shoulder.

Amana politely said hello but looked directly at Parvathi. She clasped a hand to her chest.

Meena's father looked between them. 'What is wrong?'

'Your daughter, sir. She has the same eyes as my dear mother who passed just over six years ago. The same soul.

They look just like my mother's did when she was younger. A mirror image.'

Parvathi edged forward. She turned to Meena.

'I told you I used to live here. You didn't believe me.'

She went up to the counter, though she was not tall enough to see over it.

'How old was your mother when she died?' she asked with a confidence she had never possessed before.

'She was not old, only in her fifties. How old are you?'

'Six.'

The man and his sister clung to each other. They looked like they had seen a ghost.

'Our little Parvathi must be a reincarnation of your dear mother, my friend,' stated their ma. 'She knew exactly where your shop was, and she has never been here before. God is looking over you, brother. He has blessed this world with your dear mother once again. She must have been a remarkable woman.' Her ma clutched the hands of the two strangers they had just met, yet knew so much about.

Meena felt incredulous. Himet and Mohan's mouths were open in pure shock, their eyes darting between them all. Himet was too shocked even to make a wise remark!

Her sister was a reincarnation. She wondered if she was too. Or maybe Parvathi was just too special to be reincarnated as an animal or a tree. She was needed on this Earth as a human to bring joy to everyone around her. She felt an overwhelming protectiveness for her baby sister. What if these people wanted their mother back? Parvathi was hers now. She put an arm over Parvathi's shoulder, asserting her place.

The man looked between the two sisters.

'I see you have found another special family. The bond between you two sisters will stand the test of time and distance. No matter what, you two will have each other in this world.'

He looked at Parvathi, tears threatening to spill out of his slightly bloodshot eyes.

'You, my dear, please live a life as full as you can. Spread your light. This world needs it. Look after your sister; she will need you more than either of you know. I will let you and your beautiful family continue your journey now. You were so loved here, and I know you are so loved with them. Maybe we will reunite again in another life.'

He leant over the counter and pressed a gentle kiss on her forehead. Meena looked around and noticed tears in everyone's eyes. She wondered if she would one day have to see someone she loved reborn with another family. She hoped not. This was difficult enough. She couldn't imagine losing any of her family. They all walked back to the station and let out a collective sigh. Her father crammed them onto the next train and they got off a few stops away in his hometown.

'Meena! Meena!'

She awoke with a start. Rajvir was calling her name. She rubbed the sleep from her eyes and looked around. Where was he shouting from? She held onto the tree trunk to help herself up and then walked over to the house.

'Oh, I should have known you were over there. The phone was ringing for you. It woke up the baby.'

She noticed for the first time how tired Rajvir was. His eyes were surrounded by dark circles and a puffiness that had never been present before. That thought was quickly replaced by the fact that somebody had called on the phone for her.

'Who was it?'

'They are still on the line. Your parents, I think.'

Meena ran to the phone, flying past Rajvir. She picked it up.

'Ma? Pa? Is anyone there?'

'Meena, *beti*. It's your father. I have bad news, my *beti*.'

Meena's heart stopped. Her ma. Was she sick? Was Parvathi OK? What about all of her other siblings? Was her father ill?

'What is it?'

'It's your brother, *beti*. Your brother Himet. He was out on his motorcycle and he . . . had an accident. His heart stopped while he was riding. He didn't make it, Meena. Your brother has left us.'

Her father's sobs echoed down the line. Meena's body seized up, her fists tightened so hard it felt like they would explode. Her brother. Gone. He had been the one to kiss her cheek before she left home. He had been the one to sneak her bits of food when she was hungry. Her kind, yet mischievous brother. She felt emotionless. How much loss could one human take?

'Are you there, Meena? Did you hear what I said?'

'I'm coming home. I am coming home to you all. I will get there as soon as I can. I promise. I love you. Tell Ma I love her too.'

She hung up the phone and turned to Rajvir who was standing in the doorway.

When he saw her face, he straightened his posture.

'Are you OK, Meena?'

Meena tried to take a step forward but her legs gave way beneath her.

'Meena! Meena! Please get up. Are you OK? What happened?'

She sat against the wall. 'My brother, Rajvir. My brother Himet is dead.'

Saying the words out loud made it all seem so real. She felt a sickness in her stomach, and a migraine threatening to rob her of thought.

'Come. We'll get you home. I'll help you.'

She looked at him and felt a gratitude she had never felt towards him before.

Rajvir sorted everything for them, despite not travelling with them himself. He tried to find flights but they were rare and extremely expensive. Only the British and rich Kenyans and Indians could travel that way. Instead, they found a boat leaving the next day that they could board. Amar held her tight when she told him the news. He lay with her, listening to her talk about her childhood, playing with her siblings, until nightfall. He agreed to go with her to India without hesitation.

Asmita didn't say anything when Meena told her. Though, she did give Meena a small pat on the shoulder.

Lakshmi was her rock. She held her while she cried, she fed her, and made sure she was drinking enough water in the sickening heat.

Meena knew the journey took several days, although this time it would be quicker than her first voyage to Kenya. Ships had come a long way since then, Amar told her. The next day, they would be boarding the SS *Karanja*. She knew it set out from Mombasa originally and then came to Nairobi.

She was finally going home.

Chapter Fifteen

The next morning, she awoke at 4 a.m., the sky still a dark blue, covering the world in a warm blanket. She gently shook Amar awake.

'Come, we need to get going.'

Amar rolled over.

'Amar! We need to leave now, otherwise we won't make it.'

He made a grunting noise and kept his eyes closed. Fear gripped her stomach at the thought of missing the ship. She stared at his closed eyes intensely, waiting for a sign of movement. Suddenly, without saying a word, he opened his eyes, swung his legs off the bed and went to the bathroom.

Meena didn't care if he refused to say a word to her for the whole trip. As long as he got her to her family. She dressed quickly and waited for him to be done in the bathroom. Sweat dripped from her brow as she double-checked their bags were packed. A mixture of the summer heat and her anxiety was causing her to perspire. Her brown saree felt sticky against her legs. Her ma always used to tell her to dress in bright colours. She stared at the dull brown colour and began to unravel it. The shrieking ring of the phone stopped her and she ran to get it before it woke the baby.

'*Namaste*,' she said.

'*Namaste, beti.*' It was her pa. 'I know you said you were coming today so I was hoping to catch you before you left. Are you taking a plane?'

'No, Pa, we cannot afford it. I am coming by ship. Why are you even awake at this time?'

There was silence on the end of the line.

'Pa?'

'Sorry. It's two and a half hours ahead in time here, remember?'

She heard a shuffling sound at the other end of the line. A grunting cough followed.

'Meena. I'm sorry. Please still come. We . . . we can't wait for you. We need to burn . . . we need to cremate the body today. As soon as possible. I hoped you'd be able to fly here to make it.'

Meena leant on the wall, the heaviness of the situation fully settling in. She pulled a stray bit of skin from around her fingernail.

'Meena. Please still come.'

'Of course. I would do anything to see you all again. I should be there in a week, maximum. I love you, Pa.'

She heard his soft cries on the other end of the line and her hand tightened around the phone. His gentle sobs ran through her body, causing her to shiver.

'Meena, have you been OK?'

Meena nearly dropped the phone.

'What do you mean?'

'I . . . Your mother and I just feel like something is wrong. No children after all these years . . .'

She sighed and repeated her usual answer.

'We just haven't found the right time yet. I need to leave now to get the boat.'

'OK. Be safe.'

She hung up the phone and stared at the receiver, wishing it had never rung with such terrible news the day before. She thought back to her second pregnancy. She had been so excited that she had written a letter to her parents, telling them of the news. Amar was being gentle with her, and she had known that it would be different. She would become a mother.

The first time had just been an accident because of Amar. This time she would be extra careful. There would be no reason why the baby wouldn't survive. That's what she had told herself. Nothing would happen this time. And nothing did happen. She didn't fall. Amar didn't hurt her. She just felt a pain in her stomach on the way to the post office and saw the blood dripping down her legs. Twenty minutes more and the letter wouldn't have been in her hands anymore. Her parents would have celebrated a baby that no longer lived.

'Who was that? Who rings the phone at this time?'

She moved away from the wall.

'Oh, it was just a mistake. They rang the wrong number.'

Amar's forehead creased. He stared at her, sizing her up. His face relaxed.

'That's odd. Did Rajvir talk to them?'

Meena quickly stepped in front of the phone.

'No need! I handled it. We need to get going or we won't make it. Come. Finish getting ready.'

He suddenly grabbed her. Her heart lurched and she automatically hunched over in defence. He pulled her in for a hug and kissed her forehead.

'I know I haven't always been the best husband. I hope me taking you to India shows how devoted I am to you. Make sure you pack some of the nice sarees to show your family all the things I've bought you.'

She smiled. She gently kissed him on the cheek, and he brushed his fingertips across her face. The sound of beeping outside signalled the car was ready and told them it was time to go.

The ship was far more crowded than the one from her first journey. She wondered how many people could fit on this huge boat. Throngs of Indians and Africans swarmed the deck, trying to find their rooms. There was little order. A man was shouting 'Tickets,' yet everyone was focused on making sure they had their whole family with them and finding their rooms. They had already passed the first stage to board the boat and presented their documents and tickets. She didn't know why this gentleman was asking for tickets again.

She lugged her suitcase along and eventually found their room. They couldn't afford the more expensive tickets, so they had to share a room with two other people. They all had bunk beds. She was secretly glad not to have to share a bed with Amar. She missed her own space, although back home she had often awoken to Parvathi cuddled in her armpit. Amar had decided to take the top bunk, but his height prevented him from even reaching the bunk without hitting his head. Her eyes sized up the height of the bed. If she were to fall from the top bunk, she wouldn't die. She calmed herself down and told herself not to make a fuss. Amar had bothered to join her on this journey. He didn't need to hear her complaints.

The room was simple, with dark oak flooring and wall panelling. Light blue curtains covered a tiny window, the deck below offering a questionable view. The bedsheets were thin and white, with small tears in them. She wondered what had caused such little holes. Goosebumps travelled up her arms at the possibilities. A small rug sat in the middle of the room, offering little purpose. A small wardrobe was bolted to the floor, yet it was missing one door. There was a communal bathroom down the hall she had been told. She would do her best to avoid it.

She remembered their first journey. They had a room to themselves – a honeymoon present from Amar's brother, he had said. The room had been bigger, with bedsheets covered in tiny, embroidered flowers decorating the strong oak frame. They had a small bathroom to themselves, with a bucket for washing. The window had been big enough to look out of and see the vast sea stretching out, assuring her there was no chance of escape.

Those little luxuries had removed some of the anxiety

and fear she had felt that day. Yet, as she stood in this enclosed room, she felt more settled than she had back then.

She climbed to the top bunk and tried not to look down. She spoke to herself internally, taking deep breaths to calm her nerves. *Don't complain, Meena. Deal with it. It's only about a week. Then you will see them all again. You will be reunited with the people you love most.*

As the ship rocked on the waves, she felt her stomach move with it. She closed her eyes. Why did it feel so hot in here? As she was fanning herself with her hand, she longed for ice and cold air.

As she lay on the bed, she imagined what the rooms in the rest of the boat were like. Those reserved for white people were surely more elegant. Even during meals, the passengers would be split – the white people would eat first, and then everyone else would eat what was left. However, the cooks on the boat were also people of colour, so they frequently saved the best bits for them.

Thinking of food made Meena's mouth water. It must only be morning still, but she hadn't eaten yet. They had brought some fruit with them, but she didn't want to risk eating it all now and being hungry for the rest of the trip. The vegetarian food selection was plentiful, with a lot of customers being Indian, but it always lacked a certain spice or flavour.

A loud boom signalled that the ship was about to leave the dock. It was about time. They didn't seem to have any roommates, which had positive and negative aspects. It meant they had the space to themselves and more privacy; however, it also meant that nobody was present to make sure Amar was on his best behaviour.

A yawn escaped her lips and she decided to have some rest. She closed her eyes, feeling the gentle movement of the boat. She found her mind drifting to Lakshmi's new baby, Ash. Her chubby little cheeks, the bubbles of spit that erupted from her lips every now and again. Everything she did was cute. She would soil herself and everyone thought it was adorable. She was cute, but the screaming and constant need for attention was enough to make Meena glad for a break. She missed Lakshmi. She missed spending time with her without another person in the way. She missed the both of them being childless together.

Guilt caused her to shift her body. She shouldn't envy a baby for taking her sister and friend away from her. Or did she envy Lakshmi for having someone else to love and adore?

Suddenly she heard the creak of footsteps on the bed's ladder. Her body froze over. Her breathing got quicker, and she felt her arms begin to shake.

'Meena? Are you awake?'

'Amar?'

He lay down next to her on the small bed, his large frame barely fitting in such a constrained space. His body was almost crushing hers, space but she didn't mind. They lay there quietly for a while until a baby's cry from an adjoining room broke the silence.

'It's like we're back home!' Amar exclaimed.

'I know. I was hoping for some peace and quiet on this journey' Meena muttered.

Amar pulled back from her, his body tense. 'Do you not like living with Lakshmi and my family, Meena?'

She looked into his eyes, hoping he would see the truth in hers.

'I love seeing the baby every day. I love holding her close and smelling her scalp. It can just be . . . hard sometimes. You wouldn't understand, Amar.'

'I find it hard too. I want a child too. Yet, through every miscarriage, you act like you are the only one who has lost something. You aren't. I lost something too. I lost the chance of being a father. Yet you keep your loss to yourself. You hide away. You lie in bed. You don't tell me how you feel. I'm supposed to just carry on as normal, while you get to grieve. I want to grieve too.'

Looking at his tired face, his eyes full of defeat, Meena couldn't help but feel guilty. She had always seen the losses as her own because she was the one to experience them. To grow the baby inside of her. To then see the blood and know it was gone. Amar never seemed to care. In fact, he grew more despondent each time. To hear his perspective, to see his pain, made Meena close her eyes and sigh.

'I'm sorry, Amar. I should have been there for you too. I was too busy focusing on myself. My own selfish needs and pain. We should have been there for each other. I'm sorry.'

He held her tight and they spent the night lying on the bunk bed, completely entwined.

Chapter Sixteen

On the boat back to Kenya, Meena felt a sense of peace. She had been with her family as they had sprinkled her brother's ashes in the Ganges, watching his remains float alongside those of other lost souls. Her brothers bathed in the river, tears mixing with the holy water.

Meena and Amar had arrived late and been greeted by Nita's wealthy husband. He hadn't been the most welcoming person, but he had driven them to Meena's home at a late hour. He spent the car journey talking about his superiority in the community, all the while flashing his gold watch to them. Meena had zoned out after around fifteen minutes. She noticed that Amar had shifted in his seat several times, his eyes glued to the car's flashy interior and integrated radio.

As soon as they had arrived home, Meena had run to the door, straight into her parents' arms. That had been the best feeling in the world.

Parvathi had emerged from her room, clearly wide awake. Meena knew she had been waiting up for her. Her ma had shown Amar to their room, which looked substantially tidier than it used to. The first night, Meena hadn't slept there. Amar had passed out as soon as he lay on the bed, exhausted from their long journey. The tiredness Meena felt had been overtaken by her joy. The adrenaline had rushed through her body and she had spent hours talking to Parvathi in hushed tones until they had fallen asleep in each other's arms.

The next morning, the reality of why she was there had hit her. Her brother. In the daylight, she could see the clear torment on her parents' faces. She assumed they hadn't slept much the night before or any night in the last week. She had hugged them both tight, wishing she didn't have to let go.

Amar had woken up in a great mood. He hadn't shown any sign of anger that Meena hadn't shared a bed with him. In fact, he said he had slept better than he had in years. 'India is your home, that's why,' Meena's ma had said to him. Amar had managed a half-smile but Meena could tell he didn't appreciate the comment. Nairobi was his home and always had been.

They had spent the morning talking about anything other than death. They spoke of independence, autonomy for their land. Meena was surprised at how eloquently Parvathi spoke about politics. They had discovered that the British hadn't truly left. While they didn't exercise control and power like they used to, they still owned large numbers of rice fields and tea plantations. Many Indians were still treated as slaves, doing the work while the British reaped the rewards.

Her parents asked her countless questions about Nairobi, but she was limited in her answers with Amar standing over her. She had told Parvathi everything the previous night. Parvathi had held her tight for hours, mending Meena's broken pieces and gluing her back together. Parvathi had also told her that while her parents had been initially happy at the words she had written in her letters, they had gradually become suspicious.

'They know how you write, Meena. They know you write with your heart. Your heart wasn't in those words. It was like a robot had written them. Father even said he was going to Kenya to see you. To see what was happening. Ma stopped him though. She said you are married now. You have a new family. You don't need them interfering. I told father to go, though. I think he was too scared of Ma to do it in the end. I wanted to see you. I knew something was wrong. It's been six years, *didi*. Why did you wait six years?'

Silent teardrops painted Parvathi's face and Meena sensed that she felt betrayed. She felt abandoned. She had begun to plait her sister's hair, soaking the strands with *tel*, falling back into old habits.

'I wanted to come home. They didn't let me. I missed weddings. Funerals. I couldn't miss this one. I couldn't go without seeing your face for a minute longer.'

Now, looking at Parvathi's face in the morning light, Meena felt a pain in her chest at the thought of not seeing it every day.

The conversation around the table had grown more strained as the time came for them to leave for their trip to the River Ganges. They had held onto the ashes for longer than usual so Meena could join them. Their train left at 2 p.m. The journey would take nearly a day, but they wanted the best departure for their son. Amar had decided to stay at the house. He said he had some business to take care of and some of his own family to see. Nobody had protested. In fact, Meena noticed the relief on her ma's face. She guessed they just wanted their own family there. Their own flesh and blood.

After bathing in the Ganges, Meena and her family had decided to go to dinner and eat her brother's favourite food. They had found a local restaurant serving *thalis* of *daal*, *bangaan*, pickle, *rotis* and rice. They also served *kheer* – her brother's favourite pudding. In fact, he often skipped dinner and just ate *kheer* for dessert – a rich, creamy rice pudding seasoned with saffron and delicate spices. As they all laughed around the table, reminiscing about their brother's goofy ways, Meena wished she could stay. She knew leaving would be even harder now than the first time. Now she knew what she was going back to.

She noticed the way her father looked at her mother. His eyes were full of adoration and love. All these years together and she had never seen him raise a fist to her. Never seen him insult her with sharp words. Never seen him torment her. She struggled to peel her eyes away from them.

It hadn't taken long for conversation to turn back to politics. Everyone spoke over each other, their previous manners dissipating as the family fell back into old habits.

She soon learnt that British atrocities hadn't stopped on 15 August 1947. Rather, tensions between Muslims and Hindus had reached a peak. Hundreds of people were killed in the days following independence. The British had sparked the conflict to maintain their control over the land, but when chaos erupted, they ran. It wasn't their problem anymore and they no longer cared. Not only had hundreds of innocent people died during the demonstrations – Gandhi had also been murdered. She vaguely remembered Amar telling her of Gandhi's death, but it was all a blur. She figured it must have happened around the time she had lost a baby. After that, she had tuned everything else out. In fact, she had tuned everything out in the last few years. She had become a shadow of herself, doing the basic human movements to seem alive but having no soul to guide her.

Praise around the table erupted for Gandhi. 'He was the epitome of what a man should be. Of what a human should be. He was the saviour of India,' Meena's ma stated, in a tone as if she were addressing the whole nation.

'A man who appears so charming and good must have a dark side,' Meena said. 'They all do.'

With that, she looked at her lap, suddenly nervous at the strength behind her own words.

'Come, let's go,' her pa said. 'Has everyone finished eating?'

All eyes darted to Parvathi, who was still shovelling food into her mouth using both hands, with speckles of *daal* staining her saree.

'Not yet!' she exclaimed.

Laughter erupted around the table. Light insults and gentle pokes went around the table as they quibbled.

Her brother Mohan took her hand into his and the rest of the family followed. They all said a silent prayer together, quiet tears drifting down their faces. As they got up to leave the table, Meena noticed that the tears hadn't stopped flowing from her mother's eyes.

During her trip, she had discovered that her father had fallen ill only weeks after she had first left for Nairobi. He had complained of chest pains and a throbbing in his right arm. Eventually, a knock on the door from the police had told her mother that he had collapsed at work and was in hospital. He had suffered a heart attack but, thankfully, he had recovered in a few weeks. The hospital bill had been steep, but her sister's new husband had helped pay for it. Apparently, he came from a wealthy family. It seemed Nita's childhood daydreams of marrying a rich man had been fruitful.

Her ma had remained the core of the household. She had looked after her husband, as well as the children she had left at home. She had been the one to find them suitable partners to marry. She had been the one to hold them all together. Yet, when Meena laid eyes on her mother, she knew that this time, her ma was the one who needed holding together. She had lost a son. No mother should have to lose her child. To watch their young body burn into ash. Her ma looked like she had aged ten years in the week following the death. Meena had held her tight for hours, never wanting to forget the feeling of her mother's touch.

Amar had seemed out of place. He never knew quite what to say, who to talk to. His usual charm was shrouded in uncertainty. Now that he had to adjust to being in her home, with her family, Meena wondered if he would understand how she felt living with his family every day. Being on his turf. Seeing him look so lost was almost amusing. However, her parents had welcomed him with open arms. In her letters, she had written only positive things, not wanting to worry her parents. Yet, she could see the hesitation in her ma's eyes, see the way her pa kept Amar at a slight distance, always watching him.

Her reunion with Parvathi had been everything she had wanted and more. Parvathi had grown into a beautiful woman, with flowing, thick hair down past her hips. Meena had no doubt that it would be easy to find her a husband. Just as long as he was every bit as kind and special as Parvathi was.

Chapter Seventeen

<u>Nairobi, 1951</u>

Screaming. Harsh cries ripped through the silence. Meena rolled over in the bed, trying to block out the noise. She heard Amar sigh and put the pillow over his head. His days of getting up to comfort the cries had been short-lived. Yet the shrieks showed no sign of quietening. In fact, they appeared to be getting louder. Meena grumbled to herself and sat up. As she swung her legs off the bed, she thought back to quieter days and nights. Oh, those quiet nights. She shuffled over to the door and opened it, hoping the crying would abruptly stop and she could go back to bed. She should have known better by now.

As she walked over to the crib, her head began to throb. *How can one small thing create so much noise?* She picked up the child and held her to her chest. Immediately, the baby stopped crying and looked at Meena with eyes that shone as bright as the moon. That was why Meena dealt with the cries. For those eyes. The baby didn't look at anyone else that way. Only her. This time, she was the special one. She had begun to sing a Hindi lullaby to her when she heard footsteps approach.

'Meena, sorry. As soon as she started crying, the other one started fussing. Rajvir was knocked out, I couldn't even wake him. He's tired, poor thing. Right, I can take her now.'

Meena went to hand baby Ash back to Lakshmi but as soon as her hands let go, the shrieks started again. Lakshmi's eyes sparkled with tears. She quickly handed Ash back to Meena and sat down.

'She loves you more than me. Why does she love you more than me?'

Meena couldn't help but feel a sense of pride.. The baby loved her. For once, she was the favourite. The pain in Lakshmi's eyes told her to hide her own glee and say the words Lakshmi needed to hear.

'She doesn't love me more than you. You are her mother, not me.'

'It doesn't feel like it. She clings to you. She yearns for you. When I try and pick her up, she fusses and dribbles. When you pick her up, her whole face lights up.'

Lakshmi walked over to the kitchen and began fumbling around, looking for something to comfort her. She settled on some homemade *barfi* Meena had made the day before. Meena looked at her sister and struggled to keep the look of disbelief off her face. Lakshmi still managed to look beautiful even after months of little sleep. A small gurgle distracted her and Meena noticed that the baby's eyes were closing, as she fell into a blissful sleep.

'Here, take her. You just need to connect with her more, that's all. You spend so much time with Ameera. Maybe the baby just wants some company.'

Lakshmi took the now fast asleep baby and held her close. There was no doubting that the baby was Lakshmi's. Despite her closeness to Meena, it was very clear who her mother was. Meena bid Lakshmi good night and walked back to her room.

In the past two years, Meena had suffered one more miscarriage. Shortly after returning from India, she had discovered she was pregnant again. That time, she had convinced herself it would last. It hadn't.

The arrival of Lakshmi's new baby had transformed Meena's life. With Lakshmi being so preoccupied with two-year-old Ameera, she didn't have as much time with this baby. Meena had taken to the small child straight away, caressing her small cheeks and whispering words of love into her tiny ears.

When they went for walks, taking one pram each, people would stop and ask them how old each of their babies were. Lakshmi never corrected them. She never made a point to say both were hers. The first time it happened, Meena felt her face flush. She took an involuntary step back and muttered something about the baby not being hers. The poor ladies had walked away, frightened and confused by her reaction. Now, she went along with it, proudly showing the baby off as her own, watching the Kenyan women coo and ask questions about her niece's eating and sleeping habits.

At first, Meena had taught herself Swahili by, reading signs and books, slowly sounding out every word until she got it right. However, she had really started to become fluent when she had begun to go outside more. She started going to the markets on a Saturday with a local group of Kenyan women who had helped her learn key phrases, which soon became full conversations. She had even been spending time in an allotment with them recently. They told their husbands they were going to grow fruit and vegetables, but actually they went to have a laugh and gossip about the other groups of women they saw at the Saturday market. Lakshmi had joined her once, but with two babies keeping her company, she had left Meena to continue on her own.

In the past two years, Asmita had taught her how to cook a variety of dishes, complaining that she was too old to continue cooking herself. Meena was now shaping up to be quite the cook.

As Lakshmi consumed the whole box of *barfi,* she watched baby Ash murmur in her sleep and smiled to herself.

Chapter Eighteen

<u>Nairobi, 1952</u>

It was happening again. She had been so careful. She had done everything to avoid this moment. Her hands shook with anxiety and fear. She didn't think she could go through it again. Mentally and physically. It was too much.

She was pregnant. It had started off with the usual sickness and cramping in her stomach. She had so desperately wanted to pretend it wasn't happening, so she hadn't told anyone. Lakshmi was horrendously busy with two children; she didn't notice anything was wrong. Amar had been preoccupied with work and woke up early so he usually missed the first round of sickness. Asmita was in her own world as always, but Meena sensed she knew, just by the way her eyes began following her around again, watching her every move. Rajvir was also busy at work, and with his two children. So, she kept her secret to herself for three months. She didn't even visit a doctor. What was the point when she knew she would lose it shortly after?

The first three months passed, and she stopped feeling nauseated. Rather, she just felt sluggish. However, the cries of baby Ash were enough to get her moving and doing all the things she needed to do. She told her secret to Ash, short for Aishwarya. Nobody called her by her full name, not even Asmita. Ash giggled in response, having no idea what Meena was saying. She wondered how words sounded to a baby's ears. Did they understand any of it? At such a young age, she doubted Ash had any idea what was going on. All she knew was cuddles, feeding and bath time.

Her belly started to slowly expand, and three months turned to four. When she was nearly five months along, she couldn't pretend anymore. Her belly was rapidly growing, and she craved foods she hadn't eaten since she was a child. Hope had begun to creep in, filling her veins with a renewed energy.

She had told Lakshmi first. Her sister-in-law had bounded off the bed with an energy that Meena hadn't seen in years. They had held each other for an unknown amount of time, crying silent tears. The joy on Lakshmi's face made Meena feel positive for the first time in a long time. It had been the longest period of time that she had managed to keep a baby. Once she had reached the four-month mark, she had secretly gone to a doctor twice, confirming that she was still pregnant, and the baby was healthy.

When she broke the news to Amar, she had been careful. She had spent hours practising her expression of disbelief in the mirror.

She had held his hands and looked into his eyes.

'Amar, I have something to tell you. I'm pregnant.'

'What are you saying, Meena?' he asked, his eyes looking beyond hers at the television.

'Listen. Please. I am pregnant. Five months pregnant.'

Silence ensued. She looked away from his face, scared in case his expression changed. Suddenly, his arms were around her, holding her in, kissing her cheeks with his lips. Tears stained her saree, causing the material to become transparent.

'Are you happy, Amar? Please say you're happy.'

'I am the happiest man in the world. I hope this one lasts Meena. It will, I can feel it.'

Meena half-smiled. He said that every time. It never lasted. However, something inside her told her this time it might. This time, she might have her own baby.

Lakshmi had come bounding into the room, too excited to stay away. They all squealed and cried, and Lakshmi began singing a Hindi love song, dancing around the room like a crazy person. Rajvir entered the room with the two children, looking utterly bewildered. Meena wondered why he always looked so bewildered, even after all these years. Once he managed to decipher their words, his expression changed to one that Meena rarely saw. Absolute joy. He hugged her and whispered a blessing in her ear. As it happened, Asmita was at a friend's house. They all decided to tell her over dinner.

Five months turned into six and six into seven. Clothes became impossible to fit into, especially her beloved silk sarees. Food quickly disappeared due to uncontrollable cravings. Phone calls were made every day to her parents and Parvathi, assuring them she was OK. Her parents struggled with the idea of talking over the phone, but they were trying to get used to it.

She promised them she would take her baby to see them in India. Everything was going so well, yet Meena's mind was wide awake every night. Something could still go wrong. She could still miscarry. She could lose the baby in childbirth. She could die in childbirth. She knew how common it was for women to die while giving birth in India. She wondered how common it was here. Baby kicks and Ash's crying kept her up, causing her to spend half of the daytime sleeping.

When she reached month nine, she went to the doctor with Amar. He told her she was due to give birth very soon. The next forty-eight hours were endless. She paced the house and garden. She stared at the time. She lay in bed plaiting and unplaiting her hair. Then it happened. Her waters broke. Amar rushed her to the hospital.

Thirteen painful hours later, she was holding a precious little girl in her arms. Her own baby girl. A daughter to call her own. Amar had cried with joy, holding her so tightly yet so delicately. Asmita had made a comment about yet another girl being born into the family, but held the baby with a look of astonishment in her eyes. Meena took in all the expressions of pure disbelief and shock on their faces.

Against all the odds, here was her baby girl for all to see. Now, she could walk along the street with Lakshmi, with her own baby in a pram. When people asked how old her child was, she would tell them with pride.

Lakshmi had held the baby after Amar, and Meena noticed the looks between her and Rajvir. But, the sound of her child having its first sneeze took her mind away from everything else.

Aside from having her own child, the past two years had been fruitful. Parvathi had got married. Meena and Amar had gone back to India for the occasion, Meena refusing to miss her baby sister's wedding day. Surprisingly, Parvathi's husband ended up being one of the nicest men Meena had ever met. He was smart, well-dressed, and kind. Parvathi deserved nothing less. In fact, Parvathi was the witty, sharp one out of the two. Her husband just stared at her admiringly, looking completely in love. Meena couldn't be happier for them. She had left India knowing that Parvathi was safe. She had someone decent to look after her, to provide for her. Meena's parents had chosen well for their daughter.

Meena stayed in the hospital for two days. Apparently, she had low iron levels, so they had to give her a blood transfusion and monitor her. Aside from incredible tiredness, she felt absolutely fine. Her baby stayed in a crib near her bed, never too far from her reach.

Amar visited every day and stayed as long as he could. Meena was always silently thankful when he left. She hated the feeling. She liked time with her baby, all to herself. When the nurse told her she could go home, she felt scared. Her legs quivered and she began picking at the skin around her fingers again. She didn't know how to incorporate her baby into life at home. It felt safe here in a hospital. She didn't know about feeding and bath times – only what she had done for Ash, which was following instructions Lakshmi had given her. What if she hadn't been doing the right thing? What if, after all this time, she wasn't a good mother?

The anxieties crippled her. Amar's strong arms, helping her out of the bed and into the car parked outside, steadied her. She wasn't doing this alone. She would have Amar by her side, until the day they saw grandchildren running around. The thought empowered her. She would never be alone in this journey.

As they made the journey home, Meena carrying her baby in her arms, she looked out of the window. What a beautiful country to start a family in. What a beautiful place for her child to call home. As the full moon rose in the sky, Meena looked down at the sleeping bundle in her arms.

'Amar, what do you think of the name Purnima for her?'

'Like the moon?'

'Yes, it's a full moon tonight.'

'OK. We'll name her Purnima.'

As Meena held her baby tight to her chest, she felt complete.

Chapter Nineteen

'Meena, I think we should talk about our future.'

Fear gripped her stomach. Their future. Was he going to leave her? She took deep breaths like the doctor had taught her during childbirth. Deep breath in. Hold for ten seconds. Release.

'Meena?'

'Yes, Amar. What about our future?'

'I think we should leave Nairobi.'

She released the breath she had been holding in.

'You want to move to another part of Kenya?'

'No. With India achieving independence, I see Kenya doing the same soon. I think we need to find somewhere else to settle.'

'We could go back to India!' she exclaimed, suddenly excited at the thought of being back home with her family.

'No. We need to move forward, Meena. Somewhere with good prospects for our child.'

They both sat in silence, pondering what to do. If India wasn't an option, where else could they go?

'Amar . . . how about England?'

As soon as she said the words, she wished she hadn't. She knew nothing about England! All she knew of it were the British soldiers and civilians she had seen back home and here in Kenya.

'That's not a bad idea, Meena. I've seen a few other families leave for England. I hear there are good opportunities there. Purnima could have a good education, get a good job. It's a great idea,' he said, his face crinkling into that ever-so-charming smile.

She couldn't help but smile back, unsure if she had just made the best or worst decision of her life.

'What about Ma? And Lakshmi and the babies?'

'Let's talk to them tonight. I know Ma won't want to leave here. It's her home. We need a new start though, Meena. All of us do. The kids can all grow up together in England. They could start businesses! They could become academics! They don't have as many choices here or in India. You can only grow new leaves once you've cut the old, dead ones off, Meena. Let's grow!'

Meena couldn't help but feel like it was time she began to flourish and grow.

Chapter Twenty

She stepped out of Heathrow Airport and shivered. She saw a British family emerge from the airport, the teenage girls wearing tiny T-shirts that showed off their stomachs. Her mouth dropped open. She looked around and noticed other people wearing kameez without the trousers. Men walked past in shortened pants, their calves red. Ladies wore darkened glasses over their eyes and men wore hats. She held her cardigan tighter around her body and looked back at the children.

Purnima and Ash were both crying hysterically, asking for a blanket. She sighed and rummaged around in her suitcase.

'Here. Come on, stop crying. I won't make it hotter, will it?'

She was on the verge of tears too. She stood there with the two girls and looked around her. There seemed to be a slight fog in the air. The sky here was mainly white, with glimmers of blue peeping through.

She heard squeals behind her. Without even turning around, she took a deep breath.

'Ash. Purnima. Stop it, please.'

They both stopped but experience taught her that it wouldn't last long. Amar finally emerged from the airport, grunting with the weight of his suitcase.

'I thought you were going to wait for me inside. You don't know where you are going here.'

'And you do? Plus, we wanted to enjoy some of the amazing British weather.'

His face turned sour, but she was too tired to care. She was glad they had taken the plane though – that was one battle she had won. Rajvir had kindly leant them some money. The whole experience had been nauseating. Purnima was absolutely fine and loved the experience. However, Meena and Ash had felt constantly on the verge of vomiting and couldn't eat any of the food they had been served. Imagine serving food in the air! Just the thought of it was ridiculous. However, she did marvel at how huge and powerful the machines were.

As Amar started walking off, she followed him, making sure the girls were close to her. Her eyes scanned the people walking near them, her hands instinctively reaching for the children when somebody got too close.

As she walked, she began to notice some people giving her strange looks. People walked around with red faces, clothes that looked too tight for their bellies to hold, and skin that looked wrinkled and worn. She was dressed with her saree wrapped around her elegantly, keeping her legs warm in this chilly weather. She noticed two people pointing at her. Her eyes followed their fingers and she realised they weren't just pointing at her; they were pointing at her girls too. Her arms reached around them both, ushering them along. Purnima and Ash looked beautiful in the dresses she had sewn for them herself. She had lined their eyes with kohl for good luck and tied their hair up into a *choti*, delicate braids interwoven to keep the hair out of their faces.

She pulled them closer to her and noticed she could no longer see Amar. Her hands tightened and she felt her head swim. The brutal wind was making her nose cold and she felt a headache coming on. Her legs felt tired and swollen. Just as she was about to find somewhere to sit down, she noticed him waving her over. He was standing next to a car with a driver she didn't recognise. He waved again, this time signalling for them to hurry up.

'Come, Ash and Purnima, apparently we are walking too slowly.'

She lifted the suitcase onto her shoulder and walked towards him, cursing herself for suggesting they move here. What had she been thinking? She reached the car and asked Amar who the driver was.

'My brother said he was sending a driver. It must be him, I think. Come, let's get in. He said a black car would be here to pick us up.'

She hesitated but Amar's look of pride told her it would be OK. He told the driver where to go and they began to drive.

The girls clamoured to look out of the window, wanting to see their new home. Meena watched Ash, wary that she could ask for her mother at any time. But, Ash seemed completely unaware of her new situation.

Back in Kenya, they had had a family chat over dinner, discussing their options. Asmita had immediately withdrawn inside herself, tears welling in her eyes but not daring to escape. Rajvir was optimistic – it would be a good move for business. Lakshmi had seemed hesitant but open to the thought of moving somewhere where her children would have brighter futures. However, she wasn't ready to move yet.

'I need time here. I feel like I just got back into the swing of life again. Rajvir needs time to settle up his work too.' Rajvir had agreed with her. They weren't ready yet. However, Lakshmi had a suggestion which shocked them all.

'Take Ash with you. Purnima will be so lonely in a foreign country on her own. She needs someone to play with. They're similar in age and can keep each other company while you settle in.'

Rajvir's forehead had creased at the thought. He had stared at Lakshmi, his eyes questioning why she would even suggest that they part from their younger daughter. However, Meena knew. Lakshmi had struggled with connecting to Ash. Ameera and Lakshmi had an instant bond from the second Ameera was born. But, Meena had noticed that Lakshmi would often pass Ash to her or Amar when she was crying, claiming the noise was giving her a headache. Lakshmi needed time, and Meena would do anything to help her sister.

'That's fine, Lakshmi. We will take her.' A smile passed between the two sisters, sealing the deal.

Now Meena was questioning her hastiness. As much as she adored Ash, two children felt like twenty, especially on a plane journey with no space to escape.

There was a dullness to everything outside the car window. It was as if everything had been painted in bright colours, but then washed over with grey.

As the car sped down the road, Ash and Purnima became strangely quiet, not even looking out of the window anymore. Meena noticed they were holding hands.

On the other hand, Amar seemed at ease. He had the window down, copying the actions of the driver. As soon as the driver put an arm out, Amar did the same. As soon as the driver tapped his fingers on the steering wheel, Amar tapped his fingers on his knee.

The driver pulled up outside what looked like a garage but with windows. They all sat waiting for the car to continue moving.

'This is it then,' said the driver.

'Sorry, I don't think it's the right address,' Amar said.

'Trust me, I know these streets better than you. This is it.'

Meena noticed the withering look on the driver's face and quickly bundled the children out of the car. Amar followed.

'What are you doing, mate? You haven't paid me!'

She looked at Amar and noticed that his face was frozen still.

'Didn't my brother send you?'

His broken English made the driver looked confused.

'I don't know what brother you are on about, mate, but I need my money.'

Who is 'mate'? Meena wondered. Ash suddenly shouted: 'Ok, mate.' Meena needed to get out of this car. Fast.

'Pay him, Amar, so we can go inside.'

'How much is it, sir?' he asked.

The driver looked amused but Meena had no idea why. How was Amar supposed to know the price? She watched the driver fiddle with some sort of device with numbers on it located on the dashboard. Before she could ask what he was doing, the driver spoke.

'That'll be six shillings.'

Meena didn't know English currency yet but her instinct told her that was expensive. They were being scammed. The journey had only been ten minutes!

'I'll see if I have it. Could you not offer a better price?'

The driver looked astounded.

'A better price? Are you bargaining a taxi fare with me?'

Amar's hands shook as he tried to find the right currency. He managed to get it, but Meena noticed how empty his wallet looked afterwards.

Meena noticed the taxi driver's wry smile as he took the money and sped off without glancing back. Amar's face was coated in embarrassment and shame.

She picked up her suitcase and walked towards the door. She turned to see Amar still standing in the street, looking completely lost. All the resentment she had felt towards him dissipated in that moment. He was just as lost as she was. She had to be there for him.

'Come, let's go and see inside!'

Her feigned excitement surprised even her. The children perked up at the positive tone in Meena's voice and charged to the door, excited to see what lay beyond it. Amar forced a smile that didn't quite reach his eyes. He lugged his suitcase over to the door and knocked timidly. Seconds passed and nobody answered. He tried again, this time knocking with more force. Several more seconds passed and still nobody answered. Just as Meena was about to suggest trying the back garden, they heard a shuffling of footsteps. The door slowly opened to reveal an elderly white woman in a baby pink dressing gown and fluffy slippers. She looked like she hadn't yet showered. The lady stared at them until realisation dawned on her face.

'You must be the new tenants. Come on, come in then. One of your people came by yesterday to confirm you were arriving today. I get confused. All of you look the same.'

Her voice was raspy and sounded like she was struggling to breathe. Meena wondered if the fog that hung over the city was the reason. If so, she was not raising these children here.

'Yes, that would be my brother, Abhay. That is probably why we look alike!' Amar laughed as if the lady had been joking.

'Are all the other wogs your brothers and sisters too, then?'

This time it was her turn to laugh, the sound coming out distorted from her warped lungs. Meena had no idea what she had said. She had grasped the conversation so far, but that sentence had confused her. What was a 'wog'? It didn't even sound like a real word. Amar's face had turned darker, the redness of his cheeks not as apparent on darker skin.

'Well, don't just stand there then. Grab your stuff and follow me.'

Meena realised there was no rush. The pace at which this lady walked up the stairs was startling. No wonder she'd taken so long to open the door. They all politely waited for her to get at least halfway up the stairs before they picked up their luggage and followed suit. Meena made sure the girls went after Amar but before her. She was not letting them out of her sight in this place.

The hallway had vivid wallpaper in strange geometric designs. Bright yellows and pinks in circles and squares danced off the walls, hurting Meena's eyes. The house itself had a rancid smell to it, like someone had let yoghurt go off. She noticed Purnima holding her nose as they walked up the stairs and Ash promptly copied her. Meena didn't have the energy to tell them to stop. In fact, she wished she could do the same.

The stairs creaked with every step and the brown carpet was peeling off to reveal rotten wood underneath. The stained banister on the stairs wobbled when Meena put her hand on it. She sensed it wasn't the greatest protection. She made a mental note to always accompany the girls up and down the stairs.

Meena's arms hurt from holding the suitcase for so long, but eventually they reached the upper floor and walked along a landing into what appeared to be a bedroom. It was just over half the size of their bedroom at home and in much worse shape. Here, the carpet was essentially non-existent. It had become so frayed and worn with age that you could see the battered wood underneath. There was one bedframe, which had no mattress, against the dusty wall. One small cupboard was propped up against another wall, seemingly not completely assembled yet.

At least the walls were not as garish. They had a pale pink wallpaper on them, with blotches of black. It was a strange design. Purnima touched her hand against the black blotch, seemingly also confused by the weird display. As she peeled her hand away, Meena noticed it was filthy.

'Purnima! Don't touch anything. It must just be dirt.'

'Eh, what language is that now? I thought all you people spoke the same language, but it sounds different every time! Now, there is no reason to complain. This is probably nicer than the slum you came from. I read all about 'em. Untouchables and that. Anyway, I have some strict rules in this house. This room is yours. The other rooms are mine. You can use the bathroom and the kitchen but try to limit it to twice a day. I like having the space to myself. I guess you people don't know how to use a bathroom properly, but it's pretty self-explanatory. If you make any mess, then clean it up. I want this place to be as spotless as it is now. Do you understand or do I need a bloody translator?'

Meena looked around. Spotless? Was this woman visually impaired? Amar mumbled a 'yes', all the positive energy he had been carrying for the past month having vanished. Before the lady left the room, Amar cleared his throat.

'Madam. Sorry. Can we use a phone?'

She stared at him. 'You want to use my phone? Jesus, what next? You want to sleep in my bed? Lucky for you, I'm feeling generous. You can use the phone twice a week. If you start acting up, I won't let you use it at all. Oh, and keep these children quiet. I'm not a fan of them and their weird black eyes and fancy dresses. Are they child brides or something?'

Before Meena or Amar could respond, the lady had left the room, quicker than they had seen her move before. Ash instantly burst into tears, Purnima soon following suit. Meena was about to join them when she saw the vacant expression on Amar's face. He turned to face the window and Meena could tell he was crying too. This was not the future he wanted for her. For their daughter. For Ash. She walked over to him and held him tightly from behind. She tried to find words to comfort him, but none came to mind.

Chapter Twenty-one

They had been in England for a week and Meena had never felt so lost. They had done the best they could to spruce the place up. Hours of screwing and drilling meant the wardrobe now stood sturdy on its own. They had managed to buy a chest of drawers for the rest of their clothes. In order to open the bedroom door fully, you had to move the chest out of the way. It wasn't ideal but it was all they had.

Meena had found some cheap material at a market and made curtains to put over the mould-encrusted windows so they could get some darkness at night. They had all thoroughly cleaned the walls, floor and every surface before unpacking. Even the children had picked up a duster each and got to work. The majority of their stuff still lay in their suitcases. Meena felt like unpacking signalled that this was their home. Which it would never be.

At night, dehydration and insomnia often led Meena to the dingy kitchen for a glass of water. She had lost track of the number of times she been startled by a strange man either in the kitchen or going up the stairs. The next morning, he was usually gone. Meena dreaded to think what activities were happening in that old woman's room. She had heard noises nobody should ever have to hear but luckily the girls had remained fast asleep. All the upheaval had tired them out. Meena and Amar stayed awake most nights, crammed onto the small double bed with the girls in the middle. They never spoke but she had heard his muffled cries on two nights. He probably heard hers too.

Amar had thrown himself into finding work. Only two hours after they had arrived on the first day, he had gone out looking for a job. He was a worker. Indians worked. Laziness was not in their blood.

There was no luck yet, but Amar's brother, Abhay had told him there was work in the airport which was close by. Amar was going there the next day to inquire. As they sat on the thin mattress Meena had managed to find at a very cheap price, she decided to broach the topic of work.

'Amar, maybe it would be best if I looked for work too.'

'Excuse me? Why would you look for work? What can you even do?'

She cleared her throat.

'I can sew. I can cook. I can clean. We need money, Amar. Let me try.'

'No. Do not disobey me, Meena.'

They carried on eating their dinner in stony silence, the children too tired to take part in the conversation. The landlady had forbidden them from cooking anything 'smelly', which apparently meant anything with any flavour or seasoning. So, they had been living off bread and butter with a new food called baked beans. Meena wasn't a huge fan but Amar seemed to enjoy them. The girls had been excited at the prospect of new food at first but now spent more time moving the food around the plate than eating it. She missed her spices – they all did. This food hurt their stomachs and made them tired.

After they had finished eating, Meena looked at Amar with reproach.

'You wanted this, Amar. You wanted to come here and start a new life. Now look at our new home.'

'This isn't our home for ever. It's temporary.'

This revelation surprised her into silence.

'So, how long are we here for?'

'I only paid her for a month's rent. We will move in with my brother after that.'

'Why didn't we move in with him straight away?'

Amar's fists tightened and his face was turning red.

'Meena. Leave it.'

She quickly picked up their plates and peeked out of the door. It was clear. She took their dishes downstairs and scrubbed them until her hands were raw.

On their second day, they had walked to a nearby high street which had a small collection of shops. Each one had proved either too expensive or had nothing of necessity. Eventually, she had stumbled across a side road with a fresh fruit and vegetable market. The prices were a bit high, but she had never been so happy to see fresh produce. Something other than bread and beans and not covered in plastic! She didn't have any money with her, but she vowed to return the next day.

Except when she had told Amar that evening, he said they couldn't afford it. They were saving for their own house. Apparently, a house they would buy and own themselves. A home that was truly theirs. Meena couldn't believe her ears. The image of the fresh vegetables was replaced with a house she could call home.

Food was a problem. She was used to fresh fruit and vegetables, either grown herself or available to buy cheap at markets. She was accustomed to a variety of fresh herbs and spices that she could grind together and leave out in the sun to dry. These people didn't seem to eat herbs, and there was distinct lack of sun. The children were already fussy eaters – she didn't want them to forget their traditional Indian food and eat baked beans every day.

Within a week, Amar had managed to secure a position at the airport. They had been impressed with his willingness to work, and his existing labour skills. Since then his mood had drastically improved, and he came home with a big smile on his face every evening.

However, for Meena, the days began to blend into one. She felt like she was floating on a cloud, seeing everything from above and feeling detached from it all. She began to see glimpses of beauty in her new country. As she walked the girls around the area, they stumbled upon a lovely wide open green space with swings and a large slide. The emerald green grass was painted with delicate daisies, and the trees that lined the park were bursting with beautiful leaves. She laughed as the children played on the swings, kicking their feet high in the air, shrieking as Meena pushed them higher and higher. The girls patiently waited their turn on the slide, as Meena sat on a nearby bench.

A young woman with stunning blue eyes and flowing auburn hair sat next to her. Meena looked at her, afraid that she would be asked to move.

'Oh sorry, is it OK if I sit here?' the lady asked, as she began to stand up.

'Of course! Sorry, sit. Please,' Meena stammered out, cursing her broken English.

The woman smiled and sat back down, her eyes trained on a small boy who seemed more interested in pulling out grass than playing on the swings.

'Are those two girls yours?' she asked as she pointed out Purnima and Ash who had seemingly befriended a group of children in the playground and were now playing a game that involved hop ping on one leg and then two and then repeating it.

Meena nodded, afraid her poor English would scare the kind lady off.

'They are beautiful. And so polite! My son is sitting there on the grass. He prefers to play alone. I wish he was as outgoing as your daughters!'

Meena paused and tried to find the words. She had spoken English quite well at school, but the years in Kenya had made her forget.

'It's nice that your son likes to play alone. He must just enjoy his own company. I wish I had more alone time!'

The lady laughed, a musical sound escaping her lips. Meena joined in and the sun warmed their faces as they watched their children play.

Chapter Twenty-two

As they walked into the house, Meena knew. This was the one. It was only the second house they had viewed but as soon as she stepped through the door, she knew it was the house for them. It wasn't cheap – it would cost them around £2,400.

They were staying at Amar's brothers, for now, but it was not ideal. They were once again all in one room, and there was tension between Meena and Abhay's wife, Pooja. When Meena offered to cook one evening, his wife had taken it as an insult. When Meena had not offered again, his wife had called her lazy.

They had left Ash and Purnima with Abhay and Pooja. The girls had proved too difficult to watch over during the first house viewing. Ash had decided to sit on the floor and refuse to move and Purnima had found a pen and started to draw on the wall. Her curls had bounced as she had drawn a huge red circle on the house's gold and cream wallpaper. The stone-faced estate agent had been frozen in shock. After ten minutes of Meena scrubbing, the circle disappeared. Purnima had wailed at her work of art being destroyed. Meena had felt like crying too.

She had watched Amar try to compose himself in front of the estate agent. Amar had been so angry, Meena feared he would raise a hand to them. Instead, he had told Meena to watch the girls and toured the house himself. Apparently, the bedrooms were too small anyway. Meena sensed the bedrooms weren't the problem. The house had been dismissed the minute Purnima had taken her red pen to the wall.

This time, with just the two of them, Meena could sense that Amar loved this house too. She could imagine their life there. It was in Heston, so close to the airport, and she had heard that other Indian families lived not only on this road, but in the local area. Apparently, there were even Indian-owned shops opening nearby.

As they walked out into the back garden, Meena saw a lady in her garden next door. She was hanging the washing out to dry. As she turned, Meena noticed that she was Indian. An Indian next-door neighbour! Meena felt the smile begin to form on her face.

She stared. The lady had a kind face and waved at her. A little boy was sitting on the grass near her feet, and he looked up to see who his mother was waving at. She picked him up so he could see over the fence and his angelic face lit up. He wore light blue dungarees and a yellow T-shirt underneath. He looked like the sun in the sky. She also noticed a smaller child sitting in a chair, looking adorable with the afternoon glow illuminating her small face. She was wearing a white cotton dress and her little feet had frilly socks protecting them. Purnima and Ash would love to play with her. The little boy joined his mother and waved at Meena too. Meena felt like she had made a friend already.

As they left the house, the estate agent asked how they felt. Without hesitation, Meena and Amar both said they wanted it. No matter what, this was the house they wanted to live in.

After one week of putting an offer in and sorting out a mortgage, they received the news – the house would be theirs to live in. They had to wait two weeks until the old owner had finished moving and it would be all theirs. Amar began to doubt the legitimacy of the sale. Apparently, it took much longer for these things to go through usually. The estate agent assured them, however, that the seller just wanted a quick sale.

The two weeks passed in a blur and an urgency to find furniture took over their lives. Amar was away six days a week at the airport, working in the luggage department. He left for work early and came home late, tired but in a good mood. Every evening as he ate his dinner, he said that life was looking better. Meena had never seen him so happy.

As soon as they had moved into Abhay's, house, they had promptly been swept up in the family drama. Meena wasn't sure which place she preferred – the dirty room they had first lived in, where they had occasional peace and quiet, or this much cleaner, tidier house with no privacy. Amar's brother lived only two streets away from the new house they had bought. That was her one reason to doubt whether they should buy it. But, living with so many people was causing a strain on all their relationships.

Meena regularly questioned Amar about their new house. What furniture should they buy? Where should they buy it from? Should they ask Lakshmi to ship their furniture over from Africa when it was Lakshmi's turn to leave? He initially answered her questions but soon got tired of them. One evening, they were walking around their new neighbourhood when Meena asked if he was going to get a car for them soon.

'Meena, you have no idea how the world works. Things cost money. A lot of money. Money that we don't have! I would love to have a car and nice furniture like my brother, but we can't afford that. He made his money doing business in India. I am trying my best. Once we make some money, we can buy nice furniture. For now, we have to think of another way.'

She had recognised the tiredness in his voice, the defeat. After that conversation, Meena had made up her mind. She would find a way to make extra money without him knowing. The girls deserved a nice bedroom. She had seldom cared about material objects before, but this was their home. She needed it to be nice. This was where they were going to grow old together, until their children moved out and it was just the two of them left.

The day before moving in, Meena and Amar had gone to a place that sold second-hand furniture.

Abhay had insisted on going with them, but Amar had swiftly refused. She could tell he was embarrassed at how little he could afford compared to his brother. He had even made his brother drop them outside a normal furniture store down the road, and then they walked to this one. Meena had forced a huge smile onto her face, never letting Amar see her hesitancy. In Nairobi, their house had been beautiful, with flowers growing up the outside walls, and huge windows that filled the room with sunshine and moonlight. She couldn't help but wonder why they had left.

They had walked around the store, trying to find anything that wasn't filthy or broken. They settled on two double beds, one single bed and another small double bed for the girls. The single bed and one of the double beds were slightly broken, but Amar was sure he could fix them. Meena never let the wide grin leave her face.

They also managed to find two wardrobes, one sofa that looked almost new but needed repairing, and a table at which they could eat dinner together. All they had left to buy were chairs, two more chests of drawers for the girls, and furniture for the small room downstairs. The other non-essential items they could buy later. Then came the negotiation. Initially, the owner started high. His prices were equivalent to the nicer furniture shop down the road! He was a young white man, with a sly look in his eyes. She knew he saw them as an easy target. By the end of the negotiation, however, Amar had managed to get 60 per cent off the initial price as well as everything delivered for free in three days' time. Amar left the shop with his chest puffed out and a smirk on his face that she hadn't seen since they left Nairobi.

As they left the store, they walked past a little shop on the corner selling material. As they looked closer, Meena noticed it was an Indian store. Finally! They went inside and Meena ran her fingers through the delicate fabrics, smelling the lace, hearing the crinkle of the satin. The owner greeted them warmly and they talked about their home.

'My friends, you are from India?'

Meena welcomed the Hindi, finally understanding every word a stranger spoke after over a month of English. She was picking up the language fast, but nothing was quite as refreshing as her native tongue.

'Yes, we are! Well, I am. My husband, Amar was born in Kenya and we lived there for the past fifteen years. Are you from India?'

'Of course. India is my blood. My spouse and I moved here three years ago. We wanted to see where those troops came from, what their land was like. They took over ours; now we take over theirs!'

They all laughed, and the lady offered them a cup of chai. It tasted better than anything Meena had ever drunk before.

'So, what brings you here? Why come here from Kenya? I hear it is a beautiful country. I would love to visit one day.'

'We came here to start a new life. We heard things were nicer here. So, here we are! Trying to build a better life for ourselves and our family.'

They chatted while they sipped their tea, the warm spices comforting Meena's stomach. They spoke about the smell of fresh sugar cane back home, the elegant cows that walked the streets, disrupting the traffic.

As they were about to bid farewell to the kind shop-owner, Meena noticed a gorgeous material in the corner. It was a brilliant sunset orange with delicate swirls of yellow rippling through it. Tiny, embroidered flowers decorated the hem. The lady saw where Meena's eyes had settled.

'You like this? Here, have a look.'

She unfurled the material, and it became even more beautiful. She noticed Amar watching her.

'It is beautiful, but I don't need it. Thank you. We will definitely come back!'

She turned to leave, and the lady touched her arm.

'Don't worry, it is a gift from me to you. This was in the corner because nobody else had bought it. Now, it can be made into something beautiful for you. Here, I'll cut enough material to make you a lovely saree.'

Meena was so overcome with surprise that she didn't know what to say.

Amar shook his head. 'We can't accept that. You are trying to run a business here; we can't take something for free. My wife and I will come back, we promise,' he assured them, his arm around Meena.

'I know you will come back. Which is why I will give this as a gift to you, my friends. Let this be the first piece of kindness you receive here, and hopefully not the last. Come, take it.'

Meena looked to Amar. She didn't know what do. His eyes were watery, and he hesitantly took the beautifully folded material from her.

'Thank you. Words can't describe how much this means to us. We will see you again soon,' Meena said.

They left the shop and Meena felt a sense of pure happiness. Not just at her new material, but at the kindness they had encountered. Just that one conversation was enough to erase the fears that had poisoned her mind ever since they moved here. As they walked back to their house, Amar put his arm back around Meena and squeezed her shoulders. She took it as a sign that everything would be OK.

Before they knew it, it was time to move. They received the keys for the house, and Amar was the first to open the door. As they entered, they all stood together in the doorway.

The girls ran riot immediately, running from room to room. There wasn't much space to run to. They had one small living room which led into another small room at the back which looked like it had been used as a bedroom. A tiny kitchen was accessible through either the hallway or through the back room. The stairs led to one modest-sized bedroom and another bedroom. There was also a room so small Meena doubted it would even accommodate a bed. They had a bathroom at the end of the corridor which had a shower and a sink, with the toilet located in a separate little room.

All the rooms needed cleaning and decorating before they filled them with furniture. Meena couldn't wait to start.

Chapter Twenty-three

A week had gone by in their new house, and it was finally starting to look like a home. Their furniture had arrived and, together, they had spent hours putting the pieces together, their laughter filling the house. Abhay had come over to help, but his mouth did more work than his hands.

The day before, they had gone out to find wallpaper to decorate the living room and the room at the back. They had found a vibrant roll of vivid green wallpaper with pink circles. Meena had been hesitant – it wasn't her style. However, Amar and the girls had instantly fallen in love with the print and refused to leave until they bought it. Meena couldn't help but think there was a reason it had been in the clearance pile. However, the joy on their faces after they purchased it was enough to make her happy. She had been secretly hoping for lilac-coloured walls to remind her of the lilac African sky, but it was a small price to pay for their smiles.

The girls hadn't settled into having their own room yet. Every night, Meena made a point to tuck them into their own bed and kiss them good night. Within a few hours, both had snuck in next to her and Amar. Amar was not a fan of this arrangement, but Meena secretly loved it. While they slept, she rubbed their backs and smelled their scalps. It was the most comforting smell in the world.

With preparation of the house, and Amar working nearly every day, she hadn't had much chance to leave the house. One day, she decided to hang the washing outside to dry. She hadn't needed to do a wash, but she was eager to see her friend next door. However, nobody was in the garden. Meena hung each item of clothing one by one, attaching the wooden pegs at an excruciatingly slow pace, but nobody appeared.

The walls were thin between the houses, and she had already heard not one, but three children's voices coming from her neighbour's house. She thought back to the chubby boy she had seen in the garden that day. She yearned to see the others. She had also heard raised voices, usually later at night. Sometimes she heard a loud thud or thump, and silence afterwards. She prayed that the noises weren't what she thought they were.

Amar had become a changed man. He hadn't had a drink, nor lost his temper in the time they had been in their home. She found herself relaxing in his presence, and even laughing at his silly jokes.

She called Lakshmi nearly every day to update her on how Ash was doing. Ash sometimes spoke to her parents on the phone, but she always got bored and ran off to play after a few minutes. The first time Ash had done this, Meena had spoken to her afterwards.

'Ash, why did you not talk to your parents?'

'I did!'

'Not for long. Don't you miss them?'

Ash shrugged and stared at her dolls. Meena couldn't help but notice the small tear that escaped her eyelid.

Purnima and Ash went from best friends to mortal enemies within minutes. They would be playing together peacefully and then Ash would pull Purnima's hair, or Purnima would insult Ash and then the battle would commence. Meena usually watched them with a tired stare.

The shrill sound of the phone ringing sent Meena running. It was 10 a.m., which meant it was time for her daily conversation with Parvathi. They had fallen out of touch while she had been in Kenya, but Meena had made it a priority to resurrect their bond once they had moved to England. Their conversations ranged from ten minutes to an hour – it just depended on the day! She grabbed the phone and held it to her ear.

'Meena! How are you?'

'I'm doing well. We're getting there with the house, but it still needs work. I just want the girls to be comfortable and for it to feel like home. How are you?'

'We are all fine. I can't wait for you to come out here, Meena. Our house is so beautiful, and you'll love the flowers I planted. I miss seeing your face, *didi*. Remember when we would play outside all day and come home to Ma's freshly made *rotis*?'

Meena sighed, the memory causing tears to come to her eyes. She would do anything to relive those years with her family. They had gone by so fast, and she had taken them for granted at the time. She also missed her old adventurous nature, when so little scared her.

'I can't wait to see you, Parvathi. I miss you so much. I think I'm going to go out on my own today and explore my new home.'

'That sounds like a great idea, Meena. Have fun and I'll talk to you tomorrow.' And with that, they hung up, their love for each other still floating in the air.

It was Amar's day off, so she left him at home with the children and went out for a walk. After finding the Indian material store, she was intent on discovering more. There must be a *sabzi* shop somewhere. As she stepped onto the pavement, she heard a door open. She turned back, expecting to see Amar standing there, but saw her door was closed. Rather, the white door to their neighbour's house had swung open. But, nobody was there.

Meena wondered whether she should knock and tell them that their door was open. She stood on the street, staring at the door, willing it to close on its own. Just as she had finally summoned enough courage to walk up to the door, the lady emerged from the house, with a pram in tow. Meena felt her cheeks redden and her face turned into an involuntarily grin.

Her feet felt frozen to the ground. She willed them to move, walked upto the kind-faced lady and introduced herself.

'*Namaste.* I am Meena. I live next door to you with my husband, daughter and niece.'

'*Namaste*. It is nice to meet you! My name is Kanika. This is my daughter, Rani, and I have two sons also. I live here with my husband too.'

Meena looked at the baby's tiny face and felt a pang in her chest. The baby was adorable, with a full head of hair and rosy cheeks. She was very fair skinned, with a tiny button nose.

'She is beautiful, your Rani!'

'Thank you. She was a surprise – I wasn't planning on having more children. Then, out she came!'

Kanika's face beamed as she talked about her daughter. The baby looked at her mother with eyes that sparkled.

They walked down the street together and Meena found herself naturally opening up to Kanika. The arranged marriage back in India, having to move to Kenya with a stranger, the miscarriages, finally having a baby of her own. Meena was only halfway through her story when they reached a small vegetable shop. It was down a side road but had bright lights. They went inside. An elderly Sikh man with an open face greeted them. Meena was grateful to hear the Punjabi. She hadn't heard Punjabi since she had lived in India. Amar's family predominantly spoke Hindi or Swahili. She was surprised at Kanika's fluent Punjabi response. It was clear by her accent and dialect that Kanika was Sikh. Meena had assumed she was Hindu too.

As they picked their vegetables, Meena continued her story. Kanika listened intently and looked appropriately sad or happy at the right moments. Even Rani's face had the appropriate expression at the right times. As they paid for their purchases and walked down the street, Meena finished her story. Kanika had tears in her eyes.

'You have been through so much already, and you are so young. I'm sorry all this has happened to you.'

Meena put her arm through Kanika's and smiled. There were no words to express her gratitude.

'What about you?' she asked. 'What is your story? I can see you are a Sikh – did you move here from India?'

Kanika looked uncomfortable at the spotlight being shifted to her. She cleared her throat but didn't say a word. Meena was about to change the subject when Kanika opened her mouth.

'Why don't we sit somewhere? There is a nice chai place five minutes down the road. They sell the best samosas.'

Meena nodded in agreement. Oh, how she missed samosas. The crispy pastry mixed with the spicy potato and pea filling. Her stomach began to rumble at the thought.

Later, as they sat in the little café, munching on the best samosa Meena had tasted outside of India, Meena waited for Kanika to talk. She sensed that nobody had let this woman talk before.

Rani was fast asleep, exhausted from the day. Kanika fussed over her, covering her with a blanket, and stroking her little cheeks. Meena waited patiently, happy enough just eating the samosa in silence.

'My story is not too different to yours. I grew up in the Punjab with three sisters and two brothers. My parents didn't have much but worked hard to feed us and make sure we went to school. However, my mother grew sick when I was twelve years old. I had to give up school to look after her. I wasn't particularly academic anyway, so it made sense at the time. Unfortunately, my mother passed away when I was fifteen after suffering an illness that shut down her organs. We don't know what it was. Doctors are expensive and medicine even more so. My father couldn't cope with the medical bills, as well being the sole earner in the household. Eventually, my sisters had to drop out of school too. He just couldn't afford it.'

Meena grasped Kanika's hand but did not speak.

'Around a year after my mother had died, my father told me I was to be married. He couldn't afford to have me in his house anymore. He didn't have enough money for a decent dowry, so he settled for a man who was desperate. He was twelve years my senior. I married him the next day. We moved to the house he shared with his mother. She was a kind woman but worshipped her son. He was so used to having everything done for him, that he expected that from me too. I cooked whatever he wanted when he wanted it, whether it was midnight or 6 a.m. I cleaned up after him, making sure he always had clean clothes to wear and clean shoes on his feet. I even helped him bathe when he was tired. I am essentially a servant to him, Meena. Do you know what that is like?'

Meena shook her head in sadness.

'Anyway, we lived in that house for two years. One day, he came home and told us we were moving. I thought we would be moving into our own house. Next thing I knew, I was on a boat to Kenya with him and his mother. We lived there for about seven years and then he decided he wanted to move here. More opportunities apparently. On the boat, I was pregnant with my first child. A few years later, I had my second son and now I have my daughter. They give me a reason to keep going.'

Meena hesitated. She sensed that Kanika had finished with her story, but she didn't quite know what to say. Before she could think it through, the words blurted out of her mouth.

'I don't mean to pry. We hear loud noises from your house sometimes. Are the children OK?'

Kanika's face had the expression of someone who had seen too much pain to bear any more. She coughed into a napkin and began fussing over Rani again. She took a sip of the now-cold chai and then began tidying the napkins on the table. With her eyes cast downwards, she spoke.

'Yes, they are fine. He . . . hurts me. He never does it in front of the children. Only when we are alone, and I've done something stupid. Which seems to be often. I would never let the children see. To them, their dad is their world. They can't wait until he comes home from work. They sit by the door and greet him with hugs as soon as he walks in. Whereas I dread it. As soon as it nears 6 p.m., my hands begin to shake, and I feel sick. Sick at what he might do to me today. I know I do stupid things sometimes. It is my fault too.'

Meena looked down at her hands, trying to disguise her tears.

'How about we go for walks?' she suggested. 'Every evening, when he is home, we can go for a walk together. That way you get time away from him and he gets time with the children.'

'That is a lovely idea, Meena, but what about dinner? He doesn't like me going out by myself or without him often.'

'Can't you make dinner earlier? Or we walk until 8 p.m. and then eat dinner with our families?'

'OK. Let's try it. When shall we start?'

'Tonight. Let's start tonight.'

They stood up and walked out of the little café. Meena helped her friend navigate the pushchair down the little stairs outside and they walked back to their homes. As they bid each other farewell, Meena told her they would meet outside their houses at 6.30 p.m., She couldn't wait to see her friend again.

Chapter Twenty-four

Meena and Kanika walked around the block every day together for the next few months. They somehow never grew tired of conversation and neither struggled for words. When they weren't walking in the evening, they would talk over the fence during the day while gardening or putting the washing out. Meena's hands were rubbed red with the constant need to wash clothes. Sometimes, Kanika would come over with her children in tow. Her children would play with Ash and Purnima. Meena noticed a close bond between Purnima and baby Rani beginning to blossom.

Meena had also discovered a common dessert people ate in England – cream cakes. One day, she had walked past a bakery and seen the most beautiful-looking desserts covered in a rich-looking foam. Purnima had begged to go in, but Meena knew these delights would be expensive. Money was one thing they still lacked. She had promised Purnima she would buy one for her one day. Then, as she scoured the supermarket aisle for milk, she stumbled across them. Cream cakes in the supermarket! They were a much more reasonable price, although far less ornate. She had bought two of them – one was called an éclair, and the other was an apple turnover. In her bid to regain her old English language skills, she had walked around the supermarket sounding the words out. She ignored all the strange looks thrown her way, and smiled back at the people who had given her friendly smiles.

She had shared the treats with the girls. Ash had eaten two bites and claimed she didn't like cream. Purnima had eaten what Ash hadn't touched, as well as her own. Meena claimed it as a success. She also enjoyed the taste. The sugary pastry sprinkled with white powder, which engulfed a filling of tart apple and sweet cream. The éclair was also nice – the pastry was heavier with a layer of chocolate on top – although she wasn't too big a fan of chocolate.

The next time she went to the supermarket, she bought two cakes again. This time, one was for her, and one was for Kanika. She couldn't wait to share it with her on their walk.

That evening she waited outside, hiding the treats in her bag. She felt like a mischievous ten-year-old again! However, 6.30 p.m. came and went. Ten more minutes ticked by, and Meena knew something was wrong. Kanika was always on time. She knew Kanika's husband had come home – she had seen his car arrive forty-five minutes before. Amar opened the door to their house.

'Meena, why are you still standing outside? Where's Kanika?'

'I don't know. Something is wrong. She's never late.'

'Come inside. Maybe she's busy.'

He walked away and left the door open.

'Meena! Meena! Up here!'

She looked up and saw Kanika's husband from the window of their bedroom.

'My dear, Kanika is not feeling well today. She will join you tomorrow. Sorry. Please, come over for tea with your husband on Sunday. Then we can meet properly.'

This man was lovely. His eyes crinkled like Amar's and he had a broad smile. It was hard to think that he could hurt anyone, let alone his wife. Meena smiled broadly back at him and agreed. Sunday it was.

She walked back inside but as soon as she closed the front door behind her, the effect of his charm wore off. She scolded herself for being so easy to manipulate.

She heard footsteps come down the stairs.

'Meena, are you OK? I heard the door slam.'

Amar's tall frame in the hallway gave her comfort.

'It's nothing. I just wanted to walk with Kanika.'

'It's OK. Come, we can play with the children before we put them to bed.'

She smiled and followed him into the living room. She watched the girls play with their toys, Amar making them giggle with his antics. She couldn't help but smile along with them, her eyes taking in her goofy, charming husband.

After they put the children to bed, they lay together in their new bedroom, their bare skin touching with a tenderness it had never achieved before.

Chapter Twenty-five

Sunday couldn't have come quicker. Meena realised that she hadn't actually been in her friend's house yet. She got the children dressed and they walked the twenty or so steps to her friend's front door. Purnima and Ash were strangely quiet. They had been told to be on their best behaviour.

Kanika's husband opened the door and gave them a beaming smile. Meena wondered if he practised it in the mirror. They all exchanged greetings and walked inside the house. Among the kerfuffle of taking shoes off and finding somewhere for the treats Meena had brought with her, Meena noticed how clean the house was. Everything was in order. She wondered if it was for their benefit.

Kanika emerged from the kitchen, her face plastered with a smile Meena knew to be fake. She had seen Kanika's real smile that showed her entire set of teeth. This smile was false and timid. She also noticed a purple stain on Kanika's neck. Noticing her eyeline, Kanika's husband quickly put his arm around his wife, while simultaneously pulling the chunni over her neck tighter. Meena couldn't help but notice Kanika flinch at his touch.

The tense exchange seemed to go unnoticed by Amar. He followed Kanika's husband into the living room and remarked at how lovely the house was. Further pleasantries were exchanged but Meena was eager to talk to Kanika alone. She put the children together and they automatically started playing. The men relaxed on the sofa and the ladies went to the kitchen. As soon as they had walked into the kitchen, Kanika shut the door and sobbed.

Her tears were strong but silent. Meena held her friend. There was no need for words yet. Kanika quickly regained her composure and started making the chai.

'Here, let me do it,' said Meena. 'Sit down and tell me what happened.'

Kanika obeyed. She sat, and Meena noticed the pain ripple across her face as she tried to make herself comfortable. How hard had he beaten her? Rage clouded Meena's mind and she accidentally poured boiling water onto the counter instead. Hot drips cascaded down the cabinet door and onto the floor. Meena stared at it for a few moments, willing for it to stop. She regained her composure and cleaned it up, waiting for Kanika to speak. In a lowered voice, the truth came to light.

Kanika had been getting ready for her walk when he had stopped her. He told her that he was opening his own shop and it would be in Birmingham. She had no choice but to follow him wherever he went. The children too, of course. Kanika had protested. They were settled here. The children had school. She had

Meena. The next thing she knew, she was being hurled across the room. He hit her so many times that she lost count. He left her there and went to play with the kids. She had heard their excited squeals at his return.

Meena's hand shook, her eyes burning with angry tears.

Meena understood from her own experience. She would do anything to protect her children and their love for their father. No matter what he did to her, he was their father. They had to maintain the image they had of him.

'Meena, as long as he is alive, and I am alive, they will never see the monster he is. They must always see him as the great, loving father he is, not the abusive husband he can be.'

'I understand Kanika. Now, I will carry all of this inside. You must rest. Are you allowed to keep going for walks with me?'

'Let's try today after this. Then we can have some privacy.'

Meena took the tea inside.

'Kanika! Why is our guest doing the work?'

'No, I offered. Kanika should be resting, as she wasn't feeling well.'

Meena gave a pointed look. She wanted him to know that she knew.

'Kanika, I'm sorry to hear that. Are you better now?' Amar's blatant misunderstanding of the reality of the situation almost made Meena smile.

'Yes, I am feeling better,' she said. 'Better enough to walk with my dear Meena later!'

'Oh, good,' he replied. 'You should have seen the way she was moping out the window, waiting for you.'

'Amar! Don't tell her that! I wasn't moping. I missed my friend.'

As the reality of it hit her, she realised that soon, she would be without her friend permanently. Two days had been painful enough. Amar and Kanika's husband continued their conversation while the women sat in silence, pretending to listen. Meena noticed Kanika's quickly empty mug, and Meena followed suit. As soon as the mugs were empty, Meena cleared up and took Kanika's arm. They were going for a walk.

As they walked, Meena wondered if there was a way to stop this happening. They walked in silence, Kanika's body leaning on Meena's, with Meena's strong arms carrying her friend's weight. Their minds played over the same fears, and the silence said far more than words could ever articulate. As they both silently reached the same helpless conclusion, they held hands tightly.

Chapter Twenty-six

<u>London, 1958</u>

Meena was standing at her stove, making *halwa* for the girls. They were starting a new school the next day and the tension made the air crackle and twist. Luckily, Amar had raised them to speak English fluently, as well as Hindi. The *halwa* formed in the pan, the sweet aroma calming Meena's nerves. She took a deep breath and turned to see the back door leading to the garden swinging open. Before she could register surprise, Kanika entered the room so fast Meena dropped the wooden spoon she had been holding.

'What are you doing here? How did you get in the back? We have a fence!'

'Meena, there is a small door at the end of the fence. You can hardly notice it – the old owner made it, I believe. Anyway, that doesn't matter. I have to tell you the news! I'm not leaving! He's decided to go to Birmingham by himself. He will live there in the week and come back on the weekends. I'll have five days a week without him, Meena. I don't know how it happened, but he announced it just now. I had to come and tell you. I'm not leaving you!'

The friends hugged tightly, and Meena tried to cover her tears. They held each other tight, the burning *halwa* not bothering either of them in the slightest. It was only when the smoke began to rise from the pan, that Meena turned the gas off.

They chatted as Meena attempted to rescue the *halwa*, the once beige mixture now settling into a deep brown. Kanika soon went back to her house to prepare dinner. Meena glanced up and saw Amar standing in the doorway, smiling. She looked straight back at the pan. When she looked up again, she noticed he hadn't moved. She cleared her throat.

'How was your day?' he asked, his arms crossed, his tall frame blocking the exit.

'It was OK. How was yours?'

His face fell and she noticed his brow had wrinkled.

'It was OK. I saw Kanika's husband, Jagdeep at lunch. He was in the terminal, so we decided to have lunch together.'

Ah, now his questioning made sense.

'OK. I don't know why you would want to have lunch with someone like him. Did you have fun?'

'Meena, he is not that bad. He is just a man. Men have different emotions to women. Sometimes we lose our temper. Anyway, have you spoken to Kanika today?'

'Yes, she popped round just before you came back.'

He looked puzzled. His eyes sized her up, looking for any sign of emotion.

'What's wrong, Amar?'

'Nothing. Just thought I had spoken some sense into the man.'

He looked frustrated and Meena could tell a bad mood was on the horizon. She instinctively wrapped her arms around herself.

'Kanika did mention she was staying. I wasn't sure why, but I think I know now.'

She waited for his response, anxious to know if she had waited too long. There was no way to reverse Amar's bad moods. His face brightened and the deep frown lines that once plagued his forehead cleared.

'So, you do know! I thought you'd be happier. I met Jagdeep at lunch as I told you. He started asking my opinion. He said Kanika has barely said a word since he told them they were leaving for Birmingham. He also said the children sense her bad mood and act up too. He can't even stand to go into his own home after a hard day at work! I know how miserable you have been too, so I convinced him to let them stay here. I told him, it's the best of both worlds. You get to stay married but not live all the time with your wife and children!'

He roared, laughing at his own joke. Meena forced a small laugh to keep him company.

'After thirty minutes of talking to him, he had made his mind up. He said Kanika gets on his nerves a lot. This way, she's happy and he is happy. Now, you are also happy as your friend is here to stay. Aren't I your hero, Meena?' Amar asked, taking her chunni and wrapping it around his shoulders like a cape.

She couldn't help but burst into laughter and the sound caused the girls to run into the kitchen, hoping to join in the excitement. They squealed in delight as Amar carried them, one in each arm, swirling them around the small kitchen as Meena tried to shoo them away from the stove, her laughter echoing around the house.

The following week, Jagdeep left for Birmingham. Meena placed a smile on her face and waved him goodbye, the smile dropping as soon as his car was out of sight.

The girls had settled into school well. Purnima was the year below Ash, but she dropped them off together and picked them up at the same time. Meena also learnt that Kanika's son, Sunny was in the same year as Purnima so at least she had one familiar face.

Some days, Kanika and Meena would walk to the school to drop the children off. On the way back, they would take an extra-long route, or walk to the nearest shops. Every time Meena walked past the clothing store she had entered when she had first arrived, she felt a glimmer of hope. They would be able to afford to buy something from that lovely lady one day. Meena had dropped off homemade treats every now and again to show her gratitude at their kindness.

One morning, as they walked back from the school, Meena noticed a van outside one of her neighbour's houses. A man was walking back to the van with a box in his hands. She couldn't help but be nosy and stopped to take a closer look. Her neighbour waved at them, and Meena walked over. Kanika walked a few steps behind, her feet dragging along the pavement.

'*Namaste*,' the neighbour said, her hands clasped in a prayer.

'*Namaste*. How are you?' Meena replied.

'I am well. How are you both?'

'We are good. That was a big van that man had,' Meena said, gesturing towards the van now driving away.

'Oh yes. He picks up my parcels.'

'That's good. You don't have to carry them to the post office then!'

'No, they aren't for the post office. They are items I stitch. Then companies like Marks & Spencer sell them,' the neighbour replied.

Meena was astounded. She looked at the cash the woman was holding in her hands and almost felt her knees give way.

'How can I join?'

'Sorry. They have enough people. I asked for another friend last time. Apparently, a lot of Indians have moved here so they don't need as many staff. We do double the work, for half of the pay, eh!'

Meena couldn't stop the disappointment appearing on her face. They bid farewell to their neighbour and walked to their own houses.

'Meena, why don't you stitch things yourself?'

'Nobody would buy it, Kanika. I am a nobody here. No British person would buy from me anyway, and they are the ones with money to spend.'

'No, the Indians here work hard, Meena. They are getting money. They just spend it a bit more wisely. Why not try? You sew your daughter's dresses. Tell the other mothers in the playground. Spread the word.'

Meena shook her head.

'Why, Meena?'

'It's not for me.'

'Meena.'

'I'm not that good at it. There's a different standard here. Please leave it, Kanika.'

Kanika shook her head and walked to her own front door.

Throughout the rest of the day, all Meena could think about was money. As she scrubbed the floors on her hands and knees, while her hands turned sponge-like after washing their clothes, and when she prepared the spice mixture for their dinner that night, it consumed her every thought. Her mind kept returning to sewing. It was the one thing she could do. She had become a decent cook over the years, but people here wouldn't eat her food. Indian families made their own food just as well in their own kitchens. British people might be afraid of her flavourful, vibrant food. It certainly did not look like toast and baked beans, or those beloved chips Purnima talked about non-stop.

As she looked at the sunshine-shaped clock Amar had hung on the wall, she realised she was running late to pick up the children. She had promised Kanika she would do it today. Kanika was currently enjoying her newfound freedom. She would sit on the sofa and listen to Hindi songs on the radio. She would watch Bollywood blockbusters on their television. She had found a way to make time for herself, for what Meena imagined to be the first time in her life.

Meena went to grab her keys and the phone rang. She was about to ignore it, but curiosity got to her. The phone didn't ring very often. As she answered, she made out the first few sentences the person was saying. She felt tears in her eyes, and her hand froze on the machine. Then everything sounded like white noise in her mind.

She put the phone down abruptly and left the house. As she rushed to the school, she felt a pang in her ribs. Sometimes she got a throbbing pain there, ever since Amar had pushed her that day. The pain would go away on its own. As she walked to the school, the pain increased. She leant against a wall and doubled over.

'Hey, what are you doing? Are you OK?' a man's voice asked as his hand grabbed her shoulder.

Meena could make out the words, but the world was spinning. Her body refused to move. She felt arms grabbing at her and tried to will her body to run away. She managed to stumble forward, out of his grasp.

As she lurched another step forward, the pain spreading throughout her limbs and up to her head, she could think only of the children not being picked up from school on time.

Her ribs felt as if they were on fire and her body ached all over. She forced herself up and tried to take another step. A kind lady placed her hands around her,

comforting her with words Meena couldn't comprehend. Snatches of English reached her ears, and she
struggled away from this woman's grasp. The lady's
face looked confused, but she didn't attempt to touch
her again.

The school was only another three-minute walk
away. She could make it. One more step. Then another.
One foot in front of the other. She would make it.
She had no choice. She managed to get close enough
to see the gates. She saw her girls waving at her from
the playground. She had made it. As she reached the
gate, her body collapsed. The last thing she thought
before everything went black was that at least she had
made it to the school on time.

Chapter Twenty-seven

It was so bright. Everything was just so bright. She closed her eyes, hoping to block it out, but the light seeped through her eyelids like poison in her blood. *Somebody, please make it dark.* This brightness was nauseating. As she re-opened her eyes, she saw a blur of faces above her. She couldn't quite make out who they were. Were her family here? Was that . . . her brother? He passed away years ago. It couldn't be.

She closed her eyes again. This couldn't be real. She felt a hand in hers, small and warm. It felt so hot against her icy skin. She wanted to know whose hand it was, giving her such warmth and comfort. She opened her eyes again, this time trying to blink away the blaring lights. She concentrated on the face nearest to hers, linked to the hand that was tightly holding her own. As the haze melted away, she saw it was Purnima. Her daughter. She gave out a cry and sat up, eager to hold her child close to her. Hands pushed her back down. Why wouldn't they let her hold her child?

She leant back into the pillow and let her eyes close again. It felt so painful to keep them open. Soon, the brightness stopped, and she slipped back into darkness.

Chapter Twenty-eight

She was sitting up in the bed she shared with Amar. The past two days had been a mixture of a nightmare entwined with a dream she couldn't seem to wake up from. From the afternoon when she had collapsed in front of the school gates to now, she had experienced more ups and downs than she thought possible.

She had awoken in the hospital later that day, surrounded by beeping machines and lights that made her head and eyes scream. When she was fully awake, the doctor came to talk to her. It turned out she had a condition she wasn't aware of. She was pregnant. Four months pregnant. She had experienced no side effects. No nausea. No backache. No weight gain. She had still got her period, although it had been much lighter than usual. The doctor explained that was normal. It was called 'spotting' and was nothing to be afraid of.

Sheer joy had set in, and she had begun crying uncontrollably. She was having another baby. She didn't even think it was possible.

The doctor had looked at her with kind eyes and explained that nothing was wrong with the baby, and it looked to be healthy. However, Meena had been over-exerting herself. Amar told the doctor about Meena's past miscarriages. The doctor explained that experiencing so many miscarriages is a sign of an underlying health condition. The fact that she had made it to four months safely was not something to take lightly. She warned Meena and Amar that they needed to be careful. Although they were past the 'safe' point, they were not out of the woods yet. Meena needed to relax more and not do activities that included bending over too much. As the doctor had said those words, Meena had thought back to what she had been doing that day. Bending over the bucket, scrubbing the clothes. On her hands and knees, wiping the floor. She shut her eyes at the thought of losing a baby because she had been doing household chores.

When the doctor left, instructing Meena to stay the night in the hospital, Amar had let his tears fall. He cupped his arms around her belly and prayed for a boy. Meena let him talk, not taking in his words.

As she walked through the front door of their home, she noticed the phone hanging on the wall. Suddenly, the words spoken on the phone came back to her. She sat on the stairs and tried to breathe. Amar came in, carrying Meena's hospital bag. He saw her staring at the phone.

'Oh, it rang for you yesterday. It was your ma. I told them you weren't feeling well and would call back.'

He went into the living room, and she heard him settle into the sofa. So, he didn't know the news. She got up from the stairs and walked to the kitchen. She turned the tap, watching the water splash into the glass. She still marvelled at how quickly you could have access to water here. She left the tap on as she began to cry, the sobs shaking her body.

'What's wrong? What happened? Is it the baby?'

Once she found the strength to speak in between the cries erupting from her chest, she told him the news. The news she couldn't bear to comprehend.

'Amar. The phone rang two days ago. The day I collapsed.'

The words wouldn't come out. She breathed in and struggled to breathe out.

'Meena, please tell me. Is it my mum? Is she OK?'

'It's not your moth . . . mum. It's my pa. He. He's sick, Amar. He's really sick.'

She felt his body relax. Her body stiffened further, and she moved her head away from his chest. She needed her friend. She needed her now.

Meena walked into the garden, through the fence opening and over to Kanika's kitchen door. She knocked politely. She heard footsteps and Kanika opened the door. Before she could say a word, she felt her friend's arms wrap tightly around her. Her body sunk into Kanika's.

She told Kanika what had happened as Kanika made chai, brewing the teabags with spices that made her mouth water. She also saw the evident pain in Kanika's eyes when she broke the news about her father.

'Meena, why don't you go? Go to India. Say goodbye. You haven't been back for years. Your parents would love to see Purnima. And Ash, of course.'

The thought hadn't even crossed Meena's mind. They barely had any money. Amar wouldn't be able to get time off work. It was impossible.

'We can't afford it, Kanika. It won't happen. I'm pregnant anyway. I shouldn't be travelling.'

'Meena, you can travel. You are only four months along. I travelled when I was pregnant. This is your only chance to say goodbye. You don't want to spend the rest of your life regretting this, Meena. Trust me.'

Kanika's words hung heavy in the air, spoken with the pain of experience. She then walked out of the kitchen and returned with a small ladder.

'What are you doing now?'

Kanika didn't reply. She climbed the silver ladder steps, her tiny feet decorated in purple, floral slippers, taking one step at a time. She reached into a cupboard and brought out an old biscuit tin.

'Are you going to sew something now?'

Meena knew every Indian had at least one biscuit tin with buttons, thread and needles in it. Kanika brought the tin over and, sure enough, there was a lot of thread. Meena rolled her eyes, beginning to worry about the sanity of her friend. Kanika took the threads out, placing them neatly on the kitchen table. She took out a little plastic wrapper. Kanika had a mixture of coins and notes in her sewing tin.

'Kanika! How did you get all that?'

'I have my ways,' she said with a smirk on her face.

Meena couldn't help but laugh.

'Tell me. How do you have all this? Why are you showing me?'

'I am showing you because we are going to use it. We're going to India. Me and you. Together.'

Meena was about to protest but she saw Kanika wasn't done yet.

'Every time Jagdeep gave me money for the groceries or supplies, I would spend less and keep the rest in here. I needed to save for an escape plan. He was getting more and more violent, Meena. I know I've done a bad thing. I just needed to save, in case I had to run with the kids. You understand, don't you?'

'Of course, I understand, Kanika. How did you save all of that with just spare change, though?'

Kanika's cheeks reddened slightly under her dark brown skin.

'It's not as bad as you think, Meena. I started selling things. My parents gave me some gold before I left home. He took most of it, of course. He has it kept safely somewhere, he says, but won't tell me where. Luckily, I kept a small collection for myself. I sold some pieces off to a pawnbroker. That gave me quite a lot of cash. I had to spend some of it getting the children things. They needed new shoes, new school uniforms. You know how frugal Jagdeep is. He wouldn't give me anything to spend on them. So, I used some of this.'

'How much is there, Kanika?'

'Enough for both of us to go to India and have some left over. I know that much.'

Meena refused. She wasn't using Kanika's hard-saved money.

'I'll make some money of my own, then we can go. Or I can ask my sister Parvathi. Her husband is quite wealthy. I'm sure they would help.'

'Meena, your dad is sick. You have to go now. I want to do this for you. If it wasn't for your kindness and friendship, I don't know how I would have kept going. You bring joy into my life, Meena. This is just a small way for me to repay you. Please, Meena. Accept my gift. We can book flights to leave tomorrow. Just take my help.'

Meena felt her mind run through all the possibilities. She shook her head slowly.

'You have to decide today, Meena, or it will be too late. I can call a friend; he works for an airline. He usually gets us flights quite cheap. Amar could ask too as he works at the airport. Go home and ask him, Meena. Persuade him.'

After they had finished talking, Meena walked back to her house and thought about how to ask Amar. She found him in the kitchen, attempting to steal some cookies without her noticing.

'Amar, my father is sick. I need to go and see him.'

He stopped with his hand frozen in the tin.

'To India?'

'Yes. Kanika says she will go with me.'

He held her close, his tall body providing comfort to her small frame. He supported her decision to go, but he had to work. The decision was made. She was going to India with Kanika.

Two days later, Kanika, Purnima and Meena boarded a plane to India together.

Chapter Twenty-nine

<u>India, 1958</u>

As soon as they landed in India, Meena immediately felt at peace. She had made it in time. They were picked up by Parvathi's husband who quickly took them straight to her pa's side. Meena's hands shook as she took in her pa's appearance. His once vibrant smile and sparkly eyes were now dim and grey. Yet, as she took his hand in hers, he squeezed it with a strength she didn't expect.

She stayed by his bedside, with Parvathi, Nita and her ma, taking it in turns to keep them company, holding each other tightly. Kanika had said a prayer for them and politely given them their space to be together as a family.

Meena had also brought Purnima with her, so she could spend time with her family. She didn't want Purnima to see her grandpa so sick, so she left her to play with Nita's children.

As the clock struck 11 p.m., her pa took his last breath. She silently thanked Kanika for bringing her here just in time.

The following day, rains poured relentlessly, the sky sobbing down on them with hot tears. During a break in the monsoon, they lay her pa's body on a holy fire, and she watched as her family slowly became smaller. They all held each other, their white kameez stained with a fresh downpour of rain.

That evening, Parvathi, Nita, Kanika, Meena and her ma slept in bed together, their sobs keeping each other company. Purnima slept next door with Nita's daughter, their small snores carrying down the corridor.

Kanika, Purnima and Meena flew home three days later, with tearful goodbyes and promises to see each other soon. Parvathi and Kanika also seemed to have formed a bond and shared an extra-long hug goodbye. On the plane journey home, Meena couldn't help but be glad she would soon be back with Ash and Amar.

Chapter Thirty

London, 1958

'Finally!'

Two months since her return from India and life had been slowly going back to what had become normal. Amar greeted Meena with a huge hug that lifted her off her feet. He didn't usually greet her like this, not even when she had returned from India two months before.

'What are you talking about?'

As soon as she spoke the words, she realised the answer. She had known this day would come. It filled her with intense anxiety, mixed with joy, sprinkled with apprehension. There were days when even the thought of it made her want to run away. There were other days when she couldn't wait for it to happen.

'Lakshmi, Rajvir, Ameera and Mum are coming! They will be here next week. You know how Rajvir visited while you were in India? I didn't want to tell you why he came, but it was to buy a house. They will be living across the street from us, Meena. Isn't it great news?'

He didn't wait for a response. Instead, he danced his way to the living room, holding a plate of biscuits in one hand.

She had three months of pregnancy left. If they were arriving next week, they would all be here for the birth of her second child. Conflicted thoughts scattered her brain. Her heart beat faster at the thought of seeing Lakshmi's beautiful face again. On the other hand, she had Asmita to deal with. At least she wouldn't have to live with her.

She closed her eyes and sighed. All of this stress was making her even more tired. She sat down and leant back in her chair, and felt the sun hit her skin through the window. Her eyes fluttered as her mind relaxed.

Meena groaned. Her neck screamed at her, a constant reminder of the pain Amar had inflicted on her years before. She stretched out and thought back to her time back home in India. Her eyes closed again, too tired to fight the urge.

Her inner alarm clock woke her up again, and she looked at the time. Only ten minutes had passed. She had to pick the children up from school. She looked over at Amar and remarked on the time. He looked towards her and shrugged, too busy with his plate of biscuits. She slowly got up and nodded a goodbye. As she walked towards the school, all Meena could think about was the impending arrival of Amar's family and what may come next.

Chapter Thirty-one

Two days before his family were due to arrive, Amar bought a car. He came home one day in a shiny red vehicle that made a questionable purring noise when it was ignited. Meena stared at it from the doorstep, her mouth open in shock.

'Amar. How did you get this?'

'I bought it.'

Meena's throat felt thick with smog, breath struggling to escape her mouth and nose.

'How? We don't have any money.'

'I have been saving some.'

All these months of going without. Of sacrificing her own food to feed the children and Amar. Of walking past the beloved material store they had visited when they had first arrived and staring at the gorgeous materials she couldn't afford.

'Why now?'

She asked the question, but she knew the answer. He shrugged and walked past her into the house, knocking her against the doorframe, despite there being enough space for him to walk by. She rubbed her shoulder, willing the soreness to ease.

Amar's family flew in on a Tuesday. He took the day off work and drove to the airport to pick them up. He wanted to take Ash with him, but Meena refused. She wanted to enjoy her last precious moments as Ash's carer. The girls had something called 'half-term'. Meena didn't quite understand the school system here. There seemed to be a lot of holidays and breaks compared to the Indian system. Also, the schoolwork was significantly simpler. They just seemed to colour and paint for a lot of the day. By their age, she had already started learning subtractions and basic equations.

As she saw Amar's car pull up in the driveway, her heart sank and sang at the same time. Her beautiful sister-in-law was here. Yet, she could sense Asmita's coldness already. It contributed to the icy air, causing goosebumps on Meena's arms. She greeted them and was surprised to see Amar lifting their bags from the car and bringing them inside their house. She followed him into the living room and whispered.

'Amar, why are you bringing their bags in here?'

'Be quiet, Meena. You are being rude. She might hear you.'

'Meena! It's so nice to see you again!'

Warm arms hugged her tightly and her previous worry was forgotten. As Lakshmi let her go and hugged her daughter, Meena's fists tightened at the sight of their baggage in her living room.

They would move into their house across the street later, she was told. She didn't know what that meant. She tried to control her shaking hands as she brought out the chai she had prepared for them. She winced as the glasses on the tray she was carrying clinked against each other. She plastered a smile onto her face and greeted Rajvir, Asmita and Ameera with an enthusiastic '*namaste*'. They all hugged and kissed. Asmita greeted her with a wry smile and a kiss that felt like a snakebite.

Ameera was very quiet, clearly wary of her new surroundings. The girls all sat together, but Meena could sense the uncertainty. Ameera and Ash stared at each other, suspiciously sizing each other up. Purnima watched with jealous eyes.

Lakshmi looked as stunning as ever, despite just coming off a long plane journey. Rajvir looked refreshed too. Asmita, on the other hand, looked perplexed and unsettled. As they all sat in the living room, conversation turned to their sleeping arrangements.

'So, how is our house looking, Amar?' Rajvir asked.

'It looks lovely. I bought some furniture, so it won't be completely bare. You have beds and sofas. You'll just need to buy a dining table and bookshelves.'

Meena turned to look at Amar. She struggled to keep the look of shock from her face. She felt Asmita's eyes on her and rearranged her facial expression. She didn't want to show that she hadn't known what Amar had done.

'That is so nice of you, thank you. We will go there soon and settle in. I'm sure Ameera can't wait to see her room.'

'What about my room?' Asmita asked.

'Don't worry, Ma, I have it ready.'

Meena had been looking at Rajvir, expecting him to reply. Except the words had come from Amar. Betrayal made her stand. She noticed all eyes on her and excused herself from the room. She heard footsteps follow her into the kitchen.

'Meena, did he not tell you?' It was Lakshmi. 'Mum wanted to stay with Amar . . . well, all of you. She said she felt more comfortable being near him.'

'Nobody told me, Lakshmi. He doesn't tell me anything.'

Lakshmi put a comforting arm around her, and Meena resisted the urge to shrug it away, her stubbornness clouding her judgement.

From the window, Meena could see Kanika in her garden, hanging out her washing. Her feet instinctively moved towardss the back door, but Lakshmi's words prevented her from leaving.

'Meena, come. It'll be fine. I know things were hard in Nairobi, but this is your home. Yours and Amar's. Plus, you have your sister back. You must have been soooo lonely without me!'

Meena laughed and hugged Lakshmi close. Despite talking on the phone every week, she felt like she hadn't really talked to her sister-in-law in a long time.

'I have missed you a lot! Have you thought about Ash? Is she going to stay with you?'

'Of course. Not right away though. We need to get Ameera settled first. Well, I would rather have Ameera settled first – Rajvir thinks Ash should move in with us right away, but we need time to figure things out, don't you think? We were thinking you could have her for another two weeks or so. Is that OK?'

Meena knew it wasn't for her benefit. Lakshmi was just scared to suddenly have two children under one roof again. But, she was thankful. Two more weeks with Ash to herself was a blessing. Rajvir called them back into the living room. He was ready to go.

They all walked to the new house, carrying suitcases between them. Meena struggled, worried that lifting may hurt the baby. Amar didn't offer to help her, his attention focused on his sister and his mum.

As they walked in, Meena noticed how nice their house was compared to her own. It had a small extension at the back, so their kitchen was bigger. The walls in the hallway were already painted a lovely mellow yellow. The living room had retro wallpaper, not dissimilar to theirs but not quite as garish. Amar had decorated it with nice furniture.

Ameera excitedly bounded up the stairs, eager to choose her room. Meena went to investigate the rest of the house. Ash had walked off by herself earlier. Little legs dangled from a stool in the kitchen. The frilly socks and patent shoes gave away the owner. Meena picked Ash up from the stool, took her hand and led her up the stairs too. It was time for Ash to choose her room. Ameera had already made herself comfortable in the middle-largest room, leaving the smallest room free. Ash looked at it and shrugged. She walked over to the small single bed and sat on it. Her gingham red and white dress crumpled as she hunched over and hugged her arms around herself.

Meena forced herself to leave the room and went back downstairs. Purnima was standing in the hallway with a look of bewilderment.

'I'm not living here, am I?'

'No, you'll live with me and your dad. And your grandma.'

Purnima made a face at the mention of her grandmother. Meena smiled at her and took her hand. At least she had one ally. They walked out into the garden. Amar snuck up behind her, followed by Rajvir. They surveyed the garden, picking out areas where they could grow fresh vegetables and flowers.

Amar and Rajvir went back inside. Meena stayed outside and watched Purnima play with the daisies in the grass. She was deep in thought when she felt a light tap on her shoulder.

Lakshmi wrapped her arms around Meena. They watched as the sky began to darken. The skies here in London could be beautiful at night. She loved the sudden transformation from light to dark, the way the moon suddenly appeared with a dusting of stars gracing the sky.

'It gets dark so quickly here,' Meena whispered.

'I guess I'll have to get used to it. It's quite early for it to get dark.'

Meena shrugged. She had become accustomed to the early darkness.

'Why is Asmita living with us, Lakshmi? Why isn't this house enough for her?'

'Meena, there is a valid reason. You must understand. She's so close to Amar and he loves being near her. He must have been a different person without her, huh? Now she's back, she wants to live with her son again. That's not a bad thing, is it?'

'It is when you know the way she treats me. She doesn't treat you or Rajvir that way. We have been happy, Lakshmi. Amar has changed. He's been a better husband. When she's around, he changes. I don't want things to change. I like the way they are.'

She surprised herself at how honest she was being, not just to Lakshmi, but to herself. She was terrified of change. She had experienced it too many times. She had seen it go wrong. However, she had also seen it go right.

'Meena, please don't look at me like that. There is another reason Ma can't stay with us. We didn't want to say yet.'

Meena waited anxiously. Lakshmi was staring at the floor, biting her lip. Meena knew to wait while Lakshmi was like this. Any pressure to speak and she would walk away.

'I didn't want to say. It's early, and with your experi- ence . . . Meena, I'm pregnant. We never planned on three children, but it happened. It's very early. Only seven weeks. Rajvir is praying it's a boy. I secretly want another girl. They can all be best friends! With Purnima, of course. Meena, look at me.'

Meena's eyes had glazed over. Lakshmi was preg- nant. Another baby. A third. She hadn't told Lakshmi her own big news yet. Should she wait for Amar? Surely, he would want to be the one to tell his sister.

Although Lakshmi had told her about her pregnancy first.

She suddenly hugged her sister close. They would get to experience this together. It wasn't a competition. It wasn't about who had more children. Those days were long gone now that Meena had her own. She broke away from the hug. She wanted to see Lakshmi's face as she told her.

'Lakshmi, I have some news . . .'

Asmita walked out into the garden. Meena met her gaze and her words disappeared into the wind.

'Yes, Meena. Continue. Don't let me stop you.'

Meena hesitated. All the good times she had shared with Asmita, cooking together, or sitting in the garden in Nairobi, they all paled in comparison to the dark shadows, the negative memories Asmita had cast over her. She had a way of making you like her for a limited amount of time, and then just as you had decided she wasn't a bad person, she did something to show you that you were in fact right all along. Her games had affected Meena so greatly that she felt like a child being bullied in the playground when Asmita spoke to her, or even looked her way.

'Silent, I see. I am just a harmless old lady, Meena. You don't need to look at me like that. Anyway, I will be the one to tell Lakshmi the news if you don't want to. Meena is pregnant, Lakshmi. You thought this was your time to shine. Well, it turns out Meena is sharing the spotlight with you.'

Lakshmi turned from her mother to Meena.

226

'Is this true?'

'Yes, Lakshmi. I was going to say! It's still early too, only just over four months . . .'

Before she could continue, arms were wrapped tightly around her, and her feet were nearly lifted off the ground.

'Lakshmi, put me down! You could hurt yourself!'

Despite her stern words, she couldn't help but laugh. Imagine what the neighbours were thinking if they were watching from their windows. They looked like two madwomen. For a few blissful seconds, she forgot that Asmita was still there, casting a dark shadow over her happiness.

'Let's hope for two boys, eh?' said Asmita. 'Enough of these girls! We need a strong man to look after us.'

Meena tried to pretend that she hadn't heard. Lakshmi smiled, but her eyes were dark. Meena had no doubt that Lakshmi loved her mother. However, she wasn't sure she always liked her mother. Amar, on the other hand, was blind to his mother's mischievous ways. He doted on her. Maybe that was why Asmita wanted a son. She wanted a younger, unmarried version of Amar to cater to her every need.

The two men and children came out to the garden. Meena could tell Amar was already begin to go back to his old ways. The way he barely looked at her. How he hung on his mother's every word. She hugged her arms around her stomach, silently telling her baby that they would be just fine.

Chapter Thirty-two

The next five months passed by in a blur. In between looking after Purnima, and often Ash as well, and preparing for the new baby, Meena soon became exhausted.

Financial worries kept her up at night. Three weeks before the baby was due, Meena convinced Amar to go shopping for the new baby. He had resisted for weeks, but she managed to wear him down. She had planned it perfectly. Asmita was out of the house, having made new friends to gossip with in the mandir. Purnima was at Lakshmi's, playing with her cousins.

They had gone to two stores before Amar turned around and said: 'Meena, we should stop looking.'

'Why? We haven't even bought anything yet.'

'It doesn't matter. The baby can have Purnima's old clothes.'

'What if it's a boy? Also, we left some of her clothes back home.'

'Meena, we can't afford it.'

'What do you mean? You bought Lakshmi's furniture and you bought a car. We can buy our baby things it needs.'

He turned to her with a glint in his eye that she hadn't seen since they left Nairobi. She ground her teeth and they left the store empty-handed.

On her daily walk with Kanika, Meena had told her friend that they needed money, and.

Kanika had reiterated her previous point. 'Sew. Use your skills and sew, Meena!' Kanika had exclaimed. Meena had shaken her head, while Kanika rolled her eyes.

Yet, she started asking the other Indian parents in the playground if their children needed clothes, or if they had any material that needed stitching. She got two customers just from one conversation. They both asked her to make dresses for their daughters. However, before Meena could discuss measurements, the girls ran up to their mothers, ready to go home. Meena had seen them before. One was quite petite, and the other was taller, with a bigger build. As their mothers walked away, they called back, asking her to make the dresses by Friday. They wanted them ready for one of the kids' birthday parties.

Meena stared after them, questions frozen on her tongue. Purnima, Ameera and Ash ran out, greeting her legs with hugs. On the way home, she took the girls with her to the material shop they had passed when they had first arrived. She had secretly visited the shop window every week, her fingertips pressed onto the glass, aching to go inside.

As the girls played around with some spare fabric, the owner showed her some clearance material she was trying to get rid of.

'See, it is such nice quality. I don't have enough for an adult saree or kameez, so it is heavily reduced. What do you need the material for?'

'Just for a child's dress. This should work. I need another material for another dress though. Slightly more than this. She is a bit bigger.'

'Oh, for these two girls then? You don't normally buy material from me for them.'

Meena felt her cheeks go hot and her fingernails pressed into the palm of her hands. She looked at the owner's kind, worn face and relaxed her hands.

'I just use my old kameez to make their outfits. This is for two of their friends at school.'

The owner smiled at her.

'There is nothing wrong with being resourceful. Come, we can find something that will work.'

Meena couldn't stop the smile from painting her face. They selected another material, which was slightly more expensive than the other. After she heard the total, her heart sank. She didn't have enough. She fumbled in her pockets, hoping to find some spare change. After seeing her unease, the owner took her hands in his.

'Pay me back later. You don't need to pay now. You are sewing these for other people? You'll make money from them?'

'Yes.'

'Then once you have made your money, you come back and pay me. I trust you. Now go, your girls are destroying my spare fabric,' he said with a smile.

Meena brushed away her tears. In a place that could sometimes feel so brutally cruel, she was grateful for these small acts of kindness. She told the girls off and dragged them out the door. When they got home, she gave them some *chevda* and sketched out what the dresses should look like, her eyes flickering to the doorway every so often. Luckily, Asmita was at Lakshmi's and usually stayed there for dinner. Just as she sat down to cut the material, the phone rang.

'*Namast*— hello.'

'Meena, it's me. I am calling from work. I'll be eating at Lakshmi's tonight. I'll see you after dinner,' Amar said quickly.

The phone beeped, signalling the end of the call. She smiled to herself and felt her tight shoulders relax. She had time.

She examined the first material for the smaller girl. She pictured the girl in her head. From that image, she wrote down rough measurements. The girl had very fair skin, with dark, thick hair. The material was a pale peach, with small white flowers printed on it. She decided to design it with a white collar and two buttons on the front. Her hands flew as they created the garment, her eyes hyper-focused on the soft material. Purnima, Ameera and Ash were glued to the television, watching a show that starred a cat wearing some kind of turban. It also had another feline friend.

The sound of voices approaching the house sparked her attention and she quickly packed everything away. The sudden movement caused the existing cramps in her stomach to intensify. Just as the front door opened, she shut the door to the cupboard that contained her sewing machine. She walked into the living room and saw Amar, Asmita and the girls on the sofa. Amar had a girl each on his legs, with Ameera sitting on the floor at his feet. Asmita was staring at her son.

'Look at what a good parent he is, Meena. You are so blessed. It is difficult to find a good husband. You are so lucky to have my son.'

She smiled in agreement and got Ash and Ameera ready to go home. As she wrapped them up in coats and boots, she could feel Asmita's eyes burning into her, watching her every move. She kept her eyes fixed on the children, her back to Asmita and Amar.

She walked the girls over to Lakshmi's, her stomach still cramping. As Lakshmi opened the door, Meena ushered the children inside. She felt tiny droplets of sweat drip down her face.

'Meena, what's wrong?'

Meena's hand flew to her stomach, and she looked at Lakshmi with wide eyes.

'I think . . . I'm not sure. It can't be happening already.'

She felt another sharp contraction.

'Lakshmi, I think the baby's coming!'

Lakshmi squealed with joy. She shouted for Rajvir. He came over in a hurry, nursing a cup of spilling tea in his hand. Once he understood the situation, his face froze in panic, and he ran over to Meena's house to tell Amar. Despite the intense cramps, Meena couldn't help but laugh at Rajvir's comical run, his slippers slipping off his feet and the mug he had forgotten to put down splashing brown liquid down the street. Lakshmi took Meena inside and sat her on the sofa.

'You are about to become a mother of two, Meena. It's happening!'

Chapter Thirty-three

Fifteen hours later and Meena was holding a tiny baby in her arms. Much to her joy, it was a baby boy. He already had a thick head of hair and big almond eyes. When the doctors told them it was a boy, she saw tears stream down Amar's face. She held her child close, feeling his warm body on her chest.

A few minutes later, Lakshmi, Rajvir and Asmita came to see her and the baby. The nurse tried explaining there was a rule of two visitors only. None of them listened. Asmita came hobbling over, her dodgy knee causing her to wobble more than usual. She looked at Amar and their eyes locked. They exchanged a look and a wide smile erupted on Asmita's face. She took her grandson in her arms and held him. Meena ached to have her baby back on her chest. She looked at Amar, but he was too busy looking at his mother. Lakshmi came over and kissed her forehead.

'You did so well, Meena. A little baby boy. Now we just have to wait and see what mine is!'

Meena smiled at her, holding her hand tightly. Rajvir looked lost and stood near the door. She saw Lakshmi catch his eye, warning him to stay. She watched as

Amar took the baby from his mother and cradled him. They looked alike already.

Meena held her arms out, wanting to hold her son again. Those past fifteen hours had been brutal. She felt like this birth had been worse than the first. It wasn't like the Bollywood movies, where the woman would cry a few times and the baby would pop out. No, this had been hours of cramps and pain and blood and waiting for it to be over. Now, she deserved to hold her son.

Amar ignored her for a few more minutes, and then reluctantly gave her the baby. She examined her son's face, her eyes tracing over his small, closed eyes and fluffy black hair. She decided to take a few days to see which name suited best.

The nurse came back into the room and said everyone but the father had to leave. Meena smiled warmly at the nurse, and he winked back at her.

Begrudgingly, Asmita and Lakshmi left. Rajvir was out the door before the nurse had finished his sentence. Asmita kissed the baby goodbye and patted Meena on the arm. She then went and hugged Amar for what felt like minutes. The nurse even gave what sounded like a fake cough to signal for them to leave. Lakshmi kissed both Meena and the baby goodbye and hugged her brother. Meena told her to tell the girls that she loved them and would see them tomorrow. They were all having a sleepover at Lakshmi's house.

Amar stood in the room as the nurse helped Meena sit up in a more comfortable position. Amar mumbled something about being back in a minute and left. Meena guessed he was going to catch up with his mother and walk her to the car. Never mind that their new-born baby was here. The nurse rolled his eyes as he saw Amar leave.

'Sorry, honey, I had to tell them to go. They were making a lot of noise and the rule is two visitors.'

He leaned in closer, and Meena noticed how good he smelt, like cocoa butter and mangoes. Her mouth salivated at the thought of mangoes. She hadn't found any here.

'I could tell you were a bit uncomfortable with so many people. Forgive me if I was wrong. I think you could do with some alone time with your baby.'

As if on cue, the baby started shrieking from his tiny cot. The nurse smiled at Meena and passed her a glass of water.

'I may not be your family, but I am here to look after you. So, if you need anything, just ask. OK, honey?'

She smiled at him. Her English had greatly improved, and she understood every word he said. As he brought the baby over to her, she wondered if she should ask him where to get mangoes from. She knew the smell well, and he smelt distinctively of fresh mango.

She took her baby in her arms, and he stopped crying. The nurse smiled and made his way to the door.

'Wait! Sorry. Could you tell me where you can buy mangoes from around here?'

She saw by the expression on his face that he was confused. She replayed the English words back in her head, trying to figure out which word she had said wrong. He looked at her, his forehead creased with worry.

'Are you feeling all right, honey?'

'Yes, I am. I just love mangoes. I grew up in India and spent the last ten years or so in Nairobi. I could smell the mango scent on you. Sorry, sorry. It's an . . . odd question.'

He stared at her for a few seconds more then burst into laughter.

'You just gave birth, and you want mangoes? I grew up not too far from Kenya, in Uganda. I know a good mango when I see one. I'll bring you some mangoes after my shift. There's a corner shop down the road from here that sells the best mangoes. It's Pakistani, I think. I'll be back later, honey. Rest up.'

She laughed to herself. At her laughter, the baby moved his lips. He was laughing already! She giggled to herself. She couldn't wait for her mangoes. Another nurse entered the room, carrying a tray of food. She put it on the table and walked away without saying a word. Meena looked at the plate and saw that it was a limp chicken mayonnaise sandwich with a pot of a vivid orange-coloured dessert next to it. She had told them she was vegetarian. She pushed the tray away and her eyes remained fixated on her son.

His tiny outfit was decorated with silver stars. She remembered buying this outfit in a clearance sale. It was still more than Amar would have wanted her to spend, but she fell in love with it as soon as she saw it. She traced the stars with her finger and the baby gurgled in response. His outfit reminded her that she'd been sewing. She had to make the two dresses for those ladies. Worry cramped her mind, and the baby became agitated in response. She calmed him down, singing sweet lullabies into his ear.

> *Sunio jee araj mhari o babula hamar,*
> *Sunio jee araj mhari o babula hamar,*
> *Savan aayo, ghar le jaihyo.*

He settled back down, and his eyelids fluttered. A loud noise outside caused his eyes to flash open and wails erupted from his tiny mouth.

She offered her breast. At the first touch of his lips on her nipple, she hissed with pain. She leant back and watched him feed. When he was done, she leant him on her chest and gently rubbed his back. This brought her back to memories of Purnima. How sweet and tiny she had been. She was still small, but she had developed a fiery personality, not unlike her father. As her hands moved up and down her son's small back, she wondered who he would take after.

Lost in her thoughts, she was surprised when Amar walked back into the room, and let out a squeal. He walked over and kissed her lightly on her forehead. Without a word, he took the baby from her and walked around the room. The baby instantly started crying. This hadn't happened with Purnima. She had loved being in father's arms, crying sometimes at her mother's touch.

He quickly gave the baby back to her and he settled down again. She couldn't help but notice the hurt in Amar's eyes.

'Don't worry. He just needs some time with his mummy for now. You can hold him later.'

Amar grunted and sat down in the chair next to the bed. He crossed his arms tightly, his eyes fixed on the two of them. He tapped his foot on the floor impatiently, the sound giving Meena a headache.

She felt her eyes start to close. She felt hands brush her skin as they took the warm bundle on her chest, leaving her heart cold.

Chapter Thirty-four

Meena phoned her sisters straight away the day she came home from the hospital, but it turned out Kanika had beaten her to it. After their trip to India, Kanika had become close with Parvathi. Except, how had Kanika had known that Meena had gone into labour?

'Kanika, you phoned Parvathi?' she asked.

'Sorry. Is that OK?' Kanika asked, worry creasing her brow.

'Of course! How did you know I was in labour?'

'I saw Rajvir running down the road with tea splashing everywhere. I then saw you being put into a car, and I realised what was happening.'

'Oh, Kanika, I'm sorry I didn't come and tell you that I had gone into labour. It all happened so fast.'

'Don't worry, Meena, you had enough going on!'

Kanika smiled, but Meena noticed how the smile didn't quite reach her eyes.

Nevertheless, Kanika had silently taken the dresses Meena had been sewing and finished them. She even gave them to the mothers who had ordered them and took the payment. Meena told her to keep the money. She had been the one to finish the dresses and get the job done. She wouldn't have received any payment without her. Kanika agreed to take half, but Meena noticed the envelope felt full.

The next day Kanika turned up with a gift for the baby. It was a hamper, tied with a giant blue ribbon. Inside was a blanket that was as soft as the sand on the beaches of Mombasa. Packaged in a lovely, small woven box was a white rattle, which made a lovely tinkly noise that excited the children no end. There were also two tiny outfits to dress her son in. The stripy dungarees were Meena's favourite. At first, she had shaken her head, refusing to accept such a lovely gift. However, Kanika's gentle hand covered hers and she knew that she had to accept it.

Just three weeks after giving birth, Meena started to sew again and managed to make some money to contribute to the house. Word had spread about the dresses Kanika had finished making for her, and other mums across the playground had asked for their items to be sewed too. She kept some of the money aside for her own personal savings, copying Kanika's method of hiding it in an old biscuit tin. The only problem was that Purnima had a big sweet tooth, and was constantly looking for something to snack on. Meena had to hide the tin behind the *chapati* flour!

Asmita's behaviour had changed since the birth of her grandson. She wasn't a particularly maternal woman, but every time she saw her grandson gurgle in his cot, her face lit up and she watched him with happy eyes. She helped around the house, cooking and cleaning most days. Meena even started to be thankful that she was there. The feeling quickly waned, however, as Asmita got back to her old ways, criticising Meena for breastfeeding too little or too much, bathing the children not often, or too often and changing nappies too delicately or not delicately enough.

Just a few days after they arrived home, they decided on a name. They would call their son Neeraj. It meant 'lotus flower'. Asmita had quibbled at first, but after calling the baby Neeraj a few times, she agreed. It was the perfect name for their perfect boy.

Lakshmi remained a source of comfort. As her belly grew, she began to come round less, too tired to do much other than sleep. When she did come round with the girls, she helped Meena with Neeraj, changing his nappy when it was needed and rocking him to sleep when he refused to settle.

Only a few months later, Lakshmi gave birth to a baby girl, who immediately captivated Amar's heart. She had eyes the size of saucers and delicate pink cheeks which made them all swoon. Rajvir was completely overcome with joy, and never seemed to put his newborn baby down, his arms never growing tired.

Chapter Thirty-five

The next four years passed by in a blur. After the birth of Neeraj, Purnima became suddenly very needy, constantly wanting attention from her mother, but most of all, from her father.

On the days when it felt like too much to bear, Meena thought of how hard she had fought to become a mother, let alone a mother of two. The strength pulsated through her veins, lifting her body up to clean up the mess in the kitchen, or calm Purnima's incessant wailing.

Amar had been hypnotised by his new son. The baby still preferred his mother's arms, but he began to settle into his father within a few weeks of his birth. Still, Meena liked it when he started gurgling, signalling that he wanted her.

At four years old, Neeraj had definitely developed a naughty streak. The problem was, Meena found it so hard to discipline him. He had a charm about him already. Like father, like son. He got away with a lot more than his sister, much to Purnima's dislike. She had grown into a cute, but still fiery, eleven-year-old with a full head of curly, dark hair. She had also become best friends with Rani, Kanika's daughter, despite their age gap. Purnima became almost an older sister to Rani. They played outside for hours, Rani's little feet following Purnima everywhere she went.

Meena thought her treatment of the children was fair. Whenever Purnima wanted something, she would go straight to her father, mastering an expression that never failed to work on Amar. But, Amar was strict on their son from the time he could crawl. Meena couldn't help but be kinder to their boy, careful to give him the same treatment that Amar gave Purnima.

As Meena gazed out of the window, reflecting on the past four years, the sun began to settle in the sky. Neeraj had decided to shriek at the top of his lungs for the past half-hour and Meena's head was thumping. She set about making dinner, Neeraj glued to her leg, stirring a pot of *cholay* with the one hand and holding a cold towel to her head with the other. She set him down on the floor and carried on chopping chillies. One minute later, he started shrieking again. This time, ten decibels louder.

Amar strode into the room and glared at her.

'If you can't stop him crying, then what is your purpose as a mother? Answer me! Why is he like this? You spoil him too much. How he cries when he is not with you! Stop him crying now!'

She went to pick him up, her hands shaking. Amar never usually raised his voice in front of the children. She saw the wild look in his eyes. She stood in front of her son, blocking Neeraj from his father's view.

'Amar, go into the living room. I will handle it. Please, just go.'

At seeing his father's anger, Neeraj's shrieks grew more high-pitched. Amar pushed Meena to the side and grabbed Neeraj's arm. He pulled. Before Meena could think, she hit Amar with the nearest object to her, a white, plastic rolling pin. He turned to her.

'What do you think you are doing? Raising a rolling pin to your husband? Do you have no respect for me?'

So many words flew to Meena's lips, yet she kept them sealed. Where was his respect for her? For his wife? For his child? Why must men demand respect when they show so little to their women? Neeraj had stopped crying. Meena noticed how red his arm was from Amar's violent grip. She looked into Neeraj's eyes and saw genuine fear. He was a baby. He shouldn't know fear yet. All he should know is love.

She picked Neeraj up and walked out of the back door to the garden. A beautiful oak tree had grown leaves in their garden and she sat down under it. The grass was still damp from the rain earlier and she felt it soak through her clothes, causing her to shiver. But, she took comfort from the sturdy oak supporting her, its leaves protecting her. She rocked Neeraj from side to side and kissed his arm.

Motherhood was the most beautiful thing ever to happen to her. As she cradled her son, her mind drifted to her own ma who had suddenly passed six months ago. Although Meena had felt sadness, she had also felt at peace. Her ma had never been the same since she had lost her son and her husband. Meena had an overwhelming sense of calm after she heard the news. She was devastated for her own loss, but happy that her ma didn't have to suffer in grief anymore.

The sky was getting darker and she decided to take Neeraj back inside.

Dinner ensued in silence, even Asmita not bothering to add gasoline to the fire. Later, as they climbed into bed, Amar apologised. He said it wouldn't happen again. Except, it always happened again. Always.

Her bruises paled, however, in comparison to Kanika's. On their evening walks and chats over the fence, they would confide in each other. Meena was always sickened by the way her friend was treated. Her husband might only have been home on weekends, but he made up for his absence during the week. If he thought something was out of order, he would make it known. Meena had lost track of how many times she had held her friend close, rubbing Vaseline on her cuts and bruises. She noticed how he was careful to do it in less visible places now. But each time, Kanika silently showed her the new bruises blossoming across her body.

Chapter Thirty-six

As Meena was heating some *halwa* for Purnima, she heard a banging sound next door. She had just finished talking to Parvathi for the past half hour, their phone call much later than usual due to a wedding in India. They rarely ever missed their daily chat.

'Mum, what was that?'

'Purnima, stay in the living room. I don't know what it was but stay there in case.'

Meena turned off the gas and wiped her hands on her clothes. Just as she opened the back door to see what was happening outside, Kanika came flying at her and ran into the house. There was blood leaking out of her head, spilling down her face in a ruby waterfall. Meena slammed the door shut and locked it from the inside.

'Mum, are you OK?'

'Purnima, stay in the living room. Please. Watch your programme. It's OK, *beti*. I'm OK.'

She grabbed a chair from the back room and dragged it into the kitchen. She sat her friend down. Silent tears were cascading down Kanika's face, but she didn't say

247

a word. Meena held a tea towel to her face and tried to stop the bleeding. She gently the wiped the blood stains from her friend's sweet face and forced herself to refrain from crying.

Fumbling around, she searched for the first-aid kit Amar had insisted they had. Finally, she found it in a cupboard and examined the wound. It looked like it would need stitches.

'Kanika, we must go to the hospital. It needs stitches. I can't do it.'

Kanika silently shook her head. Meena knew there was no way she could persuade her to go. That would mean explaining how this had happened. Meena had no need to ask, but Kanika would never tell a doctor or nurse. She would take this secret to the grave. She would never put her children through the hurt and pain of seeing their father for what he truly was. A monster.

Meena did her best to clean the wound and bandaged it. Kanika didn't even wince.

She put some chai to boil on the stove and held her friend in her arms. After they had finished silently drinking their tea, both slurping it out of bowls, Kanika began to speak.

'He told me that the business was failing. He said we need to move to Nairobi. That things will be better there. I said no. We have built a life here. We have our family here. I have you here. I don't want to move. He lost it, Meena. He said I have no choice. I have to go, or he will kill me. He said he'd rather I was dead than in a different country to him. I walked out of the room and he ran after me. After that, I don't remember much. Just his hands hitting me. Then suddenly something sharp hit my head and I felt the blood running down. I ran. I just ran to the safest place I know. Here.'

Then the sobs began. Rage filled Meena at the thought of this man having such control over her friend. Beating her until she agreed with every word he said. She held her friend, lightly rocking her in her arms.

'You can stay here with us. The kids too, of course. Let him go. You have us. I won't let him hurt you. I know you don't want to go to the police, but maybe now is the time.'

'You know I will never do that, Meena. I must go to Kenya. I have no choice. Rani and Purnima will be broken, Meena. They are more than friends, they have become like sisters. It might be best not to tell them. After we've gone, just tell Purnima that we had to go. Please.'

Meena agreed, salty water stinging her lips as it ran down her face. She couldn't bear to lose her friend. Their daily walks, their talks over the fence. Everything was about to change. She felt sick at the thought of leaving her friend with such a terrible man. Kanika would have nowhere to run in Nairobi. No one to fix up her cuts, or to hold her close. Meena was losing not only her best friend, but a sister.

'When do you go?'

The silence made the house seem eerily quiet, Purnima's TV show seemingly the only noise for miles around.

'In two days, Meena. He had already planned it all. He wasn't asking me. He was telling me. I wouldn't be surprised if Amar already knew.'

Meena felt betrayed at the thought of her husband knowing this news and not telling her. She heard the familiar sounds of Neeraj waking up from his nap.

'Go to him, Meena.'

She quickly went to check on him upstairs. She was so thankful that Amar and Asmita had decided to go out, only thirty minutes before Kanika had run into their kitchen. She dreaded to think what it would have been like if they had both been there, standing over Kanika, making judgements about her life. The same way they judged hers.

She settled Neeraj next to his sister and told Purnima to keep an eye on him. Purnima sighed but put her arm around her baby brother, stroking his forearm with her thumb.

She grabbed another chair from the back room and dragged it into the small kitchen next to Kanika. She shut the kitchen door and opened the fridge. The bright light welcomed her. She took two cream cakes out of the box and set them on a plate. She sat down and put the plate on her lap. They took a cake each and silently chewed. There weren't any words left to say.

Chapter Thirty-seven

Meena would never forget the look on her daughter's face two days later when she found out Rani had gone. Purnima came home from school, her little feet tapping along the pavement. She dropped her bag off inside as Meena made her a snack. As per usual, within moments Purnima was back outside and knocking on her friend's door. Meena had told her to stay inside today. She was hoping to tell her over a cup of chai.

Meena ran outside and called Purnima back in. Purnima stomped across the driveway and looked up at Meena with cold eyes.

'Where is my friend?'

'Purnima, she's gone. Come inside. Let me explain. I told you to stay inside anyway.'

Purnima's eyes filled with tears and she rushed into the living room. Meena slowly shut the door and leaned against it. This was not going to be an easy conversation. It was hard enough for her to get her head around. Her best friend was gone. Now she was missing half of her soul.

After a huge inhalation, she walked into the living room. She sat next to Purnima and put her arm around her.

'*Beti*, I'm sorry. They had no choice. They had to go.'

'Are they coming back?'

'I don't know, Purnima. I don't know.'

'Where did they go? Can we visit them?'

'No. We can't. They have gone back to Kenya. Where you were born, remember? I told you all about it. They decided to go back.'

After a few moments of silence, Meena felt Purnima's body tighten.

'So, we will go too,' her daughter said. 'We have lived there before. We can go again now.'

Meena almost laughed at the mind of her child. How simple things seemed to them. They didn't have to worry about money or bills or jobs. They went to school, came home, ate food, played, ate more food, and then went to bed. They didn't have to worry where that food came from. Where the school books came from. Meena was glad they didn't have to worry about these things. When she was growing up, she did. She watched her mother go without food. She saw the ceiling in their tiny house leak. She saw the struggle on her parents' faces. She didn't want her children to live the same way.

'We can't go. We live here. We have lives here. Your cousins are down the road. We can't leave them, can we?'

'They can come too!'

'I wish I could make Rani and her family come back, Purnima, but I can't. It's not in my power. I miss my friend too. We'll have to make do with each other for now.'

Purnima squirmed away. Meena's arms felt empty without her child in them. She tried to reach out again, but Purnima moved further away, her arms crossed. Yet, when her father used to pick her up and swing her around, she laughed until she cried. As if on cue, Neeraj began wailing.

She gave Purnima one quick cuddle before she moved away and went to check on Neeraj. Considering his age, he was still extremely needy. Purnima had been a very needy child too, but had become less so after the age of five. Neeraj, however, needed attention all the time. Especially from her. She fixed a smile on her face and took a deep breath.

She heard the front door open and Asmita's voice. A trio of other high-pitched female voices streamed into the house, filling Meena's ears.

'Meena, bring us some chai!'

She picked Neeraj up and took him downstairs. Purnima seemed to have disappeared to her room. *Give her time*, she told herself. *She'll make new friends*. She was a child. Meena, on the other hand, wouldn't make any new friends. None like Kanika anyway. While she had become friendly with some of the local mothers through her sewing business, none of them shared the bond that she and Kanika shared.

She put the cinnamon, cardamom, ajwain and fennel into the pot and began to boil them in water. She added the teabags and left it to simmer for a few minutes. Neeraj played on the floor at her feet. She picked him up and took him into the living room, noting that the door joining the living room to the back room was shut. Abruptly, the door to the back room sprung open and Asmita was staring at her.

'Bring the baby here. Stop hiding him all the time. He is my grandson, you know. My baby. Come, bring him.'

Meena hesitantly carried him over. Asmita took him out of her hands almost aggressively. Meena watched as Asmita's friends started poking his cheeks and rubbing his head. They passed him around like a parcel.

'Meena, the chai. Please. We are thirsty.'

She left the room and walked to the kitchen.

'Biscuits too, Meena. We are hungry. Quickly, please.'

She poured milk into the chai and got out some biscuits. Malted milk. She ate one as she turned the gas off and let the tea cool slightly. As she poured the tea into mugs, she took a sip out of one. There wasn't enough for her. She decided to give that mug to Asmita.

As she served the biscuits and chai, one of Asmita's friends told her to sit down. 'Join us,' she said. Meena reluctantly sat perched on the edge of the seat, already planning her escape.

'Meena, tell us about Kanika. What happened?'

'Nothing. What do you mean?'

'Meena, don't be slow. Poorna saw her face. It was swollen. She had a cut too, apparently.'

'I heard her leg was broken.'

'I heard her back was broken and she was in a wheelchair.'

The ladies continued to speak over each other, their words becoming more and more outlandish.

'She is fine,' Meena said. 'She had a slight fall. Now, I had better get Neeraj ready for a bath.'

'Meena, his bath can wait. We need to know what happened. We are very concerned, you see.'

She almost laughed. Concerned! They knew nothing of concern. If Asmita was so concerned about Kanika, why didn't she ever ask how Meena was after her beloved son had left bruises on her body? Why had she never bothered giving Kanika more than a glance when she had come round with visible bruises and cuts? It was all a show. These women had nothing better to do with their lives than to gossip about others. Except this wasn't an Indian drama. This was real life. She and Kanika weren't actors in a show. They were real people experiencing real pain.

'I have nothing to say about my friend. Especially when she isn't here to say anything for herself.'

Asmita took that as a cue to ask where Kanika had gone.

'You know where she went. Amar told you. They have gone to Kenya. Nairobi. They needed a fresh start.'

The ladies all looked at each other, smirking. Meena had had enough. She took Neeraj and carried him out the room. As she left, she paused in the hallway, listening to their conversation.

'She is a weird one, Asmita. Why did you choose her for Amar? He is such a handsome man. She is tired-looking. Not in good shape either. Look at how she dresses as well. He could have done so much better.'

'I agree, Asmita. She is trouble. Did you see the way she served the chai? She almost spilled mine with her clumsiness.'

'Can she still not cook, Asmita? I remember you saying she is a terrible cook.'

She could almost hear Asmita smile.

'Yes, I tried teaching her. I mean, she has improved a lot under my guidance. My son still cooks. It's ridiculous. A grown man cooking for his wife. She should be ashamed, but she doesn't say anything. I told him to cook meat when he cooks. She doesn't eat it, so she has to make herself something separate. You should see the look on her face when he has made meat!'

Meena heard their loud cackles and continued up the stairs. She saw that Purnima's bedroom door was shut, and paused outside, waiting to hear noise. There was nothing. She knocked. No answer. She opened the door. Purnima wasn't there. Panic caused Meena's throat to close, air unable to escape. Where was her daughter? She darted in and out of the other rooms, checking each twice.

She ran back to Purnima's bedroom and looked out of the window. She wasn't in the garden either. She had run away. Sweat dripped down her back. Where was her child? Neeraj began to cry, sensing his mother's panic. She didn't have time to console him now. She needed to find Purnima. Just as she was about to call Amar, she saw movement outside. It wasn't in their garden. It was in Kanika's. She moved closer to the window, almost pressing her face against it.

There she was. Purnima was playing in Kanika's garden. Her little body was half hiding under a bush, but the yellow dress gave her away. Thank God. Meena said a silent prayer. Her daughter was OK. She put Neeraj down and he instantly started shrieking.

'No, you can walk, Neeraj. You aren't a baby anymore.'

He continued to shriek. She did something she would never normally do. She walked away.

'Mummy! Mummy! Come and pick me up!'

She sighed. She paused at the door, her back to Neeraj.

'Neeraj, walk to me. Come, we can go outside.'

She turned to him. He shook his head, his fat bottom lip sticking out. His eyes became bigger as he stared at her. He opened out his chubby little arms.

'Fine, but you need to walk more. I can't keep carrying you. My body gets tired too.'

He nestled into her chest. She walked down the stairs and out the back door. She went through the door in the fence and sat next to Purnima. Neither of them said a word. The two of them played with the toys together, Neeraj falling asleep on his mother's chest.

Chapter Thirty-eight

<u>London, 1964</u>

Asmita had been alive only five hours ago. In five hours, Amar's world had come crashing down, leaving nothing but rubble. Asmita had shown no signs of heart failure. She had been going about her day, tending to some of their potatoes in the garden. Two minutes later, Meena had watched her keel over and collapse on the cold, wet grass. It had taken her a few moments to process what had happened. Once the gravity of the situation had set in, she had run, almost weightless, to her mother-in-law. Meena had felt for her pulse. She learned that from a movie. Asmita's heartbeat was there, but only faintly. She ran back inside and called the ambulance. She then called Amar, who was at work.

His manager had answered, saying Amar was busy and he would call back later. She told the man that it was about Amar's mother. Without hesitation, the manager went to get Amar. She barely finished telling him what had happened when she heard the phone click. He had hung up on her.

Amar had arrived just as they were lifting Asmita into the ambulance. His skin looked almost translucent – like all the blood that pumped around his body was slowly draining, leaving him lifeless. Meena had remained relatively calm until she saw the state of her husband. She had never cared very much for Asmita, but her husband did. He worshipped her. If she were no longer around, he would crumble. Moving here while Asmita was in Nairobi was different. Amar had known she was safe there, with Lakshmi and Rajvir to look after her and keep her company. He had known she was going to move to England soon. This was different. None of them knew if they would ever see her again.

Meena noticed neighbours poking their heads out of doors and windows, eager to see the drama. The paramedics were oblivious to it. They operated in a calm, professional manner, paying little mind to the nosy neighbours, or even to Amar. She saw a figure running towards them and noticed it was Lakshmi. She didn't have her hair up in her usual glamorous bun or her make-up on. Only at that point did Meena realise that she had hardly ever seen Lakshmi without at least a dash of blush on her cheeks. Even during labour, her hair had been styled.

Lakshmi ran into her brother's arms. Meena envied them at that moment. Lakshmi tried to climb into the ambulance in her saree, but the paramedic told them only one person could go with Asmita. Meena looked at the floor. It wouldn't be her. Lakshmi quickly made the decision. She would go and Amar could drive to the hospital as he had a car. Rajvir was still at work.

Lakshmi then looked at Meena, remembering her existence for the first time in the last five minutes. She told her to get the children and bring them to her house. She could look after them. Meena looked to Amar for guidance. She would much rather look after the children, but surely Amar would need her with him?

He looked at her for a second. The paramedic told them to hurry. They didn't have time to waste. Lakshmi climbed in and the ambulance sped off in a hurricane of whistles and blue lights. Amar went inside and poured a shot of whisky in a glass. He downed it and walked back outside. Meena watched him through the open door, unsure of what to do. Three of the children were at school; Neeraj and Lakshmi's baby, Parina were the only ones home, as they had a half-day on Fridays.

She ran over to Lakshmi's house and saw Parina sitting on the sofa, eating a slice of mango with her hands while watching TV. She had no idea what was happening. Meena wished she could join her. They could be in their own little bubble together, away from all the pain and sadness. She gently switched the television off and stroked Parina's hair. With her little arms crossed and her bottom lip sticking out, Parina grumbled at the thought of missing her show. Oblivious to this rehearsed tactic, Meena picked her up and carried her back to her own house, careful to shut and lock the front door behind her. A robbery was the last thing they needed.

Parina fussed in her arms and then quietened down. Meena had forgotten how big these children had become. Maybe they needed holding more now than they had when they were little. The world got scarier as you got older. Maybe everyone should hug each other a little bit more. Amar was holding Neeraj in the driveway. Meena's footsteps quickened. She didn't trust Amar when he was like this. Especially not with her son. As she reached him, he put Neeraj down. She put Parina down and they looked at each other. What now?

'Meena, it is your duty to be in the hospital with us. You are her daughter-in-law. I don't care how you feel about her, but you need to be there. Now, which woman can we give these kids to?'

Meena cringed at his words. If Purnima or Ash were here, he would have insisted on them coming too. He wouldn't leave them with 'some woman'. Meena looked down the street.

'Can't we leave them at your brother's?'

'No, Meena. I already rang him, and he is going to the hospital too. All his children are at school.'

She sighed. She had made friends with a lady four doors down. They weren't close but they spoke regularly and sometimes walked to the high street together. She was their best bet. Meena took Neeraj and Parina's hands and led them down the street. Neeraj began to fuss. He liked being carried. Meena didn't have time for that right now.

She knocked on her friend's door, praying for an answer. After another urgent knock, the door flew open. Meena quickly explained the situation and her friend offered to pick the children up from school too and look after them until Meena returned. Meena smiled at her kindness, wondering why she hadn't got closer to this nice lady.

Meena rushed back down the road and found Amar sitting in his car, revving the engine to signal for her to hurry. She jumped in the car and they drove off before she could even shut the car door fully. Judging by Amar's driving, he was a bit tipsy. She wondered if he had quickly had some more whisky while she was dropping the children off. She could smell it on him.

He parked the car and they ran inside. Once they had found their way through the hospital maze, they saw Lakshmi sitting on a blue padded chair. Doctors had told them that Asmita was in surgery. Meena couldn't see Amar's brother anywhere.

An hour and a half later they were told to go to a different section of the hospital. They all walked speedily, anxious to see how Asmita was. When they arrived at the right ward, the nurse advised them that only two people could go in. Just at that point, Lakshmi noticed Rajvir staring at a sign that showed directions. She ran up to him and hugged him. The nurse sighed and allowed three people to go in. They didn't need to consult each other. Amar, Lakshmi and Rajvir all followed the nurse, while Meena stayed behind. She saw blue padded chairs down the corridor and sat on one. Then she waited.

The blue padded chair creaked as she shifted her weight from one side to the other. She stared down at the floor and noticed the tiny crack in one tile. Just a hairline crack.

Yet, just that one small crack ruined the whole tile. It tarnished it. It made it imperfect. The once white grout was blackened with age. She wondered if that's how she looked to the world – tarnished, old and broken.

Her shoes squeaked on the too-shiny floor. She wondered how many times a day this floor was cleaned. She hoped it was multiple. In a place like this, things should be cleaned often. The blue padded chair next to her also had a crack in it. How did such a crack appear? What happened to the chair to cause a big hole in the middle of it? How many times had someone abused it?

The vivid yellow light above her flickered. She wished it would go out. She hated the false brightness of these places. It was like they were trying to make the pain and anguish surrounding her more noticeable. Like they wanted everyone to see the suffering that filled in every corner and crack in this building. Yet, here she was. Sat on a blue padded chair. Waiting.

It had been two hours so far. She only knew because a big white clock had been ticking above her head for the past two hours. She had turned around to check it on occasion, but had stopped after one hour. It wasn't like she could leave. She was stuck here. So she would wait patiently, with only cracked tiles and a big clock to keep her company.

A familiar face came around the corner. Finally. Rajvir sat down heavily in the cracked chair next to her. He didn't seem to notice that the material had a rip in it. Meena decided now was not a good time to tell him.

'Is she OK?'

She watched Rajvir shake his head. She couldn't make out if he were upset or simply tired. It didn't matter either way. This wasn't in their hands. She didn't know whether to put a hand on his arm to comfort him. It didn't feel natural, so she kept her hands in her lap. She was hungry. Maybe that nice nurse with the mangoes still worked here. She could find him. She sighed. What a ludicrous idea. This was a completely different ward. Also, the poor nurse had a far more important job to do than fetch mangoes for her.

'Are you hungry, Meena? I can get us something. There is a vending machine with chocolate in it.'

She didn't care for chocolate much. She found it flavourless and sickly. She shook her head. Rajvir stood back up and went in search of food. She hoped he would be gone for a while. She never knew what to say when it was just the two of them. A cleaner walked by with a mop and bucket. It was good to know they did clean the floors.

She closed her eyes, trying to avoid thinking of food. A bowl of *channa* would go down well right now. With a dollop of yoghurt on top. She doubted they would have that in their vending machine. The sound of the clock ticking began to make her drowsy. She felt her eyes get heavier. Just as she was about to fall asleep, she felt a hand on her shoulder.

'Ma'am. Could you wake up please?'

She quickly sat up. A stranger was standing above her, their skin still touching. The nurse pulled away and smiled weakly.

'Are you Am . . . Amar's wife? Sorry if I pronounced it incorrectly.'

'Yes, I am. Is something wrong?'

'It's best you come with me. Where is the other man you were with? The husband of Lakshmi?'

Meena cringed at the woman's terrible pronunciation. She shrugged and followed the nurse down the corridor. She heard wailing coming from one of the beds. She couldn't help but pause.

'Come on now. That's not the right room.'

Meena continued. She wondered if the wailing person was alone. What if they needed someone? She noticed the nurses around her carrying on their conversation as if nothing were happening. She guessed they were used to it. She always wondered how nurses and doctors managed to sleep at night, when they spent so much time surrounded by pain and death. Did they become immune to it? She guessed the patients must all blend into one at some point. Just another person to try and fix, and if you failed, there were plenty more waiting to be fixed. What selfless professions they had.

As they entered the ward, Meena saw her husband's face. It was etched with pain and fear. She watched his hands ball up into fists. She walked up to him and felt the anguish roll off his body. It filled the room. She had never seen him so hurt. So lost. She knew he wouldn't recover from this. Not quickly anyway. Maybe not ever.

She put her arms around him, but he was a statue. She pulled away and looked past him. Lakshmi. Beautiful

Lakshmi. Meena felt tears spring to her eyes. She couldn't bear to see Lakshmi in so much pain. She couldn't take that pain away. She couldn't do anything. Where was Rajvir? He should be here.

She walked round Amar and grabbed Lakshmi. Unlike her brother, Lakshmi clung onto her. They stayed there for endless minutes. She looked past Lakshmi at the body lying in the bed. Asmita. She looked oddly peaceful in death. This was the first time Meena had ever seen her look calm. Seeing her body lying there so still made her heart hurt. Was that how Meena's own mum had looked two years ago when she had passed away?

Rajvir entered the room, nearly walking to the wrong patient's bed. Shortly afterwards, he was followed by Amar's two brothers. Meena wondered what had taken them so long. They both looked upset, but neither as traumatised as Lakshmi nor Amar. Meena noticed how one of them looked at his watch. As if he had somewhere else to be already.

They had drawn the curtains around Asmita's little cubicle and Meena wondered if the other patients knew. If they knew someone had died. If they were wondering if they were next.

Chapter Thirty-nine

They held the funeral three days later. In India, funerals took place the next day at the latest. Here, the rules were different. It took time to plan a funeral and find a slot for the cremation. It was also extremely expensive. They used fancy wooden caskets with silk lining. What a waste, Meena had thought. Asmita's death probably ended up costing more than her sixty-seven years of life.

Lakshmi had taken over the funeral planning, making sure everything would be done in the style Asmita would have wanted. Amar spent his days either at work, in bed or in front of the television. Meena was just glad he hadn't reached for the whisky yet. Just in case, she had hidden it from him. If he asked, she would say she had been tidying up and had moved it.

They brought the body back to the house first. Amar had broken down at the sight of his beloved mother in a casket, her face so pale and lifeless. Lakshmi refused to even look, her eyes carefully averted, staring at a non-existent piece of dust on the floor. Amar's brothers gave the casket a gentle tap each, their eyes quickly grazing over their dead mother. The rest of Amar's family had already been alerted by telephone, but none were able to travel from the different countries they lived in. Meena had called her siblings to let them know too. Parvathi had cut straight to the point.

'Are you honestly sad, Meena? She was a witch.'

'Parvathi! I am sad. I am sad for Amar. And for Lakshmi. I can't say I will miss her, but I am sad for them. You remember how hard it was to lose a parent.'

Parvathi had sighed on the other end and the conversation had turned to their children. Neeraj was slightly aware of what was happening, but distant. Despite Asmita coddling him for his entire life, he had little emotional connection to her. On the day of the funeral, he spent most of his time standing near Meena or playing with his toys. Purnima, Ash and Ameera had stood together. They all seemed to pick up on the atmosphere in the room, mimicking it with their small faces. Parina had come down with a terrible cold, so she was resting upstairs. One of Lakshmi's friends was going to take care of her when they left for the crematorium.

However, the show had really begun when Asmita's friends from the temple arrived at Meena's house. They had crowded the casket, crying over Asmita's body, begging God to bring her back. They had all come equipped with tissues. And tears it seemed. Meena had watched from a distance, her face passive and calm.

Meena had dutifully handed out cups of chai and water. After the ceremony at the crematorium was done, they all went back to Meena and Amar's house where a priest completed a holy ritual, setting Asmita's soul free. They burned a small fire and prayed together. Meena looked to see if the children were taking part. To her surprise, all of them were seated together, their heads bowed in prayer. She looked at them for a few moments, feeling tears in her eyes for the first time that day.

After the prayer was complete, she noticed Amar giving her a knowing look. She looked around and noticed people impatiently sitting, some looking at their watches. A few had their hands on their stomachs, politely coughing. She quickly gathered some women and they assembled in her tiny kitchen, preparing a dish each. As they served the food in the back room, she heard snippets of conversations. Asmita's friends were now completely composed, sitting in a circle together on the floor. She heard her name mentioned a few times. She paused and then smiled broadly. She quickly rearranged her face in an expression of grief and approached the women, silently handing them a cup of chai each. As she walked away, she noticed how silent they had become.

She filled the children's plates up with food and told them they could eat upstairs as a one-time treat. They all ran, scared she would take back her offer. As people started to leave and go home, she noticed Amar looking in the cupboard. His eyes had become frantic, and his hands were slightly shaking. He turned to look for her and she quickly darted upstairs. She had hidden the whisky in their cleaning cupboard in the bathroom. She moved the disinfectant out of the way and grabbed the bottle. Racing back downstairs, she found him in the kitchen, opening the cupboard doors.

He saw her and grabbed the bottle from her hands. He didn't even ask her where it had been. Meena walked into the living room and through to the back room. Only Lakshmi and Rajvir remained, but they had begun to gather their things, ready to go home. They called their children down and they left, hugging and kissing each other before they departed. Neither seemed to smell the alcohol on Amar's breath, or the see the fear in Meena's eyes. Now, she was left alone.

Chapter Forty

London, 1965

Eleven months went by and Meena had never seen so much alcohol consumed. Amar was in a permanent state of intoxication, which varied from slight incoherence to violent outbursts.

The first two weeks following Asmita's death were sombre. Amar barely spoke. Lakshmi came round every day, as did Amar's brothers. Meena didn't know why, since all they did was sit together, barely saying two words to each other. She served them chai and biscuits and *chevda* and anxiously waited for them to go. Eventually, they stopped coming every day and visited once a week. That turned into once a fortnight, which turned into once a month. Despite the relative proximity of their homes, Meena felt like the siblings had never been further apart.

She overheard Lakshmi scolding Amar's brothers, Abhay and Rishi, one evening. They had just left and were standing in her driveway. Lakshmi's raised voice enticed Meena to open her bedroom window so she could hear the conversation below.

'Why can't you two sort yourselves out? Ma is gone now. There is no need to be so hostile towards your siblings.'

'We are not hostile! It's easy for you to say. You and Amar were her favourites.'

'There is no such thing at favouritism when you have children.'

'Then why did you give your own child to Meena to look after? You wanted more time with Ameera, that's why. She is your favourite. Well, was. Now your youngest is. Parina comes first now.'

Silence ensued. Meena had to pop her head out of the window to see if they were all still there. She noticed Lakshmi wrap her arms around her stomach. She did that when she was vulnerable. When she felt attacked.

'I don't have favourites. You don't know anything about the situation with Ash! That was to help Meena, not me.'

'Come on, Lakshmi. It was for your benefit. Meena had her own daughter to look after by then. Anyway, you and Amar took all of Ma's attention. She barely spent any time with us.'

'Stop being children. We're all grown-ups now. She loved all of us.'

The conversation had been dominated by Lakshmi and her brother Rishi up until this point. Suddenly, Abhay stepped in. Despite his bold name, meaning 'fearless', Abhay was actually quite timid, and Meena was surprised to see him intervene.

'She did love of all us.'

'See, Rishi! Listen to your elder brother.'

'I'm not finished, Lakshmi. She did love all of us. In her own way. Yet, there is no denying she loved you a lot. There is also no denying that she loved Amar more than all of us combined. I can't blame Amar for that. However, I can blame him for his behaviour. He has always put Ma first. Before his children, before his siblings, even before his wife. We can all see it. Don't say you haven't seen it too, Lakshmi. They worshipped each other. Now she is gone, hopefully Amar can turn his attention to his family, including us. Hopefully, we will become stronger together. Now, let us go and we will see you in a few weeks. You know you are welcome round anytime.'

With that, she watched Abhay walk away. She noticed Rishi was still standing there. She had never liked him. He was entitled. Arrogant. Narcissistic. He acted like the universe owed him something. Amar had a few similar streaks, but not to the same level as Rishi. Lakshmi also could be entitled, but she had become humbler with age.

Despite the argument below her, Meena couldn't help but look down at the siblings with a yearning in her heart.

Her family were so different from Amar's. It was probably because her upbringing was very different. Her parents never showed favouritism or spoilt any one of them. Despite having so many mouths to feed, they made sure all were fed equally. Yet, in Amar's family, Meena had witnessed how Asmita would feed

273

seventy per cent of the food to Amar, twenty per cent to Lakshmi, and the leave the remaining ten per cent to be split between Rishi and Abhay.

As she shut her window, she thought back to Abhay's words. She and Amar had had many great days out in London, Amar putting food on his now bald head so the pigeons would sit on him. They often went to her favourite town, Windsor, which was one of the most beautiful places she had ever seen. The grey brick castle was enchanting and reminded her of the fairy-tale books she had read to Purnima when she was younger. The river was full of hungry ducks and swans, eager to chase humans for food. Amar would also drive them to see the airplanes take off into the sky at the airport, which was Purnima's favourite thing to do. In Nairobi, he had taken them on long road trips to Mombasa.

Amar always spent time with her and the children when he could. However, Asmita was usually there in the background, watching. Always watching. When Asmita had not been there, Meena had experienced some of the best days of her life. Just watching Amar play with his children and be his usual goofy self was enough to make her heart sing with joy.

Dreams of more time together had vanished alongside the whisky. Now, clear bottles littered the bin, spilling over to the floor. Beer bottles consumed the majority of her fridge. The house began to smell of liquor. So much so that one of Purnima's teachers had asked if there was a problem at home. After Meena had inquired what the issue was, she realised that the teacher had smelt whisky on Purnima's clothes. The teacher had thought Purnima, a thirteen-year-old child, had been drinking.

Meena had surprised her husband by shouting at him when he came home from work that day. Her raised voice had subdued him, and she saw fear in his eyes for the first time. He had timidly gone upstairs, and she had heard hushed voices coming from Purnima's room.

In the four months following her outburst, Amar snapped out of his state and stopped drinking. Lakshmi and her family started coming over every Saturday night and they would all sit in the back room, the adults on the bed, the children on the floor, and sing Bollywood songs and talk. Amar was sometimes reserved and retreated within himself, but a lot of the time he was present.

Until the solicitor called. They had first discussed whether Asmita had a will a few days after her death. Nobody knew if she had one. They heard nothing from solicitors at that time, and none of the siblings mentioned it. The house in Nairobi had been sold, anyway, and Asmita had apparently already given Amar money from the sale. Other than that, she had a house in India and some savings. The will remained an unspoken topic until that Tuesday when the phone rang.

It was one of Amar's days off and he had answered the call. She watched his face freeze. He hung up a few minutes later and hit his hand against the wall. Meena was too scared to get any closer. She had often been on the receiving end of those hands, and it wasn't something she cared to experience that day.

The solicitor called Rishi, Lakshmi, Abhay and Amar, and told them to meet in his office the next morning. Apparently, Asmita had made a will only a few weeks before her death.

After seeing Amar's reaction to the phone call, Meena walked into the garden, her feet stood next to the fence, her eyes looking into the garden next door, yet her mind was elsewhere. She stayed there for a few moments, her eyes gazing at the empty washing line.

The meeting did not go well. Asmita had left her savings to Amar. She had left the house in India to Rishi and Amar. Abhay had excused himself from the room. Ever the silent one. Asmita had liked strong men, often frowning at Abhay's weakness. However, in Meena's eyes, he was strongest of them all.

Lakshmi and Abhay had been left with nothing. Meena had watched Lakshmi's face closely, looking for any sign of upset or despair. Lakshmi had simply smiled and looked at her hands, her left foot tapping the floor.

Meena's eyes had then travelled to her husband. His hands were gripping the arms of the chair, and his jaw was tightly clenched. Yet, his face showed no hint of surprise, and the solicitor was looking at him with familiar eyes. Then she realised. Amar had been with Asmita when she had met this solicitor and made her will. He had known exactly how much he would get. He knew that Lakshmi and Abhay would get nothing.

Rishi had thrown his chair across the room. The solicitor had left quickly, saying he would give them a few minutes to discuss. Amar told them to calm down.

They shared the house. Now they could decide whether to keep it or sell it. Rishi had spat on him.

When the solicitor returned, Meena asked him what had happened to Asmita's gold? The solicitor cleared his throat. That went to Amar too. Everything but the house in India went solely to Amar. Rishi spat on the floor at Amar's feet.

'You are no brother of mine.'

With that, they left. Since that day, the monster inside Amar became even worse than Meena cover have ever imagined.

Chapter Forty-one

Meena knew that it was only a matter of time. The loss of his mother was going to impact Amar eventually. She was just waiting for something to trigger it. That day at the solicitors, his brother's words had shot a bullet into Amar from which he would never recover. His wound was there for all to see. Lakshmi tried to reason with him. Rajvir took him aside and told him to calm down. Told him that it would be OK. Meena tried to speak to him, but she had the least impact of them all. She had become invisible to him.

These last ten months had been the worst of her life. She thought, after having so many miscarriages, and losing her brother and parents, that life could only get better. That now, she deserved the right to live a happy, complete life. Instead, their house that had once smelt of cinnamon, turmeric and fresh linen was now overpowered by the smell of whisky, beer and vomit. Initially, it had started off with drinking every evening after work. Meena hadn't said anything at first. Amar had gone through this phase before, and he would get over it again.

However, weeks of drinking in the evening soon turned to weeks of drinking continuously on his day off as well. He was no longer present. He no longer wanted to play with the children. Family stopped coming over as much. They grimaced at the smell when they entered the house, and one look at Amar usually sent them away.

However, some Sundays, Amar would wake up in a great mood. He would wake the children up with huge plates of breakfast and play games with them all morning. He would take Meena out shopping, buying her sarees. They would all go to Preston's, the local supermarket, and he would play hide-and-seek with the kids down the aisles. On those days, Meena felt like everything was going to be OK.

Then came the next day, and he would fall right back into his old habits. He would come home from work with a face like lightning and thunder rolled into one brutal storm. After a few months, he wouldn't even wait until after dinner to have a drink. As soon as he entered the house, he went straight to the cabinet and poured himself a glass of whisky. He went from sipping it to downing it in one go.

In the last three months, Amar had been drunk nearly all the time. He woke up to a drink. He went to sleep holding a glass of whisky. He had been sent home three times in the past month for being intoxicated on the job. His boss had given him one final warning. The only reason he had lasted this long was because his boss had lost his own mother a year ago. He understood the pain.

Meena also worried about him driving. He shouldn't be driving while drunk. Sometimes, his car would swerve into their driveway, nearly hitting the brick wall that divided their house and next door's. Yet every time she saw his car, she was relieved. Relieved he had made it home alive. That relief soon disappeared when he came inside and took his anger and hatred at the world out on her. Meena often wished he would stay in his car all night.

She could tell that Neeraj and Purnima knew something was wrong with their father. At first they didn't understand. Yet, as the months passed, they started to realise that their father wasn't well. Neeraj was now eight years old, and Purnima was fourteen.

Purnima remained close to him. Meena sensed that her daughter blamed her. She wanted her mother to make it all OK again. She was too young to understand that Meena couldn't. She couldn't fix their father. She couldn't make everything go back to normal. She couldn't bring Asmita back. Nevertheless, she showered the children with enough love for both her and Amar combined. She cooked their favourite foods, bought Purnima her cream cakes, watched their television shows with them and listened to Elvis Presley on the radio while they danced around the room together.

Amar still had days of clarity. They were becoming less and less frequent, but they were still there. Days when he would take Purnima to the cinema. Days when he would kiss Meena's cheeks and tell her how much he loved her. Days when they would all go to Trafalgar

Square or Piccadilly Circus and see the lights. The city brought out an energy in Amar. He loved the hustle and bustle, the large parks, the monumental buildings that screamed stature and grace. Meena clung to those days. She saw them as beacons of hope.

Saturday movie nights still happened most weeks. Sometimes Amar was there, and other times he disappeared. Soon, people stopped asking where he had gone. Ash, who had become so close to Amar in Nairobi and when they first moved to England, still asked for him. She didn't understand what had happened to her uncle whom she adored so much. But she didn't live in the same house. She didn't see what they had all seen.

Parvathi tried consoling Meena on the phone nearly every day, shared tears muffling the phone line. She even offered to come to London several times, but Meena always quickly refused. She didn't want her sweet younger sister to witness this.

Lakshmi and Rajvir told Meena that they were always just down the road if she needed anything. She had called Rajvir over on some nights when Amar had got out of control. It was usually when the children were asleep. He would sit in his mother's room and weep. She could handle the weeping. She would hold him and stroke his back. But without warning, the weeping would sometimes turn to pure, dangerous anger. He would push her away and shout at her. Tell her it was her fault. That she had done this to him. She had killed his mother, and now she was killing him. He threw things. Shattered photo frames. Glasses. Lamps.

On those days, she called Rajvir over. At first, he came every time. Soon, he started making excuses, saying he was too busy with his children to come over. That Lakshmi needed him to be home.

Amar somehow managed to keep his job, but Meena didn't know for how much longer. So, she decided to get her own. Sewing was bringing in some money, but it wouldn't be enough to support her family. Although word about her business had spread, other Indians in the community could also sew and competition was high.

Meena had become closer to her friend who lived four doors down the road – Sheila, who was born and raised in India too. She had also made friends with two of her customers, Lisa and Anne, who often helped her with some of the trickier English words. In return, she taught them some Hindi, which they loved.

Sheila worked in a factory, Meena discovered. They made razors. Sheila told her it was the biggest razor manufacturer in the United Kingdom. Meena went with her one day. They got the bus together and Meena felt butterflies in her stomach once they stepped off the bus. The building was huge. It towered over her small frame, almost swallowing her whole.

Sheila led her inside and called her manager over. The manager agreed to hire Meena on a probationary period. Two weeks. If she passed, she could work there permanently. Sheila told her that there wasn't a minimum wage that employers had to pay their staff. They could pay them whatever they wanted. Apparently, in this factory, she would earn £1.65 an hour.

Meena decided to work part-time. She wanted to still be there for the children. She worked three days a week, sometimes four if they asked her to. She passed her probation period with no problems. She told Amar that she had got a job. He shrugged and continued to watch the television channel he had been watching for the past two hours, his glazed eyes staring at the screen.

Working was a huge lifestyle change for Meena. Suddenly, she had to balance getting the children ready for school, making their lunches, and making sure Amar wasn't too drunk to drive to work, all before 8 a.m. Once she dropped the children off to school, she caught the bus with Sheila to work. Most of the employees at the razor factory were immigrant women. Around seventy per cent of the workforce were Indian. Twenty per cent were black women, and the remaining ten per cent were white Europeans. Meena learnt that the white European women earned more than the Indians and the black women. Sheila had been livid when she found out, but Meena only shrugged. All that mattered was that she was earning money to care for her family.

She began to enjoy working. The hours could be long, and her hands began to hurt with all the labour. However, she made some friends at the factory, and the hours went by quickly. They laughed and chatted in Hindi, comparing the best way to make *rotis* and how much time their *masala* took to dry out in the sun. After work, she would go to Lakshmi's to pick the children up.

Money started coming in slowly, and Meena did her best to hide it from Amar. Whisky wasn't cheap. She had noticed the number of empty bottles increasing, beer cans overflowing the bin as well.

Every night, she checked the savings she had tucked away. She added a bit to it when she could. Except now she had to pay for the groceries and the bills. Amar was not in a position to do anything that required responsibility. She never asked where his wage went, knowing that it had all been drunk by him.

Meena closed her eyes and prayed every night, her hands clasped together. Sometimes her prayers were disrupted by the noise of Amar vomiting. Other times, they were interrupted by him coming in the room and crashing out on the bed, often still fully clothed. Sometimes, his trousers were soaked in urine. Meena undressed him slowly so she wouldn't wake him and went downstairs to wash his clothes. Her hands were rubbed raw with the effort required to clean the vomit and urine off everything before the children woke up.

Then, one evening after work, she was walking to Lakshmi's house and saw a car in Kanika's driveway. The person who had moved in after Kanika had left didn't have a car. Maybe they had got one. It seemed that cars were popping up down the street these days. She shrugged it off and sighed. She carried on walking to Lakshmi's house until she heard a sound that she had thought she would never hear again. Her name being called in a sweet, mellow voice.

Chapter Forty-two

Meena stopped outside her old best friend's house, her eyes glistening with tears. How she missed Kanika. She sighed and carried on walking to Lakshmi's house. As she knocked on the door, she was greeted by Lakshmi's exhausted face.

'Come in, Meena.'

'It's OK, Lakshmi, I can pick up the children and take them all for a bit. You can rest.'

'That would be lovely, but we need to talk.'

Something about her body language told Meena that this was serious. Her usually light-hearted, sparkling sister looked deflated. As if the weight of the world was on her shoulders. The children were all playing upstairs, leaving the living room free. Two cups of chai were steaming on the table.

'Meena, I don't want to worry you. I know things have been . . . difficult at home with my brother's behaviour. I don't know what I can do to help. I tried talking to him, but he doesn't listen. He says nobody understands his grief. I lost her too, Meena. I lost my mother too.'

Meena went to wipe her sister's big almond eyes.

'Meena, Neeraj has been acting up at school. Not only that, but he has been affecting my children. Ash swore the other day and she said she heard Neeraj say it. I also caught Parina taking money out of my purse. She said Neeraj told her to do it. I have to believe my children, Meena. I think you have to talk to him and tell him it's not OK. He can't take money. Or tell my children to take it for him. What does he need money for? He's a child!'

Meena couldn't believe her ears. Her poor innocent baby boy. He wouldn't do something like this. Lakshmi's daughters were misbehaving and blaming it on Neeraj. She could feel Lakshmi's eyes watching her. Before she could say anything, Lakshmi called Ash downstairs.

She heard Ash's feet walk down the stairs. Ash came into the room, her hair sitting in a blob on top of her head. She was wearing one of the dresses Meena had made her. The little black buttons running down the middle sparkled in the light. The pink gingham that Ash had picked out complemented her caramel skin tone. She looked like a princess, Meena thought.

'Ash, tell us what you told me earlier about Neeraj.'

Ash's eyes widened and she looked scared. In that instant, Meena knew. She was telling the truth.

'Don't worry, Ash *beti*,' Meena said. 'You don't have to say. It's OK. I will speak to Neeraj.'

She held her arms out and Ash ran into them. She gave the best hugs. Lakshmi looked at her and smiled.

Meena called her children down and saw her son in a new light for the first time. What she had always seen as a cute, unknowing smile was now full of mischief. Purnima looked moody, her lip pouting at the fact she had to go home and stop playing with her cousins. Neeraj hugged Meena's legs. Her eyes softened and she hugged him back, his cute smile gracing his face once again. Purnima rolled her eyes and hugged her aunt goodbye. They started walking back to their house when Neeraj asked her a question.

'Mum, can I have new sneakers? Mine are old.'

She looked down at his feet. She had only bought those trainers four months ago or so. They weren't cheap either. Neeraj had insisted all his friends had nicer sneakers than his, so she had bought them for him. She had used some of her savings money that she kept aside in her tin.

'Neeraj, we just bought you those not long ago. They look fine to me.'

He grunted. She hated when he made that animalistic noise. She paused outside Kanika's old house. The car she thought she had seen was no longer there, leaving the usual void space.

Purnima went straight upstairs as soon as they got home. Meena heard the sound of running water. Amar was home already. Neeraj threw his shoes off and left them in a heap in the middle of the hallway. She bent down and put them away. *Boys*, she thought. She went into the kitchen and started preparing dinner. Her feet and hands ached. In the past few weeks, she had noticed a mild pain and swelling in her hands. She forced them out of their clenched state and stretched out her fingers. She would talk to Neeraj tomorrow when she had more energy.

As she chopped the onions, she heard the creak of the stairs. Her stomach tightened into a fist. She heard Amar talk to his son, and then he emerged in the kitchen. He had shaved one cheek and had the other side still to go. Meena couldn't remember the last time he had shaved properly. His patches of hair were starting to make him look like a caveman. Sometimes, he started shaving while he was drunk. He had cut himself a few times. Meena had been there to clean up the blood.

He seemed in a great mood today. He posed and asked her if he should keep his face like that. One side with stubble, the other without. She laughed and swotted him away with her tea towel. His eyes sparkled again. She watched him out of the corner of her eye, not wanting to make Amar feel self-conscious. She saw the shake of his hands. They always started shaking when he hadn't had a drink yet.

'I had a great day, Meena. An old friend popped by at work. He said they are hiring in another part of the airport. It pays better. He's going to let me know next week if I have the job. We could be rich, Meena! We could buy a bigger, better house and a nice car, and I'll buy you the most amazing sarees and gold bangles for your wrists. We will have everything we want! I can't wait to tell the children – we can get Purnima those concert tickets she wanted!'

He called Purnima down. There was no answer. She watched his forehead crinkle. He sighed. She watched him walk up the stairs. Her hand froze as she listened for noise. She continued chopping onions. The sound of the knife slicing the hard exterior of the onion rang in her ears. She put the knife down again and listened for any signs of disturbance. With her heart pounding so loudly, she struggled to hear much else. Deep breaths, she told herself. Her heart quietened.

She heard laughing. The sound made her realise how much she missed Purnima's laugh. She often heard her daughter laughing with her friends at school, and sometimes with her cousins. She never seemed to laugh much at home anymore.

Purnima came down the stairs alone. Neeraj's foot-steps followed his sister's. She told Meena that their dad was finishing shaving his face. Purnima and Neeraj went to the living room, and she heard the familiar sound of the television. She couldn't keep up with what they watched these days. There was one show she quite liked. It was about a family of cave men and women. Amar liked that show too.

She stirred the onions in the pan, with *jeera* and chillies. A booming voice caused her to drop the spatula onto the linoleum floor. Her back creaked as she bent down to retrieve it.

'Look outside! Look outside! Purnima, look!'

Meena switched off the gas and ran to the living room window. Purnima and Neeraj were standing on the sofa, looking outside. Then she saw it. The car. It was back. Parked right in Kanika's driveway. Purnima leapt off the sofa and ran out the front door. Meena felt a rush of cold air hit her as Purnima sped past. Meena followed her daughter outside, lifting her saree and running faster than she had ever run before.

She rubbed her eyes. It was true. They were back. Kanika stood in the driveway, surrounded by her children. Meena ran over to her, nearly tripping over her saree. When she reached her, she hugged her so close, she thought she would never let go.

The house looked exactly the same. The previous occupiers hadn't changed much. Meena soon discovered that Kanika's husband had rented the property out instead of selling it. He had always planned on returning. He just hadn't wanted Kanika to know that. He had wanted her to feel helpless and trapped.

Amar and Jagdeep went outside to the garden to talk. Disgust rippled across her face at the sight of her husband greeting the man who beat her best friend on a daily basis. *Boys will be boys*, she muttered to herself.

The children all huddled outside on the street. Meena kept an eye on them from the window. The sofa creaked as she sat next to her friend. They looked at each other, lost for words. The pain they had each experienced was clear on their faces. They had both aged beyond their years, yet Meena felt like a schoolgirl sitting next to her best friend.

That evening, she confided in Kanika about the problems she was having with Neeraj. Her friend immediately told her to stop the behaviour now, before it got out of control. As if on command, Neeraj came into the room, excited to see his Kanika Auntie who always fed him treats.

'Neeraj, your ma wants to talk to you,' Kanika said. 'I'll just be in the kitchen.' She rose from the sofa and walked out of the room, leaving mother and son alone.

'Neeraj, *beti*, come sit. I hear you've been swearing and asking your cousins to steal money for you. Is that true?'

Neeraj shrugged, his eyes staring hard at the floor.

'Please talk to me, Neeraj. I know it's been difficult at home, but you never need to steal. Ever. Somebody else has worked hard for that money. The same way your dad and I work hard for ours. OK? Promise me you won't do anything like this again?'

He nodded solemnly, blinking tears away. She hugged him tight and sent him back outside to play with his cousins and friends.

As the night got darker, and once the kids were tucked into their beds, Meena and Kanika resumed their spot on the sofa. Instead of discussing all the pain the last few years had brought, Kanika told her stories about a handsome man in Nairobi who delivered the post every day, and how the neighbouring ladies all made sure to be in their front lawns every morning with their best dresses on. Meena roared with laughter as Kanika stood up, impersonating the ladies smoothing their hair and applying a fresh coat of lipstick. Meena told Kanika news about the neighbouring ladies, how Lisa was having an affair with the butcher down the road, and that Anne wanted to marry her long-term girlfriend of fifteen years. As Meena watched her friend laugh, she never wanted the evening to end.

Chapter Forty-three

Their evening walks continued seamlessly, Meena stuffing cream cakes into her handbag for them to scoff while they talked and walked.

Another benefit to Kanika's return was additional help with the children. Although Ameera, Purnima and Ash were old enough to walk to and from school themselves, Neeraj and Parina preferred being guided home. Kanika picked the children up from school and gave them snacks until Meena arrived home from work. And Meena was trying to get Kanika a job at the razor factory too.

Purnima and Rani had resumed their friendship, but Meena had noticed Ash sitting on the outside, trying to join in but being abruptly turned away. Rani was a sweet girl, open to Ash's friendship, but Purnima was quick to banish Ash to the outskirts. Meena thought to intervene but decided to let them work the issue out for themselves.

Weeks went by, and the familiar autumnal gloom crept over the country. Days became shorter and nights were frosty. Meena was so thankful for central heating in this country. However, it was expensive. Some nights, she wrapped the children up extra warm and used two duvets in bed. The children didn't feel the cold as much, having spent most of their lives here. For Neeraj, this was all he knew. Amar was a typical hot-blooded male who could walk around in the snow wearing just a shirt and not feel a chill.

The shops soon became littered with tinsel and lights and presents for the holidays. Meena wasn't a huge fan of Christmas. She found it overwhelming. She loved the day itself. The children would get so excited. She loved buying the gifts, and carefully wrapping them in gold and silver paper. However, she found the build-up to the holiday tiresome. Suddenly, the shops were busier, and everything was more expensive. She had got into a habit of buying the children's presents in the summer sales. The only problem was hiding them. Especially from Neeraj.

She had given in and bought him the sneakers he wanted. He had taken them from her with that angelic smile and run straight to his room to try them on. Her gesture had not gone unnoticed. Amar had frowned at the new shoes on his son's feet. He had asked her how they could afford them. Despite being caught in the moment, she told him she had paid for them from her wages. His eyes had narrowed, accentuating the new wrinkles around them. Lines riddles his forehead as he weighed up her answer. She could tell he wasn't happy, but it was her choice if she wanted to treat her son.

Between Purnima's Beatles obsession, and a sudden desire to dress in shorter skirts, and Neeraj's constant need for new shoes, Meena's money pot was becoming increasingly empty. She took on more sewing orders, quietly sewing into the night, the whirring of the machine keeping her company as her hands grew tired.

Chapter Forty-four

Meena was grateful for a day off on Saturday. She rarely had time to herself, and the promise of the day ahead made her giddy. She brushed her teeth and looked in the mirror. It was funny how your face could shift and change over the years. She once had clear, glowing skin and thick dark hair. Now, her hair was threaded with thin silver hairs embroidered through her scalp. Her face looked tired, with bags under her eyes that never seemed to go away. Wrinkles had appeared in the corners of her mouth and eyes. She had noticed slight discoloured spots on her face.

She brushed her hair and sighed. Maybe she should dye her hair. Ladies at the factory told her you could do it at home yourself. No need for an expensive salon appointment. One more glance in the mirror made up her mind. She was going to buy some hair dye. She dressed. Her beautiful pastel sarees shimmered as the sun hit them through the window. She hadn't worn any of her nice sarees in months.

However, their beauty captivated her once again, and her fingers traced the ornate designs. She decided to wear the last saree Amar had bought her. She had sewn the fall in and made the blouse but had never worn it. She laid the delicate material on the bed. It was simple, yet stunning. She had chosen it because it was the most beautiful shade of purple. It reminded her of the lilac sunset in Nairobi. The material subtly sparkled in the sun. Small paisleys were embroidered throughout. She put the blouse on. It was too big around her bust.

She pinned it in and wrapped the saree around herself. She looked in the mirror and smiled. She looked beautiful in it. She plaited her hair into a bun and secured it. She touched the grey hairs and sighed. As she walked down the stairs, she held on to the banister with a firm grip, the edges of her saree threatening to trip her over.

She looked at the time and decided to call Parvathi to ask her opinion. After a quick phone call, and Parvathi's attempt to persuade Meena to dye her hair blonde, Meena hung up the phone with a smile on her face.

She gathered her bag and made sure she had money in her purse. She opened the front door and abruptly shut it, the cold air startling her. Her hands fumbled for her coat among Neeraj and Purnima's jackets piled up on the banister. She put on her comfortable shoes, invisible underneath the saree. As she left the house, she thought to ask Kanika to come with her.

She knocked on her friend's door just in case. Kanika answered.

'Meena! You look so beautiful. Wow. Where are you going?'

'Just to the shops. I want to buy hair dye. Do you want to come with me?'

Kanika turned nervously, her eyes looking back into her hallway. Meena could hear the children playing in the garden.

'I wish I could, Meena. I have to look after the children. Jagdeep should be back soon, but I don't know what time.'

'Is he not at work?'

She regretted asking the question. Kanika lowered her eyes. Meena waited patiently.

'No. He told me not to tell you. He didn't want you or Amar to think less of him. Please don't say anything to Amar. Jag has been going out trying to find another way to make money. We barely have any left, Meena. He has spent it all on new business ventures that never work.'

A door creaking made Kanika stop. She turned to look into her house. Meena couldn't see anyone.

'We'll talk on our walk. See you later!'

Meena walked down the street, feeling like a queen. As she turned a corner, she passed a group of youths. Some were sitting on their bikes; others were standing and smoking. She crossed the road to avoid them. She felt them watching her. She paid no attention. As soon as she was further down the road, she exhaled. She hadn't realised she had been holding her breath.

She walked into a chemist's and found the hair aisle. Why were there so many different colours and options? How did she know what shade of brown her hair was? She began to panic. She shouldn't have done this. She knew nothing about hair dye or beauty. As she was about to turn and leave, she felt a hand on her shoulder.

'Do you need some help, lady?'

She turned. A stunning lady with skin like oiled mahogany and hair woven into an elaborate series of plaits on her head was staring at her.

'Do you work here?'

'No, but I can tell you need help. Look, I've had my hair every colour you can imagine. Let me help you out!'

Meena nodded, grateful for some assistance.

'Now, are you looking to dye your hair the same shade or lighter?'

'I don't know. I just want to get rid of the . . . you know.'

'Don't be ashamed of grey hair, honey. It comes with experience. Let's have a look for you. Here, darkest brown. That should match your hair.'

Meena took the box from her. It did look very similar to her hair colour. Her eyes skimmed the other bottles.

'Thank you. That was very kind of you to help me.'

'No worries. Have a good day and good luck with the hair dye!'

She watched the lady walk to a different aisle and smiled. She went to the cashier and paid. The aisles all promised different ways to become more beautiful, but Meena decided one product was enough for today. As she walked out of the store, she noticed a few familiar-looking boxes. The brand Fair & Lovely. She hadn't realised they sold skin-lightening creams here too. They must be for the Indian population. These British people seemed to want darker skin judging by

298

the fake tan aisle. She picked up a box of the cream that promised youth and beauty, but then put it down. She knew of many horror stories of women burning their faces using these creams. She returned the box to its position.

She left the shop and stopped. More English youths were outside, their black hoodies contrasting with their white skin. They all smiled at her as she stood, trying to see if they were the same boys or just another group. She quickly walked in the opposite direction. She walked at high speed. She turned to look behind her. Nobody seemed to be there. She slowed and breathed deeply.

As she turned into her street, she heard the rush of wind before she felt it. They were there, cycling past her, chanting something. She couldn't make out what it was. She ran to her door and fumbled for the key. Her hands shook so badly she couldn't unlock the door. She turned and saw that two boys were now in her driveway. She managed to get the key into the lock and ran inside, slamming the door behind her. She went to the living room window and looked outside. They were gone.

She took a few deep breaths, and then put some chai on the boil and walked to the fridge. She smiled at her remaining cream cake left in the box, and considered leaving it for Purnima, but she loved sweet food so much. Her stomach rumbled. She chuckled and put the cream cake on a plate. As she slurped the tea out of her bowl and ate the cream cake, the radio played old Bollywood songs in the background. Songs from her childhood. She closed her eyes as the music took over her body.

'Meena, come dance with us!' Her sisters took her hands and she swayed with them. They danced around in a circle, laughing, and falling into each other. They were playing in the street and other neighbourhood kids had come to join in. The music was blasting from a nearby house where a wedding reception was taking place. Meena's mother had told her they would go to the wedding house later and say their congratulations. She couldn't wait to see what the bride was wearing.

She noticed her father walking towards them. He looked sad. For the first time, she noticed how he walked with his eyes looking at the floor. He didn't look ahead. Only downwards. She called for him. At the sound of her voice, he looked up and smiled. She broke away from the circle and ran into his arms.

'Why do you look so sad?' she asked.

'I'm not sad, Meena. I'm happy. I get to come home to a lovely daughter like you.'

She kissed his cheek.

'Why do you look at the floor when you walk?'

'So I can see where I'm going, Meena!'

She laughed hysterically. Her sisters came rushing over, hugging their father's legs. Meena watched as his face transformed. What once looked so forlorn, now looked overcome with joy. She vowed to make sure her father always looked so happy. He joined in with their dancing, his glasses falling down his face. She looked up at her father that day and felt like the luckiest child in the world.

★

A knock on the back door brought her back to the present. Her eyes were misted over, and she felt like her body was frozen still.

Another knock on the back door made her stand. She opened it and saw her friend. Kanika asked her to come over to her house so they could keep an eye on the children. Meena went, taking her hair dye bottle with her. As they walked into Kanika's kitchen, Meena noticed how much better her friend seemed. She had a spring in her step that Meena had never seen before.

She showed Kanika the hair dye. They told the children to look after each other, and Meena and Kanika went upstairs. Forty-five minutes later, the bathroom was a mess, but Meena's locks were dark brown again. There had even been some extra in the bottle, so Kanika had touched up her hair too. The children had run in to see what they were doing, and had all laughed hysterically at the sight of their mother and her best friend with wet hair combed back and spots of brown dye on their faces.

'Do you want some, Rani? Come here, Purnima!'

Kanika had chased them out the room, as they all laughed hysterically.

Afterwards, Meena and Kanika sat in the living room, waiting for their hair to dry. Meena snacked on biscuits as Kanika found something for them to watch on the television, scrolling through the three channels, deciding which she preferred. As they sipped chai, Kanika turned to her.

'It's nearly the anniversary of Asmita's death. You told me she died about a year ago, right?'

Meena nodded. It had been on her mind too.

'Do you think Amar will be OK?'

She looked at her friend.

'He will be fine. He has me and the children. We'll probably spend time with Lakshmi and his brothers.'

Kanika nodded. She was about to ask if Jagdeep had mentioned anything about Amar's state of mind, but the sound of a car outside made them lean to look through the window. Amar was home.

Chapter Forty-five

Meena hugged her friend goodbye and walked to her front door. It looked like Amar had already gone inside. She thought about collecting Neeraj from Lakshmi but decided against it. It would be nice to have some time alone with her husband, especially with her newly dyed hair and saree. She closed the door behind her. It was eerily quiet. Amar liked to hum to himself when he came home, but she heard no sound.

She walked through to the kitchen and noticed two cupboard doors were open. She didn't remember leaving them open. She quietly shut them. A creak of floorboards told her that Amar was in the back room, the door between the back room and living room half-shut. She swung it open and went through the door. He turned to her, his eyes blazing. She involuntarily took a step back. Her husband looked like a crazed man, his lips quivering and his eyes wide open, unblinking.

'Where is the whisky, Meena?'

She had hidden it weeks ago. He hadn't noticed because he had stopped drinking it.

'We ran out. You finished it.'

His face cleared for a minute. Considering how intoxicated he had been at the time, she knew he would struggle to remember if he had finished the bottle or not. Without hesitation, he charged past her, knocking her into the wall. A few seconds later, she heard the door slam and the sound of the car engine. She walked to the window and looked outside. He was gone. A few seconds later, she saw that Jagdeep had returned. She watched him go inside his house.

She sunk down to the floor, her arms wrapped tightly around her waist, holding herself together, struggling to keep herself from falling apart. What had happened? What could have tipped Amar over the edge again? He was doing so well. He had been OK that morning. She pushed herself back up and stood waiting. When he returned, she would be there to question him. He was a father. A husband.

She didn't know how long she had been standing there, rehearsing her speech to Amar in her head, when she heard a knock at the door. She opened the door, with her head held high, ready for an argument. Except it wasn't Amar. Lakshmi was standing there, with Neeraj and Purnima by her side.

'Meena, you didn't pick Neeraj up. You said you'd pick him up at 4. It's now 5.30! Luckily Purnima came by and got him.'

She had said she would pick him up at 4 p.m., but the incident with Amar had made her lose all sense of time. She apologised and the children ran inside. She asked Lakshmi if she wanted any chai.

'I'll come inside but I don't want anything to drink.'

Lakshmi walked past her into the living room, with strong, purposeful steps.

'Meena, I'm worried about Amar. It's nearly Ma's anniversary and I'm worried it might tip him back over the edge.'

Meena simply nodded, her eyes watching the driveway, anxious for Amar's car to pull in. No matter what mood he was in, she needed him to be safe.

'Meena, are you paying attention? Stop looking outside.'

Lakshmi paced the room, words flying out of her mouth, but Meena didn't catch any of them. Her eyes never left the driveway. Lakshmi didn't seem to notice, her need to vent stronger than her need to have a reaction.

Then the car pulled in. She breathed a sigh of relief. At least he was OK. Until he came inside, she had a few precious seconds to feel relieved. Lakshmi turned and saw her brother stumble up the driveway, holding an open bottle of whisky in one hand, and a bag full of bottles in the other.

'Meena. What's happened?'

Meena didn't have time to answer her. Amar came crashing through the door, causing Lakshmi to shriek. He called out to his children. Meena leapt from the living room, aiming to block him from seeing them.

She saw Purnima and Neeraj paused on the stairs, staring at their drunk, incoherent father. Meena had no idea how he had driven in such a state. He must have bought the alcohol and drunk half the bottle before even getting back in his car.

Purnima carried on walking down the stairs. Neeraj stayed near the top. She could see the fear in his eyes. Purnima on the other hand looked slightly frightened at first, but then relaxed. She hugged her father. He picked her up, swinging her around, the bag of bottles on one arm clinking against each other. Meena was frozen. She could hear Lakshmi's heavy breathing behind her. He swung Purnima back down. Meena noticed how quickly Purnima stepped away from her father, nervous to be swung again when he was in such a state.

Amar then laid his eyes on Neeraj.

'Son! Come downstairs. Hug your father!'

Neeraj shook his head. Meena noticed he was sucking his thumb. He hadn't done that since he was four years old. Purnima beckoned her brother down the stairs. He shook his head again, this time tears clouding his eyes. Meena walked up the stairs and lifted him up in her arms, his weight making it difficult to get up each step. She felt his muffled cries against her chest. She struggled to walk the three remaining steps. Her son had got so big! She put him in his room and told him to stay on his bed and keep the door closed. He nodded obediently. She closed the door behind her and walked down the stairs. The hallway was empty.

Amar, Lakshmi and Purnima were sitting in the living room. The television had been switched on, and the programme with the cat chasing the mouse was on. Meena hoped the mouse got away again.

Purnima was cuddled into her father's armpit, and he was cuddling his bottle of whisky. Lakshmi was sitting on the edge of the sofa, never turning her eyes away from her brother. Meena searched Lakshmi's face, trying to read her expression.

She walked straight to the kitchen and started preparing dinner. Amar and the children would be hungry soon.

Thirty minutes later, and the smell of the *sabzi* told her it was ready. She put the *atta* dough in the fridge to set briefly. She strode back into the living room.

'Lakshmi, are you staying for dinner?'

Lakshmi looked up for the first time. 'Dinner?'

'Yes. It's dinner time.'

'I should go home. I need to feed the kids.'

'OK. See you later.'

Lakshmi hesitantly stood. Meena noticed how Amar rarely looked at his sister anymore. Maybe he saw his mother in her. Maybe he couldn't bear the sight of her sorrowful eyes. Maybe he just didn't care to see his sister's judgement.

'Bye, Amar. I'll see you tomorrow, maybe?'

He shrugged. Meena noticed how much the bottle of whisky had gone down. She watched as Amar's eyes began to close. He was falling asleep. Relief washed over her face, and she felt her rapidly beating heart subside.

Lakshmi left and Meena went up the stairs to get Neeraj. She found him on his bed. As she went to the shake him awake, she noticed the bedsheets were wet. She lifted him up and saw that he had also been crying.

His eyelashes shone with salt water and his cheeks were rubbed red. She gently undressed him, putting the wet clothes and bedsheets in a pile on the floor. She took him to the bathtub and poured water over his body, scrubbing his back and stomach as she softly sang Hindi songs to him. She picked him up and dried him. He got dressed in clean clothes and she started walking down the stairs, carrying the damp items in a pile. Then she heard her daughter scream.

Chapter Forty-six

She stumbled in a hurry to get down the stairs and to her daughter. She regained her balance and ran into the living room. Purnima was standing across the room from her father. She looked at Amar. He was still fast asleep.

'Purnima, what's wrong?'

'He dropped the bottle. It scared me.'

'Are you hurt? Did any glass hit you?'

'No, it was in his other hand.'

She hugged her daughter to her chest and breathed a sigh of relief. She wasn't hurt. She had just been startled. She told Purnima to go upstairs. As she watched Purnima retreat from the room, she walked over to Amar. The broken bottle littered the carpet with shattered glass. He must have either hit it against the table on purpose, or it smashed against it when it fell out of his hand. A Punjabi swear word flew from her mouth as she sliced her hand with a broken shard. Tears mixed with the blood as she continued picking up the pieces.

The floor stank of the leftover whisky, and she grimaced. Months of cleaning up vomit and urine that reeked of the light brown liquid had put her off the smell for life. She winced as another piece of glass cut through the skin of her hand. As she began walking to the kitchen to rinse her hands and bandage them, she heard Amar groan. He was having a nightmare. Well, so was she. Except she couldn't wake up from hers.

She eventually managed to clean most of the glass from the floor and then began to dab at the carpet, but it was no use. The whisky had seeped all the way in, discolouring the cream carpet. Her hands shook as she scrubbed, tears mixing with the soap mixture. As she stood up, she noticed Amar staring at her with dazed, half-lidded eyes, his mouth slightly open. She began to tiptoe away, scared to fully wake him.

Then he called her name. His voice was rough and scratchy from the alcohol. She watched him cough. She should get him a glass of water. Except, her feet stayed right where they were.

He said her name again. She moved closer to him.

'Yes?' she said.

'Meena. My Meena. My wife. Sit with me.'

She hesitated. She didn't want to be anywhere near him. She sat on the edge of the sofa, as far away from him as possible.

'Meena. It's not my fault. This is not my fault.'

His words angered her. She felt repulsed by him. She stood up to leave.

'Meena, stay. I didn't get the job. They told me I don't have the "qualifications" for it. I didn't get it. We're stuck being the way we are.'

Anger shook her body.

'You come home like this because you didn't get some job? You come home scaring your children because of a job! You should be ashamed of yourself, Amar. For the way you treat us. I didn't marry you for this.'

She watched as his eyes widened. He sat there, his hands shaking. He didn't move. She took the opportunity to leave the room, her hands clasped into tight fists.

She went into Neeraj's room and found he was already asleep. His lamp was still on, and she saw an empty packet of crisps by his bed. She closed the door softly and walked to Purnima's room. She paused outside. There were voices inside. She couldn't quite make out all the words. She put her ear to the door.

'Rani, I think my dad is drunk. You might not know what that means, but it's when someone drinks a lot of alcohol which is a bad drink. When he drank before, I used to think he just got tired because he would fall asleep or his words would come out funny. I don't think he's just tired. I think he has a problem, Rani.'

She couldn't make out Rani's response. They must be talking out of their windows again, as their bedrooms were next to each other's.

She was about to walk away when she heard words she never imagined she would never hear come out of her child's mouth.

'Rani, I think it's my mum's fault. I think Dad doesn't love her anymore and she's making him stay. I think she makes him sad. So he drinks.'

She slowly went back down the stairs. Where did Purnima even get that idea from? Why would Amar want to leave? And why would she make him stay? It would be easier if he left.

Meena paused, unable to believe she had just thought that. She didn't want Amar to leave. She loved him. Despite everything. She loved him. She didn't know what she would do if he left. She didn't know if she could bear it.

As she reached the bottom of the stairs, she noticed that the front door was open. She peered outside, unsure if somebody had left her house, or had entered. Suddenly, she saw Amar speed out of their driveway in his car. She walked out into the driveway and stood there, staring at the brick wall that separated their driveway and Kanika's. It now had a bright yellow word graffitied on it. She read it a few times. Paki. She had heard and seen that word countless times in her decade in this country. The same word those youths outside the shop had used. She knew they had been up to something. How naïve of her to think they had left her alone.

She heard a door open and saw Kanika standing in the doorway of her home. Meena didn't know what Kanika had seen from her house, but whatever it was, it forced her to come outside in the cold and wrap her arms around Meena, guiding her inside. Once they were back inside Meena's house, the tears started. They didn't stop. Kanika asked what was wrong but one look at the living room floor told her everything she needed to know. Meena cried and cried. She was powerless.

Kanika went upstairs to check on the children. She came down and told her that Purnima was in bed. Neeraj was still asleep. She then tried to clean the carpet, dabbing tea towels to soak up the stain. It didn't work, but she kept trying. Kanika always kept trying. As Meena looked at her friend dabbing the floor, on her knees with her sleeves rolled up, she noticed the marks on Kanika's arm.

'He hasn't stopped, has he?'

Kanika looked up at her. Her eyes glistened with tears that didn't spill.

'Meena, you have enough going on. Focus on finding a way to sort Amar out. You can't let him go on like this. I've seen it, Meena. I've seen his behaviour for months now.'

'How do you know how long it has been happening?'

'Sheila told me, Meena. She came round to chat when I got back. She told me how everyone on the street knows about Amar's . . . problem. It's no secret. I was just sad that you didn't tell me yourself.'

Meena pulled her friend up on the sofa. She didn't let go of her hands.

'I'm sorry I didn't tell you. I just didn't want to worry you. You had enough going on with your accident. You told me Jagdeep was treating you better. I didn't want to tarnish your happiness. Plus, he got better. There was nothing to tell.'

Kanika shook her head.

'He's sick, Meena. He won't just get better. He needs help.'

Meena nodded. She couldn't fix this one on her own. The ding of the doorbell signalled a visitor. Kanika went to answer it, and walked back into the room, Rajvir behind her.

'I just came to check everything was OK,' he said.

She saw his eyes looking at the ruined carpet. She insisted everything was fine, and Rajvir nodded and left. Meena watched him wistfully, wishing she could follow him to his cosy house that was void of this torment.

They sat up waiting for Amar to return. Eventually Jagdeep knocked on the door, asking Kanika to come home. She left, but not without hugging Meena tight. As she watched her friend leave, Meena sat in the living room in the dark alone. The half-moon shone through her window, basking her in its glow.

She thought back to the day they had brought Purnima home, the moon shining above them. She had thought her life had changed for the better that day. That the dark days were behind her. How wrong she had been. You can plan for happiness. For a better life. However, plans fail. They fall apart and all you're left with is ashes. She had a feeling someone was laughing down at her every time she felt happiness. They knew it wouldn't last. It never lasted. Hours went by and the sky turned a deep navy, with a sprinkling of stars dusting the sky, fighting through the clouds. Eventually, the moon disappeared behind the clouds and she was covered in complete darkness.

Chapter Forty-seven

Her neck protested as she tried to sit up. She had fallen asleep on the sofa. She jumped off the worn seat and looked outside. Amar's car was there. He had come home. Her body felt sore all over. Her eyes passed over their clock and she noticed the time: 6 a.m. The house was eerily quiet, except for the gentle shuffle of her feet in their slippers walking up the stairs. She eased open the door to her room and saw Amar collapsed diagonally across the bed.

Meena heard a noise coming from the bathroom. She heard a clatter and walked to the door and knocked gently. Purnima opened the door, her eyes wide with fear.

'It wasn't me. I promise.'

Meena looked past her. There was yellow-tinged sick in the bath. It looked like Purnima had been trying to clean it up but instead had caused it to splatter all over the bathroom tiles and the floor. Suddenly, Meena felt exhausted.

'Go to your room.'

'Mum, it wasn't me! I was trying to clean it.'

'I know, *beti*. Go back to bed. I'll clean it.'

Purnima ran past her, tears cascading down her face. Meena felt a pang in her chest, but her tired body gave her no other room for emotion.

She grabbed a bucket and disinfectant, and got to work.

Soon, she had managed to get rid of the stench and the bathroom looked clean again. Her footsteps took her back to her bedroom, apprehensively avoiding the creaks in the floorboards. Amar was in the same position. She could try and move him so she could get in, but it wasn't worth disturbing him. She decided to go back downstairs and sleep on the sofa.

The clattering of dishes woke her up. The children had school. Her eyes glanced at the clock hanging on the wall. 7.30 a.m. She was going to be late to drop the children off and get to work. Her brow started to sweat as panic took over her body.

She heard a knock at the front door, and a few moments later, Purnima answered it. Lakshmi's voice travelled through the house, falling on her welcome ears. She heard Lakshmi walk into the living room and Purnima whisper to her. They must think she was asleep. She called out to them from the sofa in the back room.

Lakshmi walked in, startled to see Meena sleeping on the sofa. Her expression changed as she noticed Meena's facial expression. She told Purnima to finish getting ready for school and to make sure Neeraj was ready. Purnima walked off, clearly unhappy at not being included in the adult conversation.

'What happened, Meena?'

'I waited for him. I fell asleep on the sofa. When I woke up, he was back and upstairs. The bathroom was covered in vomit. Purnima was trying to clean it. I cleaned it and went to the bedroom.'

She felt like a robot reciting a script. Lakshmi looked at her and stood taller.

'Right. I will take the children to school and call your workplace and tell them you are sick.'

'I don't have a number for them. Could you tell Sheila, please?'

'Of course, Meena. I will go to her house and tell her now. Then I'll come back and get the children to school. I'll come back and check on you afterwards. OK?'

She couldn't find words to express her gratitude. She nodded and tried not to cry. She had cried enough tears to last her several lifetimes.

She felt her eyes close again and she drifted back to sleep. She woke up to hands shaking her. She rolled over. She didn't want the sleep to end. She wanted to be left alone in her own bubble of nothingness. The hands shook her again. She wearily opened her eyes.

Amar's face loomed over hers. Her body instinctively moved away. She felt his warm hand clamp around her wrist. He quickly pulled back, clearly seeing the fear in her eyes.

'Meena, it's Neeraj. The school called. We have to go down there.'

She was up in a heartbeat. Amar looked in a terrible state. His skin was sallow. His unshaven face just added to the haphazard look. She didn't have time to make him presentable. They had to get to the school. She grabbed the car keys and shoved them in Amar's hand.

'Meena, I can't drive. I don't feel well.'

She slowly turned. She was about to respond to Amar but saw the look on his face. He couldn't drive. Not in that state.

'I'll go to the school alone,' she told him. 'You can ring your work and tell them why you aren't in today. Hopefully, they will let you go back in tomorrow.' She slipped on her shoes and grabbed a coat.

The quick walk to the school felt like it took longer than usual. As she rushed through the gates, her adrenaline was dissipating, the tiredness scrambling her mind. She tried to speak to the receptionist, but she kept mixing up English words with Hindi. After three attempts, the receptionist asked: 'Are you Neeraj's mother?'

Relief washed over her as she nodded. Exactly. She was Neeraj's mother. Even the receptionist knew Neeraj! She followed the lady down the hall, noticing how short she felt in comparison to the receptionist, who was taller and wearing high-heeled shoes – navy, with a sharp point at the toe. She was dressed in a pencil skirt that skimmed her knees and a polka dot blouse. Meena envied how professional she looked, and marvelled at the effort it must take to get ready in the morning. Receptionists must earn a lot, she thought.

She couldn't help but wonder what the receptionist thought of her appearance. She must look a mess.

She was taken to the head teacher's office and welcomed in immediately. She couldn't see Neeraj.

'Sorry, where is my son? Is he OK?'

The headteacher nodded. He was a young man with a well-groomed beard. His shoes made a slight squeaking sound as he walked over to his desk and sat in his chair. She noticed how his crisp white shirt crumpled as he sat. He offered her the chair opposite to him, on the other side of the desk, and Meena's small frame sunk into it.

'Mrs Varma, I've brought you here today to discuss Neeraj.'

'Yes, I know. What's wrong with him? Has he been hurt?'

The headteacher looked puzzled.

'No, ma'am. He is fine. He hasn't been hurt. This—'

'Oh, thank God,' she exclaimed. 'He's OK. My poor baby. I was so worried . . .'

'Sorry, ma'am. That's not why we called you in. Are you not aware of the behavioural issues your son has been experiencing?'

She froze. Behavioural issues. What did that even mean? She had lectured Neeraj, and his behaviour had improved recently.

'No, I don't understand. Neeraj is a good boy.'

'Neeraj is, frankly, a difficult child. We noticed a change in him about a year ago. He suddenly grew more mischievous. He stopped doing his homework. He picks on the other children. He doesn't have any friends. He's rude to his teachers and disobeys them. We didn't do anything for a while. We got the impression that things were difficult at home. His behaviour seemed to improve in recent months, and his grades got much better. However, this morning he has been completely out of control. We can't have him in school like this.'

Meena stood up. No longer have him at this school? He was a student here. They couldn't just kick him out.

'I don't believe the things you are saying. Neeraj is kind. He is thoughtful and loving. Things have been a bit difficult at home but he's trying. We all are. Please don't punish him.'

'I don't think you understand. We haven't expelled a child from this school in over five years. Neeraj has broken too many rules. Unfortunately, today he crossed the line completely. He tried to steal money from his classmate, and when she noticed, he pushed her to the floor. We have spoken to his other classmates, and they say he is often violent and steals their lunches and pocket money. We can't allow him to be a student here. It's not safe for the other children.'

'Not safe? He is a child!'

'Exactly. So are his classmates. They need stability and they need to be able to learn. They can't do that when Neeraj is in their class.'

'Why? What exactly has he done so wrong?'

She noticed the headteacher falter for the first time. He looked unsettled.

'He told us not to tell you the exact details. He said . . . he said he would get into trouble at home. That you might . . . hurt him. I told him we could call social services . . .'

'What? Hurt him? I would never lay a hand on my child. He wouldn't say that.'

'He did. I had a feeling he was lying, which is exactly why we chose not to call social services, but to call you in instead. Neeraj has an issue with lying, Mrs Varma. He lies about everything. He told the other students that his parents are rich and that you all live in a seven-bedroom mansion. I know it's a harmless lie, but it is one all the same. We have your address on file, so I was more than aware that this isn't the case. He also told students that his father is a drummer in a famous band. Apparently, he is on tour a lot. Is that true?'

She shook her head. Neeraj had created fantasies about their home life because he couldn't bear to come to terms with how it was in reality. She felt her chest ache. She had let her child down.

'That is not all. He also said he didn't have any siblings. His sister used to go to this school! She now goes to the secondary school next door. Surely he would know that was a terrible lie. His sister was not the . . . easiest child with her temperament, but she was definitely better behaved than her brother. Not only does he lie, Mrs Varma, but he steals. On two occasions, the dinner ladies have seen him steal lunch from another student, or steal lunch money. We have no doubt it has happened other times, while nobody was watching.'

'My son is not a thief.'

'I know this is difficult to hear, Mrs Varma. We understand you have troubles at home.'

'Why do you keep saying that? What troubles?'

The head teacher opened a file on his desk. Inside were a collection of papers. He put one piece of paper in front of her. It was a short essay.

'Would you like me to read it to you?'

She looked at the sheet again. It was an essay written by Neeraj, titled 'My Family'. The first few sentences were about her, saying how much Neeraj loved her. However, the next paragraphs made her arms shiver. He wrote about a father on tour and too busy to see his children. He wrote that his father was his best friend who didn't bother to come home, that he was an only child with nobody to play with and that he felt alone most of the time.

Her hands shook as she gave the piece of paper back. She had let her child down.

'There's more, Mrs Varma. In a family tree project, he named random celebrities as his family. Somehow, I don't think you're related to John Lennon. There's clearly an issue at home, particularly with your husband. I assume you're still married?'

'Yes, we are.'

'I'm not sure what the problem is then, but he needs someone to discipline him.'

Just as she was about to say that her son needed love, not discipline, she heard the door open. She turned around and saw Amar in the doorway. He had made himself more presentable, but nothing could hide his pale complexion.

'Sorry I'm late. I'm Mr Varma. Neeraj's father.'

'Oh, good to see you. We didn't know if you would be joining us. You're not on tour then!' He laughed at his joke. Amar looked confused.

'Amar, we've finished now anyway. I'll meet you outside.'

She didn't want him to know.

'No, no,' said the head teacher. 'I can go over it again for Mr Varma. Please sit.'

Amar sat in the empty seat next to her. She heard the head teacher go over everything again but noticed how he had shut the folder containing Amar's essay. She couldn't take her eyes off Amar. She watched as his eyes opened in surprise and then turned into slits. His hands shook and tightened into fists. She knew he was angry. In fact, beyond angry. He was livid. He managed to maintain his temper and shook hands with the head teacher. The meeting was over, it seemed. Amar walked out the door. She stood up to follow him.

'Mrs Varma, I see now that your husband is not well. I understand. He seems like such a kind man. I'm sorry you're going through this. Given the circumstances, we'll give Neeraj one more chance. If he changes his behaviour in the next two weeks, he can stay. If not, we have no choice. Have a good rest of the day.'

She walked out of the office. He thought Amar was ill, that he had a sickness, which he did. Just not in the way the headmaster thought. At least it gave Neeraj another chance. The receptionist had Neeraj waiting for them by the front door. She watched as Amar grabbed his arm and they walked to the car. She rushed to catch up with them, her hand opening the car door just as Amar started the engine. She quickly slipped into the front seat and put on her seatbelt.

When they got home, she couldn't stop Amar. He screamed at Neeraj. He turned him around and smacked his backside. Neeraj ran upstairs crying hysterically. Meena went to follow him and Amar turned to her.

'Stop it. Stop mollycoddling that boy. Stop spoiling him. He needs discipline. He was stealing, Meena. Stealing! It's not good enough. Let him cry alone. Let him think about his behaviour.'

She paused on the step. She looked at Amar. His anger was lessening. His shoulders were drooping, and he was steadying himself against the doorway. He looked weak and fragile. She turned around and carried on walking up the stairs to comfort her child.

Chapter Forty-eight

The sun burst through the window, filling the room with its heavenly light. For the first time in months, Meena felt warm. She let the warmth seep through her caramel skin, reviving her aching limbs and bones.

Purnima was now a fully-fledged young woman. Meena had caught her out with a boy on the high street a few weeks ago. She had seen them holding hands as they walked into Woolworths. When Purnima had come home that day, Meena hadn't told her she had seen her. She had hugged Purnima extra tight that night.

It had been over six months since the incident with Neeraj, and she was struggling to parent him. He refused to listen to her or Amar. He spent all of his time locked in his room, or sat in front of the television, watching shows for hours on end.

About six months ago, Amar had collapsed at work. He was rushed to the hospital, where the doctor had told him that his kidneys and liver were failing. He had discharged himself and walked home, stopping for a bottle of whisky on the way. Meena wouldn't have

325

known about it if she hadn't bumped into his colleague in the supermarket. His colleague had asked how Amar was feeling, and her confusion had shown that she hadn't known. She had looked like a fool.

She had started picking up more shifts at the factory. They needed the financial support. She was a robot, every day the same. Wake up. Check what state Amar is in. Make sure he gets up for work. Get dressed. Make lunch for Amar and the children. Check the children are ready. Make sure Amar has left for work. Go to work. Come home. Help children with homework. Cook dinner. Sew clothes. Walk with Kanika. Bathe. Go to bed. Wait for Amar to come to bed. Sleep. Repeat.

Every morning she asked herself when it would end.

She had asked Lakshmi to look for help for Amar. Anything. Lakshmi had said there wasn't much. Only counselling, and Amar would never do that. They were stuck.

Kanika's life had also taken a turn for the worse. Jagdeep's promises of kindness had soon dissipated, and his violent streak had returned. Meena has lost track of how many times she had heard thumping next door, shortly followed by Kanika crying. Her hand had frozen over the phone several times, her finger tempted to press the three digits that could save her friend's life. Except, the reality was that Jagdeep would charm his way out of the situation, and the police would leave, thinking it was another weird Indian household.

Today was full of sunshine. It was only March but surprisingly warm. Cherry blossom sprouted on the trees in their street. Her body ached, but her mind felt active, despite another sleepless night.

Amar had come home at 3 a.m., his eyes wild with grief, his clothes askew and dirty. If she hadn't known better, she would have thought he was a homeless man.

He had raided the fridge, eating the cream cakes she had saved for her tea the next day. He had downed half a bottle of vodka. She didn't even know where he had got the vodka from.

Next, Amar had thrown their wedding photos across the room. She had winced as she saw them shatter. He then turned to photos of them in Mombasa and near Lake Nakuru. He shattered them with even greater force. His anger had turned to her next. The angry bruises on her neck and arms were blossoming today, much like the spring trees outside her window.

Yet, today was a new day. It was one of her days off from the factory. Meena walked through the door in the fence and knocked quietly on Kanika's kitchen door. She watched her friend open the door, beckon Meena inside, and silently shut it behind her.

'Meena, are you OK? We heard such loud noises from your house last night. I wanted to come over and see if you were all right, but he stopped me. He said I would end up getting you into more trouble. Did he hurt you?'

The concern on her friend's kind, small face made Meena's heart lurch. She saw the moon-shaped purple marks on her friend's chest and longed to hold her.

'He hurt me a bit. It's OK, Kanika. Nothing like what Jagdeep does to you. He doesn't force himself on me. Just a few bruises.'

'Jagdeep forcing himself on me isn't a crime, Meena. We're married. A husband has needs.'

Meena looked into her friend's deep-set almond eyes and saw nothing but unfiltered, pure, raw pain. Before Indian girls got married, their mothers told them: 'A man has needs. You have to let him get it out of his system. It is your duty as a wife to satisfy your husband in everything you do.' Her mother had warned her of the expectation, but she had always told Meena: 'You have a choice.'

'I'm going to do something about it, Kanika,' she said. 'Tonight. I can't sit by anymore. I can't let him destroy his health. I can't let him destroy our children.'

'What are you going to do, Meena? Are you going to leave him?'

Meena let go of her friend's hand. She looked at Kanika with confusion etched on her face. Her mind spun out of control, Kanika's suggestion muddling her clear plan. She shook away the mist, refocusing on her goal.

'No, Kanika. I can't leave. The same way you haven't left Jagdeep. We are stuck in these marriages. Where would we go in this foreign country? Nobody would take us. But I have a plan. I am going to get rid of all the alcohol in this house. I am going to hide it and refuse to give it back.'

'Haven't you tried this before?'

It was true, she had. Except she had given in. Amar had shouted at first. Then he had turned mellow and endearing. It was scary how quickly he could turn his charm on. This time, she wouldn't give in. In fact, she would dispose of all the drink so she couldn't give in.

'I am going to pour it all away. He might shout and scream. As long as he doesn't turn to the drink. I can't take it anymore.'

Kanika smiled at her, but there was evident worry in her eyes. She knew all the ways this could go wrong.

After a promise to see each other that evening for their walk, Meena went back home. Time to get rid of everything that he could drink.

She found every bottle and put them all on the dining table. Her hand flew to her mouth upon seeing the sheer number of bottles they had accumulated, most of them half-full, or completely empty.

She took one bottle at a time and emptied its contents down the sink. When they were all empty, she took them out to the bin and threw them all in. With each sound of shattering glass, she felt free.

She stared at the bin full of bottles, some shattered, some intact. Her stomach tightened. She had told the children to go to Lakshmi's house after school and play there. She didn't want them to see the aftermath of her plan. She sat on the sofa and waited. He would be home in an hour. He had an earlier shift today.

The hour went by slowly, the hand on the clock reminding her of what was to come with each tick. Finally, she saw Amar's car pull up outside. It was time.

Chapter Forty-nine

Amar opened the front door. She tensed, ready for a battle. Then she heard it. The sound of the children's voices. Why were they home? She heard Amar taking his shoes off and the sound of the children's footsteps going up the stairs. Purnima didn't want to say hello to her mother today, then.

Neeraj bounced into the room. He was in a good mood. She was too distracted to ask why. Amar came in smiling. He bent down to kiss her forehead. He hadn't done that in weeks. Maybe she didn't need to be scared. Maybe he didn't want to drink today. Amar groaned as he sat on the sofa. She noticed how much he had aged. What was once a youthful, handsome face, was now wrinkled and pale. He looked older than his years. She knew she did too.

Neeraj nestled into his father's arms and she looked on as they watched the cat and mouse show together. She watched along with them, laughing when they laughed. Then she heard Purnima's footsteps up above, and decided to go and see if her daughter was OK.

She gave one last look at her two boys on the sofa. They looked happy. She walked up the stairs, realising as she went how much slower she was these days, her bones creaking in a way they hadn't before. She paused outside Purnima's room. There was no sound. She knocked on the door, heard Purnima's grunt of approval and opened it. 'Are you OK, *beti*?' she asked.

'What do you want?'

'Nothing,' she said and was about to turn to leave. She paused by the doorway of her daughter's bedroom. 'It's just that we are watching the television downstairs. Come and join us.'

'I don't want to.'

'Why, has something happened?'

'No, it's just girl stuff, OK?'

Raising a teenager was a battle and Meena decided to sit this one out.

'I'm here if you need me, Purnima. Always.'

She retreated from the room and closed the door behind her.

'Meena! Where is it?' Amar's voice boomed from downstairs.

'Where is what?'

'You know what! Where is my bottle? I know I had a bottle left. At least one. Maybe four. Or three. I don't know. There was at least one!'

She shook her head. She couldn't bring herself to say it. To tell him what she had done. She hurried downstairs.

'Meena, I know you have it. Give it to me. You know this won't work. I need the drink. I need it to calm my nerves.'

She shook her head again. Tears fell down her face. She couldn't bring herself to look into his eyes.

'Purnima! Neeraj! Come here now!'

'No! Leave them alone. This has nothing to do with them.'

She watched as the children paused as they approached. She couldn't help but notice Purnima's accusatory glance.

'Children, have you seen where your mother put my bottles? Hmm? Tell me now. Come on. Tell me.'

Neeraj shook his head. Purnima stared at her mother. Meena couldn't make out if she was angry or grateful to her.

'Meena. Tell me. Now.'

She had to be brave. She had to show the children not to put up with this treatment. That they deserved better than this.

'I threw them away. All of them.'

She watched Amar's face go from red to pink. He was in disbelief.

'Which bin? I'll get the bottles out. I hope you didn't break any of them.'

She watched him storm to the garden and walk to the side gate. He took out the bottles one by one. Some had smashed, but others were intact. Each one was empty. His hands were bleeding from the broken glass, a deep red staining their patio.

One bottle had a little left in it. She hadn't emptied it fully. He opened the lid and let the last few drips touch his lips. Then he threw the bottle on the ground.

'Where is the rest? Tell me *now*. We'd better have some left, Meena.'

She hugged her hands tight across her body. She felt her nails draw blood in the palm of her hand.

'It's all gone, Amar. It's for your own good. You're destroying your body. You're destroying us.'

She paused, properly looking into his eyes for the first time that evening. She watched as his face calmed down. His eyes closed. When they reopened, they looked full of regret. But just as quickly, the regret disappeared. He pushed past her and walked back into the house. Meena noticed how the children had moved into the hallway.

Amar went into the bathroom. She followed him, keeping a short distance between them. He grabbed a bottle of bleach.

'You have left me nothing else to drink now, Meena. This is what you've done. This is your doing. I don't want to live like this anymore either.'

She screamed at him to stop. She was too late. He unscrewed the cap and she watched as the bleach poured out of the bottle, past Amar's lips and down his throat. She heard Purnima cry out. The next two minutes happened in slow motion. As soon as Amar put the bottle down, his body fell to the floor. His skin turned red. He leant over the toilet and began violently throwing up. Meena ran to him and rubbed his back. Blood ran through the vomit.

She stood up and felt her heart almost beating out of her chest. She needed help. She needed a doctor.

Sweat dripped down her back. What should she do? An ambulance would take time. They didn't have time. She ran past the children, out the door and across the street. She banged on Lakshmi's door. Rajvir opened it, looking annoyed. When he saw her expression, he grabbed her elbows.

'What's wrong? What's happened?'

'It's Amar. He . . . drank bleach. He's going to die, Rajvir. Please. Drive him to the hospital.'

Within seconds, Rajvir had his shoes on and jumped into his car. He drove it in front of Meena's house and met her at the front door. He grabbed the door frame when he saw Amar lying on the floor. Blood and vomit stained his shirt and his skin had turned white. He almost looked dead.

With his hands shaking with shock, Rajvir bent down and lifted Amar up, his knees buckling under Amar's weight. Meena quickly grabbed Amar's other side and they hauled him into Rajvir's car. She watched her husband's almost limp body slump against the car seat. She tried to get in the car, but Rajvir stopped her.

'You need to stay here with the children, Meena. Let me take him. He'll be OK. Ask Kanika or Lakshmi if they can take the kids, and then meet us at the hospital.'

She watched as the car drove away, her feet not moving until the car had disappeared from sight. She then sprang into action.

She asked Lakshmi to watch the children and ran to Kanika's door, having no time to explain the whole situation. She simply said Amar had been taken to hospital and she needed to go and be with him. Jagdeep nodded straight away and drove her to the hospital, speeding past traffic lights. She was grateful for his urgency.

She ran into the emergency unit and managed to find Rajvir. They had just taken Amar in for testing. They said he would most likely need surgery.

Forty long minutes passed. Eventually, a doctor came up to them and sat them down. He explained that Amar had severe internal bleeding from drinking the bleach. His stomach lining would be destroyed, as well as his throat. With time and medicine, he would recover to a certain extent, but it would be a long road. Rajvir breathed a sigh of relief and went to phone Lakshmi. When he had gone, the doctor placed a hand on Meena's.

'Did your husband have any issues with drinking? Sorry to ask, but we noticed some severe trauma to his kidneys and liver.'

She nodded. He sighed and told her that Amar would be OK. As long as he took the time to rest and didn't drink again. He advised her to go home. They would keep Amar overnight and she could see him tomorrow. She was about to ask to see him but decided against it. It could wait until tomorrow.

Except tomorrow never came. She received a knock on the door at midnight. Abhay and Rishi stood in the doorway, the light from the lamppost casting them in an eerie glow.

Lakshmi had phoned her brothers to tell them what had happened. They had insisted on going to the hospital. They had been there when Amar's heart had stopped beating. They had been there when he was pronounced dead. Now they had come to tell Meena that she was a widow.

Chapter Fifty

Four months later and Meena still replayed that day in her head over and over again. They were now in the hottest month of the year, but she lived in cardigans and jumpers. She put vests underneath her salwar kameez. She had worn the same one for a week now. The sarees lay untouched. She didn't feel the warmth. No matter how long she stood outside, waiting for the sun to comfort her, it never did. It left her cold. She didn't think she would ever feel that warmth again.

She watched as Purnima walked down the road with Rani. They both wore summer dresses, although Purnima's would have given her father a heart attack with its short skirt and lack of sleeves. Meena let the image wash over her. Thank God for Kanika and her family. They had been the rock keeping them afloat. Without them, Meena was sure she would have drowned in the frozen water, going down until there was only darkness.

In the last few months, they had started taking weekly trips. She gave the children turns to choose where to go, with Neeraj usually choosing Oxford Street and Purnima choosing the airport. Despite Amar's absence,

337

they all sat together and watched the planes go by while munching on homemade samosas. Each child had dealt with the grief differently. Neeraj had closed himself off, and Purnima had opened up. Sometimes she took her anger out on Meena, and other times she came crawling into her bed at night, wanting cuddles. Neeraj was quieter now – he had calmed down and changed his mischievous ways. He often helped Meena in the kitchen; they would make *rotis* together while listening to the Jacksons on the radio.

Kanika's children came over most days, and Kanika and Meena continued their evening walks, the fresh air helping them to relieve their stresses. Despite having grown up in heat and warmth, Meena was starting to like the feel of the cold, crisp air as it brought her a renewed energy.

Chapter Fifty-one

Meena could hear shouting coming from Kanika's house. Jagdeep must have a day off. As Meena walked out into the garden, curious to see if her friend was OK, she heard a loud thump. She had heard similar noises over the years, particularly after a round of shouting. Each time, she had covered her ears. She couldn't stand the sound of her friend being hurt. This time, though, it sounded different. Heavier. Then she heard it. The scream.

She ran over to Kanika's house and threw the kitchen door open. Kanika was standing, every part of her body shaking uncontrollably. Jagdeep was standing next to her with a knife in his hand. Something switched in Meena, and she took her friend's hand and stood in front of her, covering her body.

'You should leave, Jagdeep. Before I call the police.'

He looked between them and put down the knife. She watched his jaw clench as he grabbed his car keys and closed the front door with a slam.

'Kanika. This is enough. You are leaving him.'

'Meena, I can't.'

'Stop! Why? What are you waiting for? Until he

kills you? Is that when you'll leave him? When you have no choice, and your kids are without a mother?'

Her sharp words cut through Kanika. With a shaking hand, Kanika took hers and they sat together, their silent tears filling the room.

Chapter Fifty-two

After Kanika had threatened legal action, surrounded by Meena; Sheila; Lakshmi; and her neighbours, Lisa and Anne – whose cousin was a divorce lawyer, Jagdeep eventually admitted defeat. He didn't go lightly, taking with him everything from the house that was of any value. Kanika told Meena that he moved to Birmingham. The kids went to see him every other weekend, and Kanika had no fears that he would hurt them. He loved them. He had never loved her. You don't hurt someone you love.

The day he left, they celebrated. Lisa bought them all pizza and Meena tried it for the first time. It was absolutely delicious! Five slices and a cream cake later, and she was loosening her salwar kameez and laughing with her group of friends, seeing genuine happiness on Kanika's face for the first time. They also celebrated Meena's success. She had begun writing again, and one of her Hindi poems had been translated into English and published in the local paper in the local talent section. It was one of the best moments of her life. She had also slowly begun to teach herself how to write poetry in English, getting used to the enchantments of the language. She wondered where her writing would take her next.

As the party wrapped up, and everyone left, Meena cleared up Kanika's home. Kanika had already planned all the work she was going to do to make it her own style. Magazines showing different sofas, carpets and wallpapers littered the coffee table. It turned out her friend had a secret passion for interior design.

As the sky began to turn a dusky blue, Kanika turned to Meena.

'Fancy our walk? We can take the kids.'

Meena smiled. They gathered all the children up and walked down their road, as the lampposts began to turn on and illuminate their way. They looked up at the sky as it turned from a light blue to a soft pink. She closed her eyes. When she opened them again, the sky was lilac.

Acknowledgements

Thank you to my late Nanny who inspired this book. Without her, this novel would not exist, and I wouldn't be the person I am today. She showed me the meaning of strength, love and perseverance. I also want to thank Rhea and Sanah, my lovely editors at Orion, for their belief in me and my book. They took a chance on a twenty-five-year-old Indian girl who had written a novel based on her Nanny's life. I am so grateful for their faith in me and my writing. A final thank you to my partner Dilesh for lending me his tablet so that I could write this novel during my lunch breaks at work, and for his support and belief in all of my crazy ideas.

Printed in Great Britain
by Amazon

15739205R00202